TABBY HAYES

C.J. PETIT

TABBY HAYES

C.J. PETIT

TABLE OF CONTENTS

TABBY HAYES

C.J. PETIT

Printed in the United States of America

First Printing, 2020

ISBN: 9798671995893

PROLOGUE

August 2, 1878
Watson, Southwest Montana Territory

Sheriff Tex Smith grabbed a shotgun from the rack on the back wall of the jail as he shouted, "Holt, grab that second scattergun!"

Deputy Sheriff Holt Archer didn't reply before he bolted from his chair and almost ran into his boss when he rushed to get the double-barreled twelve gauge.

The sheriff's only other deputy, Bill Carroll was across the street pressed against the wall in the doorway of Bob Rupert's Feed and Grain with a large blood stain on his left leg trying to avoid getting shot again.

Most of the outlaws who had just held up the Watson Bank of Montana were already mounting their horses as two of the gang kept anyone else from entering the streets. It had just been Bill's bad luck to be heading to the bank to deposit his month's pay when he spotted the unusual activity outside the bank. He hadn't even tried to confront them when one of the two men out front saw his badge and fired his Winchester.

He didn't even draw his pistol before a .44 passed through his right pants leg. He hobbled quickly to the other side of the street as they fired again and barely made it to the sanctuary of the feed and grain's recessed doorway.

5

Sheriff Smith and Deputy Archer both stopped by the door of the jail and the sheriff peeked around the doorjamb.

"Damn! We can't go out there now," he snapped, "We'd be deader than dirt after we set one foot out that door."

Holt asked, "What do we do, boss?"

"We wait for 'em to leave town. They're just about ready to make their getaway, so all we can do is mark 'em as best we can so we know who they are when we catch up with 'em."

After he revealed their only option, Sheriff Smith started studying the two outlaws. At almost two hundred yards, it wasn't easy, but he looked for anything that would mark them. The two criminals who were sitting on their horses were average size, but one had a black hat with a white band. He was riding a dark brown horse with two white stockings on his forelegs but none on his hind legs. The other outlaw was riding a lighter brown horse with a black mane and tail, had a gray Stetson on his head and wore his pistol on the left side.

He began relaying his observations to his deputy when the other outlaws bubbled out of the bank and fired two pistol shots into the building probably to keep everyone on the floor. Tex felt so damned useless as he watched the other four outlaws climb into their saddles, but he knew it was the smart move. Dead lawmen were no good to the townsfolk.

He barely had time to take notice of the other four as their jostling horses created a cloud of dust before they even set them into a gallop heading east out of town.

Once they rode away, Sheriff Smith bolted out of the jail and headed across the street to help his wounded deputy who was now sitting on the boardwalk in a daze. Deputy Holt Archer stood in the road watching the gang disappear.

As the sheriff began tearing Bill Carroll's bloody britches away to inspect the damage, he shouted, "Holt, get the doc and then start rounding up men for a posse. We're gonna need all the firepower we can get!"

"Okay, boss," Deputy Archer yelled back before taking one last look at the fading outlaws then turning and jogging toward the barbershop.

Men were already congregating as the sheriff tied a tourniquet just below his deputy's knee and then helped him to his feet.

"It ain't too bad, Bill. You'll be on your feet pretty soon."

He then turned to the closest spectator and said, "Horace, help Bill to the doc."

After Horace and another man led Deputy Carroll away, Sheriff Smith picked up his unfired shotgun and pushed through the gaggle of onlookers who were peppering him with questions.

The men who were asking wouldn't be joining him on the posse or they wouldn't be there.

Once back in his office, he wrote down the limited amount of descriptive information he had and then exchanged his shotgun for a Winchester '73 before leaving the jail to head to the telegraph office. He hadn't heard of any gangs of that size operating in the area, but he'd wire the U.S. Marshal's office in Helena to see if they had any idea who had robbed the bank.

On the way, he stopped at the bank and asked the president, Ted Francis, how much they'd stolen and to make sure that no one else had been shot. He would include the information in the message he was sending to the U.S. Marshal.

It turned out that they'd gotten away with more than three thousand dollars in cash. The only casualty was his deputy's relatively minor wound, at least so far.

By the time he returned to the jail, Holt had his horse saddled and the first members of the posse sitting in their saddles behind him.

"How many are gonna join us, Holt?" he asked as he slid the Winchester into its scabbard.

"We've got eight more coming, so we'll have a dozen to chase down those bastards."

He nodded and mounted his tall gray gelding. As he waited for the others to arrive, he was impressed with how well-planned the job was. He figured that at least one of them must have been in town for a couple of days and Watson wasn't nearly big enough for him not to notice newcomers.

He turned to Holt and asked, "Do you remember seein' any strangers around town?"

"I was just running that through my head, and I know that I haven't spotted any."

"I wonder how they could have scouted out the bank if we didn't see 'em?" he asked aloud without really expecting an answer.

As other members of the posse began collecting behind him, Sheriff Smith let that mystery fade as he concentrated on running them down. There weren't any railroads and the nearest town was Bannack, which was another forty miles west. Virginia City was about seventy miles east, which was the direction they headed, but he doubted if they'd go to either town because the telegraph was still working. If they planned to run to Bannack or Virginia City, then they would have cut the line so they wouldn't be expected. But about thirty miles down that road, there was an intersection. The north direction took them to Virginia City while the other way headed into Wyoming. It made more sense that they'd make their way out of the territory.

It was almost an hour after the robbery before the posse rode out of Watson. The sheriff let Bo Wrigley handle the tracking because he used to serve as a scout before a Sioux arrow ended his career with the army. It was most likely that they just took the road to Wyoming, but if they went cross country, then he'd need Bo.

They didn't ride five miles when Sheriff Smith's guess was proven wrong and Bo pointed out the fresh tracks that turned right off of the roadway. The sun was getting low in the sky when Bo led them off the road heading south into the hard country. The mountains, gullies and trees made for ideal ambush locations, but Sheriff Smith wasn't concerned as he and Bo led the large group of armed men who were determined to find and punish the outlaws.

———

Less than a mile ahead of the large posse, Cash Locklear had positioned his five men in a semicircle leaving a gap for the posse to enter their killing zone. They'd left a clear trail behind them and he wasn't worried in the least of the number of men who would follow it. They could have had an entire company of cavalry and they'd be decimated by the massive firepower the six men could unleash with their Winchesters.

Each man had his repeater fully loaded and cocked as they hid behind rocks and trees. Their horses were all tethered four hundred yards down the trail and hidden in a small canyon. Cash expected to add more saddled animals to their collection after the posse arrived. His only real concern was the possibility of a bad ricochet when they had the posse in their crossfire.

He expected that not a single member of the posse would return to their town.

———

The posse had to form two columns as the terrain became more difficult, but they were still making good time. Bo said that they were only a mile or two back now and might even spot them soon.

They were just four hundred yards from the waiting outlaws when Bo gave his opinion to the sheriff who rode beside him.

Sheriff Smith may have believed that his large posse was immune from ambush, but that didn't mean he wasn't scanning the ground in front of him. It was second nature to any lawman who had to chase bad men through the rough terrain.

He may have been looking, but by the time he realized they were targets, it was too late.

Cash had been checking each of his men since they'd heard the loud hoofbeats of the large posse and knew they were not only ready but had the patience to hold their fire until the last man was well within range. Cash would be the first to open the gates of hell with his powerful Winchester '76.

He looked over at his number two man, Max Johnson and when their eyes met, each man grinned before looking back down the trail.

It was Deputy Archer who ignited the storm when he caught sight of Harry Brown's Winchester muzzle moving to settle his sights on a target.

He pointed and shouted, "Ambush!"

As the men in the posse began either pulling their pistols or wrestling their assorted repeaters from their scabbards, the six outlaws opened fire.

Two members of the posse immediately fell from their saddles with the first volley and another two absorbed .44s but remained upright. As the outlaws began to quickly bring fresh cartridges into their breeches, Sheriff Smith and Deputy Sheriff Archer were cocking the hammers of their Winchesters to return fire. Four of the others in the posse were about to pull their triggers as the second round of fire from the ambushers began slamming into the men who'd chased after the outlaws.

Bo Wrigley never got a shot off before a bullet drilled into his chest and he rolled off the side of his saddle with his unfired Colt still in his hand.

Sheriff Smith felt a .44 rip his jacket's right sleeve just after he fired, but before he even bothered to lever in a new round, he knew the situation was hopeless.

He shouted, "Get out of here!", and whipped his horse around as bullets whizzed past him. He soon realized that his order had been obeyed before it was given when he saw that four members of his posse were already almost four hundred yards away.

He had to ignore the men on the ground because they'd all be dead if he tried to help. As his gelding moved quickly back along the trail, he glanced back at the carnage behind him and felt sick. He counted six bodies on the ground and one of them was his deputy. He didn't know if they were dead and he fought an angry urge to turn his horse back around and face those bastards. But he knew it would be a futile gesture. He wasn't sure if the townsfolk would label him a coward, but it didn't matter now.

Once the posse had gone, Cash had his boys enter the site of the massacre and collect what they could. He stood guard at the edge facing the trail where the remnants of the posse had gone and doubted if any would return.

After they'd taken the guns and whatever else of value they could find on the bodies, the gang made a long trail rope for the six horses before they resumed their ride south through the difficult terrain.

The gang wasn't just meandering into the unknown. They knew where they were going. It was also the answer to the sheriff's unanswered question of how they had been able to scout the bank without being spotted. One of his boys had lived there.

———

When Sheriff Smith led his battered group into Watson, it was obvious to the people who lined the main street what had happened. They'd probably heard the gunfire and when the decimated posse returned without any prisoners or bodies, they knew that the sheriff's men had met with disaster. It was just a matter of details.

It took the rest of the day to reach a minimal level of recovery. There had been four new widows created in the debacle, including Holt's young wife. The only good news was that Bill Carroll would be back on the job tomorrow.

The bank was on shaky ground because of the loss and the town's confidence in Sheriff Smith was even shakier.

Despite the horrible results, Tex Smith wasn't about to turn in his badge. When he walked into his house after sunset, his wife Rosalie hadn't tried to make any excuses for the disaster, but she understood how much it had affected her husband. She and their eight-year-old son did all they could to restore his belief that he was still a good man.

———

August 31, 1878

Buster Nye handed the Colt Model 1873 to Tabby Hayes as he asked, "Are you sure you don't want a Remington? I've got three of them that fire the same .44 cartridge that your Winchester uses."

Tabby pulled the hammer to the loading position and rotated the cylinder checking to make sure the gun was empty. He then snapped the hammer all the way back before pointing it at the back wall of the shop and pulling the trigger. He repeated it twice more before he set the new revolver back on the counter and looked at the gunsmith.

"I'm a Colt man, Buster. I'll take this one and give me two boxes of those .45 Long Colts. I'll need a new gunbelt, too."

"If you're gonna trade in your Walker, then you can use your old holster if you don't mind not having any spares on the belt."

Tabby grinned before replying, "That cartridge pistol would get lost in this holster after my Walker spent all those years stretching the leather. I'm not trading it anyway. It's never let me down and I'd feel like a traitor if I gave it up. I've got to admit, that '73 sure feels better. It's a lot lighter and it's better balanced, too."

"Good enough, Tabby. Sorry to hear that you lost your job."

"It's the way of a cowhand, Buster. I've been working at the Slant 6 longer than most of the other spreads, but the boss really didn't have much of a choice. Cattle prices have been low for too long now. After we culled out that much of the herds to keep the ranch going, he had to let a lot of us go. I still reckoned I'd be staying, but he had to send more of us packing than I expected."

Buster laid a new gunbelt with eight cartridge loops next to the Colt then placed two boxes of the .45 Long Colt cartridges beside it.

"You need anything else, Tabby?"

"Give me two boxes of .44s for my Winchester."

Buster reached below the counter, retrieved two boxes of the biggest selling ammunition and set them beside the Colt cartridges.

"Where are you headed, Tabby?"

"I'm going to ride to Bannack. I'll stop at every ranch along the way and see if I can find a new place to hang my hat, but it's not very likely. I'll probably have to ride the grub line for a while until beef prices come back."

"Well, now that you've got that new Colt, don't go thinking you're a bounty hunter and try to chase down those killers that robbed the bank in Watson."

"I heard about that, but it's been a while. I reckon they're long gone by now. Besides, I'm not a bounty hunter. I'm just a cowhand."

"Five of those boys that they killed in the posse weren't lawmen, either."

"I know, but they were chasing those bad boys and I'm not about to do anything that stupid. I've got no intention of being a

16

bounty hunter. I'll bet that almost every man that comes through your door is a better shot than I am and probably any lady, for that matter."

Buster snickered and after Tabby paid his tab, he watched as Tabby took off his old gunbelt and laid it on the counter. After filling the loops of the new one with eight .45 Long Colt cartridges, he transferred the sheath carrying his razor-sharp foot-long knife to the fresh leather gunbelt.

Tabby filled five of the chambers and then pushed the pistol hard into the holster before taking it out again then returning it to its new home and securing it with the hammer loop.

As his customer outfitted himself with his new Colt, Buster put the rest of his ammunition into a cloth sack.

Tabby shook the gunsmith's hand as he said, "Thanks, Buster."

"You take care, Tabby. Hope you find another job soon."

Tabby smiled as he picked up his ammunition and his old gunbelt then replied, "Maybe I'll have to start selling ladies frocks in Bannack to make a living."

Buster was still laughing as Tabby left his shop.

Once outside, Tabby dropped the bag of ammunition in one of his enormous saddlebags and then wrapped his old gunbelt around the Walker and put it in the other. With all of his clothes and personal gear, even the voluminous saddlebags were getting full and he still had to make one more stop before he rode out of Virginia City.

After making that stop at the dry good store and greengrocer to buy some trail food, Tabby Hayes mounted his dark gelding and headed south out of town. He guessed that there were at least four or five ranches between here and Bannack, but he doubted that any would be hiring. It was the life of the cowhand.

He was only twenty-six, and that way of life was all he'd known after leaving his father's house. It was uncertain, but it was a good life. He had no real responsibilities other than taking care of cattle and the only worries that he had were trying to avoid angry bulls, rattlesnakes, or being caught in a blizzard. As he rode along the well-traveled roadway, he suspected that his preferred way of life wouldn't be around much longer.

He just hoped that he really wouldn't find himself selling frilly dresses to women just to put food in his belly. At least he still had a good amount of savings because he didn't waste his pay in the saloons in Virginia City or any of the other establishments in town that thrived on fast-spending cowhands.

CHAPTER 1

September 4, 1878

After leaving Virginia City, Tabby had stopped at four other ranches, but each of them was in the same shape and wasn't hiring. He had spent a day at each of them working for his chow and sleeping in their bunkhouses in the hope that they'd see how good he was and still offer him a job, but that didn't happen.

He had his chaps rolled up around his bedroll and blanket and they were covered by his slicker. It made for a large but soft cylinder behind his saddle that came in handy when he felt the urge to lean back and stretch his spine.

The road had turned south out of Virginia City, then after forty miles or so, he had reached the intersection that headed west toward Bannack. He almost thought about heading south into Wyoming, but he stuck with his original plan and turned his gelding to the right.

He still wasn't optimistic of his chances. The further he rode away from the Slant 6, the newer the territory and the less likely he'd find a rancher who might give him a job. He figured if he didn't find a place soon, he'd have to start working just for chow and a place to stay warm. He was surprised that he hadn't seen any snow yet but knew it wouldn't be long.

He was already wearing his heavy, wool-lined coat but hadn't started wearing one of his two flannel Union suits yet. He just didn't want to have to wash them. His coat had an inside pocket that where he kept his life's savings of almost six hundred dollars. He knew he could live on that money for almost two years but hated the idea of spending any of it. He hated subtracting from his savings unless he felt it was absolutely necessary.

It was just around noon when he rounded a curve and saw some buildings ahead. He knew it was Watson, which was the only town of any size between Virginia City and Bannack. He kept the same pace and figured he'd be able to ask around town if there were any ranches hiring. If that didn't work, he might see if he could get a job in town, at least to get him through the winter. He just hoped he could avoid that dress shop.

He kept Philly at a walk as he neared the town and began looking for the barbershop or an eatery. Which one caught his eye first would be where he would dismount.

His first stop was set when he passed the bank and spotted a diner named Arnie's.

As he angled his gelding toward the café, he said aloud, "Well, Philly, it looks like I'll be eating before I get cleaned up."

TABBY HAYES

He began to snicker when he noticed a man staring at him from the boardwalk. He'd received funny looks before when he was new to a town, but this was much different. The man's eyes were as big as pie tins as if he'd seen a ghost.

Tabby then smiled and loudly said, "Howdy!"

Instead of returning his friendly greeting, the man's right arm jerked up and his index finger jutted out at him as he shouted, "You're one of them!"

Tabby was too confused to answer before the man then yelled, "You robbed the bank!"

Tabby shook his head and showed him his empty palms as he exclaimed, "I'm not a bank robber, mister! I'm just a cowhand!"

His denial had barely left his mouth when he heard a second shout come from the other side of the street.

"He's one of them killers!"

Tabby felt as if he was living a nightmare as he whipped his head around to make the same protest to his new accuser. But when he finally saw the man, his nightmare became much worse as the man on his left was pulling his pistol.

As the man's revolver cleared leather, Tabby didn't hesitate but dropped down to Philly's neck and slammed his heels into his gelding's flanks.

His Morgan lurched forward and just after his hooves dug into the dirt, the man fired his pistol. Tabby didn't feel any impact, so where the bullet went didn't matter as Philly began accelerating down the street leaving a cloud of Montana dust behind him.

Tabby's face was being whipped by Philly's dark mane as he flew past homes and businesses. He heard a second shot but knew he was almost out of range unless somebody else had a Winchester.

By the time he reached the western edge of town, another man had opened fire, but even with the loud echoes from Philly's hooves, Tabby knew it was from another pistol shooter.

He was about fifty yards past the last building before he sat back in the saddle and twisted around to see if anyone was chasing him. There were no riders, but an angry crowd was already gathering in the street. When he saw a man with a badge rush out to talk to them, Tabby knew he was in trouble.

He slowed Philly to a medium trot as he tried to make sense of what had just happened. That first man had accused him of being a bank robber and a killer, so they must have mistaken him for one of those men who'd robbed the town bank a month ago. Why they thought he was one of the outlaws was another question.

Tabby was sure that if he was given the chance, he could convince them that he was just a cowhand, but he doubted if they'd let him get within a hundred yards of the town before they filled the air with lead. After hearing about the massacre of the posse that tried to run down the outlaws, he could understand their anger. But going off half-cocked the way those two men had done was something else entirely. If they had taken just a few seconds to figure out that he was alone. And even if he was one of those men, he would have to be crazy to enter the town. The last place any of those outlaws would want to be was Watson.

Now he had to do something he'd never done before in his life. He'd have to run. He'd have to run from the law and run for his life.

———

As Tabby disappeared, Sheriff Smith faced the excited, jabbering crowd and shouted, "Quiet!"

He then looked at the first shooter and asked, "Al, what the hell were you shootin' at?"

"It was one of them robbers, Tex! Joe saw him, too. He was ridin' that dark brown horse with the two front white boots and had a black hat with a silver band. It was him!"

The others began yammering their agreement before the sheriff yelled, "Quiet down!"

He shook his head slowly and said, "You boys are all wrong. Whoever that feller was, he sure wasn't one of those bank robbers."

"But, Tex," Joe LaPierre asked, "how come you're sayin' that when you didn't even set eyes on him?"

"Because I got a telegram this mornin' that the same gang that robbed the bank knocked off the stage to Virginia City yesterday afternoon. They were spotted in the act by an eye witness who told Sheriff Wolfson. They're still bein' trailed by a posse. Now how do you reckon that one outlaw could ride all that way so soon? Besides, even if he was stupid enough to come back here ridin' that same horse, why would he come here without the others?"

"They coulda kicked him outta the gang and got a new man."

"Now you're just bein' silly, Joe. Y'all head back to wherever you were and forget about it. I don't reckon we'll see that feller again anyway. But if he comes back, don't start shootin'. Just ask him to talk to me first."

There was an assortment of mumbling and grousing as the crowd began to disassemble and after five minutes, only Sheriff Smith was standing in the street.

He turned and headed back to the jail wondering who the stranger was.

———

Tabby's last check of his backtrail didn't reveal the angry lynch mob he was expecting to find, so he slowed Philly to a walk as he tried to concentrate on what he would do next. This was all virgin territory to him. He'd never even been tossed into a cell to sleep off a night's revelry as almost all of his fellow cowhands had been. Now he was in danger of being shot because of his resemblance to one of those outlaws.

He knew he couldn't go back into Watson and as Philly headed west, he suspected that telegrams were already being sent along that wire that was strung along the right side of the road. He knew he was still about forty miles out of Bannack and was certain that the law would be waiting for him when he showed up. They might give him a chance to explain the mistake, but he didn't want to risk it. He'd let things cool down for a while. That meant he had to find another ranch and work for free for a few days. The further off the road the better.

Once he decided he couldn't stay on the road, he began looking for a trail that led to the north or south. It wouldn't be a proper road, but he could use it to find a ranch. Just as he had after leaving the Slant 6, he'd spot the ruts from their supply wagons and the hoofmarks from their cattle and horses and they would lead him to the ranch.

Tabby continued riding west for another few minutes checking his backtrail and the western horizon. He was getting nervous and knew that Philly was tired and was about to just leave the road and go cross country to set up a camp when he spotted a trail on the left.

It wasn't a big trail with a lot of hoofprints, but there were some markings left by hooved animals, maybe horses. There were wagons ruts as well, so he knew that there was probably a small ranch on the other end of the trail. As he turned Philly onto the trail, he thought he might really get lucky and he'd find that elusive job at the ranch. Even if he had to work for food and a roof over his head, it would be a lot better than getting hanged.

The trail wasn't exactly a finished highway, but it wasn't as bad as riding over untouched ground. As Philly walked south on the trail, Tabby scanned the landscape for the first signs of a ranch. He was surprised that the trail had gone south because south of the roadway, the land was a lot more difficult than that to the north. There was good pasture land on the north side of the highway and while the south might have some clear spaces, it had a lot more granite and trees than grazing land.

The sun was touching the tops of the mountains when the trail made a sudden turn to the west. He pulled his dark brown Morgan gelding to a stop and scanned the area.

To his left, he saw about a half a mile of clear ground before the forests blocked the way. There was about a mile of reasonably flat ground ahead and almost double that to his right where the wagon ruts and hoofprints went. He still didn't see any buildings or even cattle, so he wondered where the trail led. Some of those ruts and tracks were fairly recent, so it couldn't have been abandoned.

He may have still been concerned about a posse, but his curiosity was piqued. Where was the small ranch that the trail told him was nearby?

Tabby turned Philly to follow the trail, but as he rode he still didn't see any buildings. He did see a herd of antelope in the distance, so he wouldn't go hungry even if there wasn't a ranch. But the trail continued, and he was still mystified.

Just five minutes later he caught a whiff of smoke in the air but still didn't see any signs of human occupation or the source of the smoke for that matter.

The landscape was in shadows and he wondered if he would discover who had something burning when a canyon almost popped into view a few hundred yards away on the right side of the trail. As he drew closer, the smell of smoke grew more pronounced and when the canyon was close, he saw the trail enter its mouth.

When he turned Philly north into the canyon, he finally saw the ranch buried deep inside. It wasn't an impressive spread, but there was smoke coming from the cookstove pipe of a medium-sized ranch house. There was a nice barn and a corral nearby, but no horses were in sight. He didn't see a single cow either. If it hadn't been for the smoke, he would have thought it was abandoned. He almost wished it was because he could stay here for a while and live off the land.

Because of the low sun and the quiet nature of the place, Tabby's neck hairs began to tickle. It was an eerie environment and he almost pulled his Winchester, but after his recent welcome in Watson, he wasn't about to be the one to create a new problem.

The ranch house was a good mile back from the mouth of the canyon and he could see grass pastures behind the house with trees lining both sides of the canyon as far as the eye could see. He didn't know if it was a long box canyon because the trees obscured the other end. It was about eight hundred yards across at the mouth, but the mountains would protect the ranch house from the howling winter winds but might let more snow build up when the blizzards struck.

He kept Philly at a walk as he drew closer to the spooky ranch house. He knew someone must be inside, but the lack of movement by human or critter gave him the willies.

Tabby finally pulled Philly to a stop a few yards from the front of the ranch house. He was going to announce his arrival, but his mouth was too dry. So, he pulled one of his two canteens and took a long drag of water before closing the cap and hanging it back in place.

He still hesitated for almost thirty seconds before shouting, "Hello, the house!"

As he sat in his saddle waiting, he felt an urge to check his backtrail, but pushed it aside. He didn't want to start behaving like an outlaw after having been identified as one.

The front door finally swung open and he almost pulled his Winchester when the first thing he saw were the twin barrels of a shotgun slowly appear from the opening. That idea quickly evaporated when he realized that if he made that move, whoever was on the other end of the shotgun would let him have both barrels and he wouldn't live long enough to cock his repeater's hammer.

Instead, he quickly threw his open hands to the side and watched the rest of the shotgun emerged from the house.

He was surprised to discover that it was being held by a young woman. The lady soon stepped out onto the porch and leveled her scattergun at his face. He noticed both hammers were pulled back which would make his next words critical.

But before he could even compose his first sentence, she snapped, "They're not here! Go away! They don't need any more of you bastards!"

For the second time that day, Tabby found himself thoroughly confused and in danger of being killed for an unknown reason.

He quickly replied, "I'm just a cowhand looking for a job, ma'am. If you don't have any, I'll just leave if that's okay."

She still glared at him but slowly lowered the shotgun just a few inches.

"You're not looking to join up with them?"

"Who is that, ma'am? I'm kinda lost here. First some men in Watson accused me of being a bank robber and started throwing shots at me and now you seem to figure I'm looking to find somebody."

She lowered her shotgun's muzzles a few more inches and lost some of the anger in her eyes as she asked, "What's your name?"

"I was born Thom Hayes with an H, but everybody calls me Tabby."

"Tabby? Like a cat?"

"Yes, ma'am, but a lot of the boys would shorten it to Tab," he replied before he asked, "Ma'am, I'm not going to cause you any trouble, so can you ease back those hammers on the shotgun?"

She didn't reach for the hammers but pulled the trigger back and the hammers loudly snapped against empty barrels.

"It wasn't loaded anyway. Go ahead and set."

Tabby slowly dismounted and led Philly to the hitchrail where he tied him off. He didn't step onto the low porch but stayed near his gelding waiting for further instructions.

The woman looked past him to the mouth of the canyon for a few seconds before saying, "Come inside."

"Thank you, ma'am," he answered before following her into the house but leaving the door open in case he had to make a hasty exit.

The big front room was dark but no one else was inside, which gave Tabby some measure of relief. For a moment, he thought the woman might be luring him into some sort of trap. It didn't make a lot of sense, but nothing that had happened since he rode into Watson did.

He removed his Stetson and stood in place as the woman took a seat in one of the six chairs of assorted sizes, cushioning and condition.

She set the empty shotgun against the nearby wall before she said, "Go ahead and park."

"Thank you, ma'am."

Tabby selected a chair facing her, sat down and set his hat on his lap.

"You say you're a cowhand, but why did you come here? Do you see any cattle?"

"No, ma'am. It's just that when I rode into Watson, some of the townsfolk accused me of being one of those bank robbers and they didn't give me a chance to tell them any different before they started throwing lead in my direction. I skedaddled out of there and I figured they'd send a posse after me, so I was looking for someplace to stay until things quieted down. I spotted the trail that came here and followed it figuring I might be able to get a job."

She still had a curious look on her face after he finished, so Tabby quickly added, "But I can be on my way if you're afraid."

"I'm not afraid of you, Mister Hayes. You don't need to go right now, but you might not want to stay here very long, either."

"No, ma'am. I reckon your husband will be back soon and it won't look good if I'm here, so it's probably better if I just go on my way."

She didn't say anything for a few seconds and seemed to be evaluating him as he sat across from her in the shadowy room. Tabby began to feel uncomfortable even though he had a loaded pistol and she was unarmed.

After almost a full silent minute of examination, she said, "I know why those people in Watson would think you were one of the men who robbed their bank and killed six of them."

His eyebrows rose as he asked, "You do?"

"Your dark brown horse is unusual in that it has two white stockings on his forelegs, and you wear a black hat with a light band around the rim. One of those outlaws rides a horse with the same coloring and wears a hat like yours. His name is Snake O'Hara."

Tabby quietly asked, "How do you know that?"

"Because they live here when they aren't out in the territory robbing and killing."

He remained in stunned silence for what seemed like an hour before he asked, "Where are they now?"

"They went off to rob the Bannack to Virginia City stage. They're probably on their way back by now."

Tabby reflexively glanced at the closed door before saying, "I'd better get going then. I don't want to face more bullets for just being here. I'm sorry to have bothered you, ma'am."

He began to stand when she quickly said, "Wait. You don't need to leave right now. They won't be back for at least another day. They were going to stop it just after that last turn to Virginia City and they were going to ride east after robbing the stagecoach to throw off the law."

"Why do you know all this? Why are you alone?"

She didn't answer his question, but said, "I was cooking my dinner when you showed up. Go ahead and bring your horse into the barn. After you take care of him then come back inside. You don't have to knock."

"Yes, ma'am," Tabby replied as he slowly stood.

She left her seat and he watched her disappear into the dark hallway before he slowly left the house.

As he was untying Philly, he looked toward the mouth of the canyon a mile away and couldn't see much in the dying light. He was debating about just riding away, but a combination of curiosity and concern about who he may run into in the dark made him lead his gelding toward the barn.

When he entered the dark interior, he found six empty stalls that needed cleaning, so he chose the cleanest of them and led Philly inside. He began removing his gear and after setting them on a clear area of the floor, he began unsaddling his horse.

The woman's unusual behavior had him flummoxed. He'd been taught to always treat women with deference as each of them could be a mother, yet this lady seemed hard and calculating, almost to the point of being a man. She surely didn't look like a man, but maybe living with six outlaws had made her that way.

Then there was the most glaring question of what her purpose was for being here. He realized what her primary job would probably be, *but why was she alone if there were six of them? How long had she been living with them and how did she get here?*

She was a very attractive woman with the kind of figure that would attract any man. He guessed her age to be mid-twenties and if she'd been living with them for very long, where were the children?

He didn't brush Philly down, but made sure he had water and some grain before hanging his saddlebags over his shoulder and grabbing his Winchester. He patted his white-booted gelding on the neck before leaving the barn.

As he walked to the house, at least now he understood what had caused the mistaken identity problem in Watson that had almost gotten him killed. When he'd bought Philly four years ago, it was his unusual two white stockings on his forelegs more than anything else that had spurred the purchase. He was a strong Morgan and even now was only nine years old, but it was those half-white forelegs that had attracted him. He'd never seen another horse with them before but now he knew that someone else rode another dark brown horse with the same distinctive markings.

That revelation may have answered one question, but he had a lot more now and wasn't sure he wanted to know the answers. He was still debating about getting out of the canyon before daybreak. He was at best an average shot with his guns, but doubted he was as accurate as the worst of those outlaws. And he hadn't even put a single round through his new pistol.

After entering the house through the front door, he passed through the front room and headed down the hallway to the kitchen where a lamp was now burning.

When he reached the kitchen, he found the woman scooping something out of a skillet onto two plates, but she didn't even look at him as he entered. He leaned his Winchester against the nearest wall, then slid his saddlebags from his shoulder and lowered them to the floor. As he was removing his hat, she finally turned and carried the two plates to the large table and set them down.

Tabby laid his hat on one of the six empty chairs and asked, "Do you need any help, ma'am?"

"Just sit down and we'll talk."

"Yes, ma'am," he replied and took a seat behind one of the plates.

She returned with two large mugs of coffee and placed them on the table before sitting down in the next chair.

"You didn't ask my name," she said before cutting into her beefsteak.

"It's not my place to ask, ma'am. I'm the visitor here."

"My name is Monique Dubois."

Tabby was cutting his own meat when he said, "That's a very pretty name, ma'am. I've never heard it before."

"Well, now you have. You said you were looking for a job. Have you always been a cowhand?"

"Most of my life, ma'am. My father was a wheelwright and my two older brothers were apprenticed to him. I left when I was seventeen because I wasn't fond of working indoors. It took a few years to figure out what I wanted to do, and I've been working with cattle ever since."

She had started eating after asking her question, so Tabby began shoving steak into his mouth. It was cooked just as he liked it and wasn't overly salted, so he at least appreciated her skills at the stove.

After she swallowed, she took a sip of her coffee before saying, "You haven't asked why I'm living with a gang of killers and thieves."

"It's not my place, ma'am."

"Will you please stop calling me ma'am? Call me Monique."

"Yes, ma'am. I'm sorry, I mean Monique. Was your father a French trapper?"

She then said, "No. He was a carpenter and owned a lumber business. He wasn't French or French Canadian."

Tabby just said, "Oh," then took a bite of his roasted potatoes.

Monique didn't move her fork as she looked at him for a few seconds before saying, "It's not the name I grew up with. I was called Rena when I was a girl."

Tabby set his fork down and asked, "Rena? I've never heard that name before either."

She exhaled then said, "I was christened Irene Anne Thomas, but I've been Monique Dubois for years. I'm sure that you can understand why I was given the more exotic name."

Tabby had a very good idea of the reason for her name change but didn't want to tell her in the chance that he might be wrong. If he gave her the answer that popped into his mind and it wasn't right, she'd most likely slap him for the insult.

"No, ma'am…I mean, Rena."

She suddenly laughed before saying, "You really don't know; do you?"

"I'm afraid not. I reckon I'm just too stupid to figure out things about ladies."

"I'm in a ranch house that's being used by six men and I tell you my name is Monique and even after I tell you that it's not my real name, you can't figure out what I am?"

Tabby thought he was safely past the slapping stage, so he answered, "I reckon I can pretty much guess, Rena."

"Then you'd be right, but maybe not about the circumstances that keeps me here."

Tabby resumed eating after she did and waited for her to tell him of her unusual situation.

They continued eating for another three minutes and Tabby had just about cleaned his plate when she began to speak again. When she did talk, she didn't explain her circumstances but startled him with a request that bordered on a demand.

She had her fork tightly gripped in her fist as she stared at him and firmly said, "Take me out of here."

A startled Tabby's eyes popped into saucers as he asked, "Ma'am?"

She quickly repeated, "Take me away from here."

Tabby simply didn't know how to react. He just got here, and this woman was asking him to take her away from the ranch.

He stared blankly at her for about thirty seconds before he replied, "Ma'am…I mean, Rena, you took me by surprise by what you just said. I don't know what's going on and you're already asking me to bring you with me when I leave."

She set her fork on her plate then said, "I suppose I owe you an explanation. I guess that I'm used to being so forward that I forget there are decent men in this world."

"Now before you even start telling me why you asked, I have to tell you just how hard that would be. I didn't see any other horses around the ranch and unless you can make one appear out of thin air, then that leaves us with just my gelding. Do you have any other horses?"

"No. They take their six and three others with them when they leave. One is used as a packhorse and the other two are spares in case they lose one. They don't want to leave one here so I can't run away. It's also why the shotgun doesn't have any shells."

"Then you must realize how hard that will be with only one horse. Now, we could ride double out to the road and I can get you most of the way to Watson, but I'm not about to head into that town again."

"I can't go back there either. But I do have a buckboard behind the barn. We could put your horse in harness."

"Why can't you go to town? I told you why I can't risk going back there."

She sighed then said, "For the same reason that I'm here, Mister Hayes."

He put his elbows on the table and rested his chin on his folded fingers as he waited for the explanation but still didn't believe it would be good enough to help her. He may have wanted to get her away from whatever situation she was in, but if she wouldn't go into Watson, then it was out of the question. *How could he bring her with him when he had no idea where he was headed?* Being a cowhand looking for a job is hard enough but having to provide for a woman made it almost impossible. *Then what would happen if she suddenly didn't want to be left at the next town?* Unlike him, she obviously didn't have to worry about finding a job.

Then there was the other, more immediate problem: the returning gang of outlaws. Even if he was able to drive her away from the ranch using her unseen buckboard, he imagined those killers wouldn't be happy to find her gone. Even if they were angry for losing their common wife, knowing she was gone and could expose their hideout would almost guarantee that they'd be hunted.

Tabby just couldn't imagine any reason for helping her. But even as he logically presented a strong case for turning her down, he knew no matter how strong the arguments were, he'd probably give in. She may be a prostitute and whatever else, but she was still a woman and needed his help. He almost cursed his weakness.

Rena slid his empty plate onto hers then pushed them away before saying, "Before I tell you about this place and why I'm here, I don't want you to believe that I'm only telling you a story to make you feel sympathetic. It's the truth and if you still want to leave in the morning by yourself, then I won't hold it against you. Okay?"

She probably didn't realize that she had actually made it less likely that Tabby would leave without her. Her selfless offer had moved her up a notch from his previous low opinion of her.

"Alright. Thank you for that. Go ahead."

She nodded and began what would be a much longer explanation than he had expected.

"I worked at Dilly's Saloon and Dance Hall in Watson for four years. I was called a dance partner, to make it sound more acceptable to the church ladies. It really didn't matter what they called it. Everyone knew I was a whore. More than two years ago, two of our regular customers, Jimmy Parsons and Mark Tinker offered to buy us from Dilly. They built this ranch and were raising horses. They were doing pretty well and wanted to have women on the ranch for more than what they were paying us for when they came to town.

"He got a good price, but never even told us what it was. Mark Tinker wanted me, and Jimmy Parsons bought Sharon Adair. The name that Dilly gave her was Elena Cortez, by the way. She was much darker than I was, and Dilly liked his whores to sound classy. After we were brought to the ranch, we did what was expected of us and Sharon and I had the benefit of not having to perform so often. Granted, we had to work around the house and didn't get paid, but we really had no choice. They didn't treat us any better or worse than most of our customers, so we just went through each day as most people do."

Rena let out a long breath before continuing.

"Then things began to change when late in the summer when Sharon discovered she was pregnant. She didn't know which of them had fathered the child as they shared our favors, but that didn't worry her. What frightened her was that she thought that once Jimmy realized she was pregnant he might just bring her back to Watson and find another girl. She asked me to help her avoid that problem because she knew that I'd been in a similar position before I started working there. I told her I could never do that to another woman. It's not for religious reasons or anything like that. It's just that I knew that if I tried, I'd more than likely kill her.

"Her belly grew as the snows got deeper and even though Jimmy didn't threaten to take her back into town, he did tell her that when the kid was born, he'd just leave it outside. When she told me what he'd said, I thought I'd be sick. As you can imagine, she felt much worse. I was expected to be the midwife, which I'd done before, so we began to come up with a way to save the baby. Even as we made our plans, we knew it was almost hopeless.

"It was the middle of February when there was a break in the weather that Sharon decided to make her escape to save her baby. One night she just disappeared. I never knew where she went or how far she'd gone, but I never saw her again. Even after the ground cleared, I never saw another sign of Sharon. I tell myself that she made it safely to Watson and had her baby, but it's just a silly notion.

"After she was gone, Jimmy and Mark began to get into fights over me. Mark would tell him to go to Watson and buy another girl, but Jimmy wouldn't hear of it. It wasn't about money, either. Almost from the day we arrived, I knew that Jimmy was jealous of his partner. Mark told me once that he had to outbid his friend so he could have his choice. I'll admit that I was the prettiest of the working girls and had more skill than most. What was odd was that Mark didn't seem to be jealous when Jimmy bedded me. After Sharon was gone, Jimmy took me even more often than Mark did, so why there was an argument at all seemed strange to me."

Tabby wasn't about to argue the bizarre nature of her entire story, but she still hadn't explained how the outlaw gang had managed to make the ranch their hideout.

Rena didn't pause for very long before she continued her monologue.

"It came to a head in late May when Jimmy and Mark had a nasty fistfight in the barn. Mark had given me their guns and knives before they left the house, which surprised me because they normally didn't let us near their weapons. I heard the loud sounds of the fight, but I wasn't sure who would emerge from the barn. To be honest, I hoped that they'd kill each other. But Mark staggered out after ten minutes of brutal, unrestricted brawling. Before he reached the house, Jimmy left the barn and I expected Mark to take his pistol and shoot Jimmy, but that didn't happen. They weren't friends, but I thought that they'd work together. It must have been worse than I thought because Mark even though he didn't take his pistol to shoot Jimmy, Mark picked up his rifle, ordered Jimmy to leave and kept it pointed at him while he packed his things.

"I don't know how they split up their money or other things, but by nightfall, Jimmy was gone. He led a heavily loaded packhorse when he left. For a couple of days, Mark thought he'd return, but when he didn't, we settled back into a routine. It was harder taking care of the herd of horses alone and he said that he'd start looking for someone to replace Jimmy but never got around to it."

"Why not?" Tabby asked quietly, finally interrupting her long story.

"Because when Jimmy did return in August, he wasn't alone. He had five men with him and all of them seemed to be much worse than Jimmy."

"It was that gang who held up the bank; wasn't it?"

She nodded then took a swallow of her cold coffee before answering.

"They showed up late one afternoon while Mark was out in the corral breaking a mare. By the time he spotted them, it was too late. I don't know which of them shot him, but he was dead by the time I left the house and saw them walking their horses in my direction."

"What happened to all of the horses?"

"Jimmy let them each pick a better horse than the ones they were riding, and that's when O'Hara chose the gelding that looked like your horse. He and Larry Brown drove them into Watson and sold the lot to Tom Henderson. He owns the biggest livery in town. I became their new distraction as well as their housekeeper. I thought Mark and Jimmy were slovenly, but this bunch were worse than pigs, and not just in their lack of cleanliness. They were planning to rob the bank in Watson and then come back here. They talked about it in front of me as if I wasn't there. It wasn't until I heard their boss, Cash Locklear, tell Jimmy that they'd be moving closer to Helena soon that I understood the danger I was in. It wasn't because they didn't know I was listening; it was because they didn't care. Either they were going to abandon me here without a horse or they were going to bury me next to Mark."

"I don't reckon that they'd let you live, ma'am. You could walk to Watson even if you didn't want to go back there."

"I know. I still didn't want to think that I had no chance to live much longer."

Tabby leaned back in his chair before he asked, "When we leave in the morning, which way do you want to go? We can head to Bannack or to Virginia City."

Rena was surprised and relieved by his question, but replied, "I can't go to Virginia City. That's where I lived for a few years."

"Is Bannack okay?"

"It's really the only direction we can go; isn't it?"

"I reckon so, ma'am. Oh. Sorry for slipping into using ma'am again, Rena. It's just that I'm not used to carrying on long talks with ladies."

"I'm hardly a lady, Tabby. So, you'll take me out of here tomorrow?"

"Yes, ma'am. But let me ask you about something else that just popped into my head. You said that this gang was planning to abandon the ranch and head to Helena. What if they do that?

Do you want to come back here? I mean, it's your ranch now; isn't it?"

She snapped, *"Why would it be my ranch?* I was just a damned whore who wasn't even getting paid. This is a man's world, Mister Hayes, in case you haven't noticed. I learned years ago that the only thing that made me valuable to men is what I have between my thighs. I should never have left Minnesota, but it wasn't up to me. First it was my father's decision to keep me from leaving home, then my uncle pushed me out of my father's house. Another man brought me here and left me with a baby growing in my belly. I have nothing now. I've never even been married because no man thought it was necessary to get what he wanted."

As soon as she spat out her last word, she stood and grabbed the empty plates then stomped to the sink.

Tabby sat at the table looking at the back of her head and had no idea what to say. It wasn't as if she was a troublesome cow that needed to be returned to her calf.

Rena pumped water into the sink while Tabby finally picked up his cup and walked to the stove to fill it with warm coffee. He took a sip and then leaned on the cooler edge of the iron cookstove.

"I'm sorry, Rena. I just did a bad job of saying what I meant. I heard that if a woman stays with a man for a while, then she becomes what they call a common law wife and she can inherit what he leaves behind if he dies."

"That may be true, Tabby, but it doesn't mean much; does it? Do you believe I can waltz into the county courthouse and tell them that I lived with Mark Tinker and that they'd just smile and hand me the deed?"

"I reckon not, ma'am. I'm sorry I brought it up."

She sighed then turned and said, "It wasn't your fault and I suppose if I wanted to ensure that you'd help me, I should have smiled or shed a few tears rather than behaving as I did."

Tabby smiled as he replied, "I don't reckon it mattered a whole lot. I probably would have been more afraid if you started crying anyway."

"Thank you for not getting angry. I need to start packing my things for tomorrow. Feel free to take anything. There aren't any guns except the empty shotgun, but they have a lot of clothes. Just avoid the ones in the big basket on the back porch. You're not a big man, so you should be able to add quite a collection."

"That's alright, Rena. I'd rather not."

She set the dishes into the drying rack on the counter as she said, "I only have two what you might call housewife dresses, and one is a much-altered dress from my days at Dilly's. I have three others that I never got around to fixing, but I'll bring them along. You might find them interesting."

"I imagine that I would, ma'am."

"I don't have any of my makeup, so you wouldn't get the full effect. I used to be quite an attraction at Dilly's."

"I don't think you need any makeup, Rena. You're a very pretty woman. Why don't you start packing and I'll go check on the buckboard? I don't know if my horse has ever been in harness, but it shouldn't be too hard for him because he won't be in a team."

"Okay. I'll light some more lamps before I begin to pack."

Tabby nodded then stood, picked up his hat and smiled at her before walking across the kitchen and exiting the back door as he pulled his black Stetson onto his head. He hadn't taken the Winchester with him because he didn't believe it was necessary. He had discounted the possibility that Rena would use the rifle to shoot him in the back then take Philly and make her own escape.

As hard-hearted as he thought her to be when he first met her, he was now trusting her with his life. Even if she didn't shoot him in the back, he was convinced that by taking her away from the ranch, he would be facing the likelihood of men trying to put bullets into all sorts of places on his carcass. And these men would be much better shots than those men in Watson's main street.

Before he looked for the buckboard, he entered the dark barn and had to light three matches to find the harness. It wasn't in

49

the best of condition, but is should be good enough to at least get them to the road.

He carried it out of the barn and soon discovered that the buckboard was in better condition than the harness. He tossed the tired leather onto the short bed then walked to the front, lifted the pulling poles and began to walk it out of its parking spot. It squeaked from the right rear wheel, but not too badly. Normally, he would have greased it, but he couldn't find a grease bucket hanging under the chassis, so he continued to tow it away hoping the squealing would lessen.

By the time he had rolled it all the way to the front of the barn, the noisy wheel had stopped complaining. He knew it still would need greasing, but in the morning, if he found the grease can in the barn, he'd just toss it in back and take care of all four wheels when he had the chance.

While Tabby had been evaluating the buckboard, Rena had been in her room which she shared with Mark while he was alive, then with each of the six outlaws after they arrived. Not even Cash Locklear had spent more than his allotted time in her bed.

She had four empty burlap sacks to serve as her travel bags and began stuffing her clothes into each one tightly. She wanted to save at least one bag for some of the pantry's stock. After her drawers were empty, she took the half-full bag, left her room then trotted into the room used by the boss and Max Johnson, his trusted lieutenant.

There were two chests in the room, but she ignored them both and hurried to the bed and dropped to her knees before lying flat on the floor and reaching under the dark space. After a few seconds of searching with her right hand, she pulled out a set of saddlebags, then sat on the bed and began to pull her clothes out of the burlap sack.

When it was empty, she slid the saddlebags into the bag then began stuffing her clothes back inside. Rena then quickly returned to her room, tossed the last empty sack over her shoulder, picked up the three full bags and walked back to the kitchen.

After she set the heavy bags in the corner, she took the last bag to the pantry and began adding tins of food and two tin plates, cups and some cutlery. She assumed that Tabby had the rest.

Satisfied that she was ready, she walked to the cookstove and touched the side of the coffeepot. It was still warm, so she filled a cup and took a seat at the table to wait for Tabby to return.

She was sipping her coffee and wondering what kind of man he really was. She had met all sorts of men over the course of her life, but Tabby seemed different from all of them. What made him different wasn't clear to her, but he was definitely different, and it wasn't just his unusual nickname.

Tabby left the buckboard then headed for the back of the house. He planned on getting Philly into the harness during the predawn and setting out by the time the sun arrived. The problem was the canyon walls that blocked out the morning sun. He didn't have a pocket watch, but his years of working cattle instilled the habit of waking very early each morning. He just hoped that tomorrow wouldn't be any different. What made that possibility more probable was Rena. He wouldn't mind spending the night with her and after their talk, he suspected that she might make the offer. But as much as he would have normally jumped at the chance, he couldn't risk the impact it would have on his built-in alarm clock.

Even if they spent a purely chaste night in the same bed, which would be remote if they were that close, he wouldn't be able to sleep. He had never spent all night with a woman and was certain that it would keep at least his mind occupied until the hours available for sleep were gone.

As he neared the house, he began to consider just staying awake all night, but he needed to be sharp tomorrow. She may not believe that the gang would return until tomorrow evening at the earliest, but he couldn't afford to take the chance that they might suddenly arrive at the canyon's mouth.

When he entered the kitchen, he found Rena at the table sipping her coffee and a pile of burlap sacks in the corner.

She smiled at him when he entered and asked, "How is the buckboard?"

"It's okay," he replied as he removed his hat and set it on the table.

He filled another cup with the last of the coffee before taking a seat at the table.

"Is that all that you'll be taking?"

"Yes. I packed some food, too."

"I want to get an early start in the morning, so as soon as I wake up, I'll go outside and harness Philly and then bring the buckboard around."

"I can make breakfast while you're doing that. Have you figured out where we'll be going?"

"There isn't really anyplace we can go besides Bannack. We can talk more on the ride out of here."

"Okay. Thank you for doing this. I know what a burden it's placing on you. I owe you more than you'll ever know."

"That's okay, Rena. Once we're on the road, I think we'll be safe."

"That's only part of the reason I'm so grateful. It's not just the danger that Cash and his men pose, it's a chance to make my life better."

To Tabby, it sounded as if she expected him to keep her with him after they reached Bannack. The idea had been churning in the back of his mind ever since he'd agreed to take her with him, and it made him uncomfortable. He was just a cowhand and had been set in that life for years. He enjoyed his time with women and that time had been his biggest expense, but he never even thought about a more permanent arrangement. He had been quite content with his life that held no real responsibilities.

He still smiled and said, "I'm glad I could help, ma'am."

She set her coffee cup down then asked, "You are joining me in my bed; aren't you?"

Even though he had been expecting the offer, the blunt nature of her question took him aback, so he didn't answer right away.

After ten seconds of silence, Rena laughed then said, "Don't tell me that you're going to act like the noble gentleman, pretend that you're surprised and then say that you won't take advantage of an innocent woman? That would be almost insulting, and you would disappoint me."

"No. I won't pretend to be some preacher because I'm just like all those other men who visited you. I just think it's a bad idea. I need to get up early and if I spend time with you, then I'll probably sleep too late. That's all."

"Are you sure? I really wouldn't think any less of you if you joined me."

"I reckon that's so, but I'm not just giving you an excuse."

"Well, if you insist. But I'm not going to start shedding tears to get you to hold me and then use my many talents to seduce you either. I'll admit that I would thoroughly enjoy spending the night with you."

Tabby's eyebrows rose as he said, "I thought you'd rather have a night off. I mean, after all those years doing what you did and even after you moved here, you still had to, you know, spend so much time in your bed. I figured you'd enjoy a peaceful night's sleep for once."

"Before I moved here, I always had a good night's sleep, but it was really a good day's sleep. I didn't have to couple with Jimmy and Mark every night, but I'll admit I've been busier since Jimmy brought his friends to the ranch. I just don't want you to look at me and feel pity or sympathy for me. When I asked you to join me, I wasn't just trying to repay you for your help. I really wanted to have you close to me, even if it was just to continue talking. I doubt if we could manage to avoid going well beyond talk, but if you're still worried about bedding me, then I can live with simple conversation."

"Maybe you could, Rena, but I wouldn't be able to sleep at all and I really need to rest. I don't want to drive the buckboard out of the canyon in the morning and bump into those outlaws."

"I told you that they won't be back until tomorrow night at the earliest. I'm sure we'd be able to sleep as late as we wanted."

"I'm probably just being too careful, but I'm just a cowhand, not some super lawman. I wouldn't stand a chance against any one of those boys. And if I'm dead, then you'll be in an even worse spot than when I found you."

Rena sighed then nodded before saying, "Alright, if you insist. I'll head to my bed, but I'll leave my door open, so if you change your mind, feel free to slide in next to me. I won't be wearing a nightdress."

It was Tabby's turn to sigh before he asked, "I'm going to find another place to get my sleep. Which bedroom is yours?"

"The one in the middle. You'll probably want to use the first one."

"Thank you, Rena," he said.

He stood then picked up his saddlebags and bedroll pack before he walked out of the kitchen leaving his hat on the table.

Once he entered the first bedroom, he closed the door, set his things on the floor near the foot of the bed then unbuckled his gunbelt and hung it over the bed's footpost. He began unbuttoning his shirt and glanced at the closed door. There wasn't any kind of lock, but despite Rena's repeated and very tempting offer, he didn't think that she'd sneak into his room. He had no reason for the belief, but it was there.

He sat on the bed and pulled off his boots before stripping his socks. He glanced at the sole of his right boot before dropping it to the floor. He needed to get the boots resoled. He left his britches on before lying on the top of the bed. It was already pretty chilly in the room and he would pull the heavy wool blanket over himself in a little while. He wasn't sure if he was an idiot for turning her down. If nothing else, he would appreciate her body's heat, but knew he would appreciate much more about her.

After Rena entered her room, she left the door open as she stripped off one of her two 'normal' dresses but did slip on her one flannel nightdress. After Tabby had turned down her offer, she knew he wouldn't change his mind and she was already covered in goosebumps from the cool air.

She slid beneath her two blankets and pulled them up to her chin while she thought about what she would have to do in the morning. Maybe it was better that he hadn't spent the night with her, and it wasn't because she was worried that Cash and his five bastards would be arriving early. She had found him to be more than just different and didn't want to get too close to Tabby knowing what was going to happen when they left the canyon tomorrow.

———

Cash and those five bastards who Rena believed were still closer to Virginia City than Watson, were sitting around a campfire less than ten miles east of the canyon. The well-planned stagecoach heist had turned into a series of small disasters courtesy of a wayward .44.

The plan had been almost perfect. The stagecoach was supposed to be carrying a strongbox with over six thousand dollars. There weren't any extra guards to keep interest at a minimum. But Cash had discovered their mild subterfuge from a talkative guard he'd befriended by buying a few rounds in Bannack five days before the stage was scheduled to depart.

That gave him enough time to design the almost fool-proof strategy for stealing the strongbox. They were familiar with the area around Virginia City and Cash had quickly selected the site for the ambush. It was about eight miles south of Virginia City and provided them with much more than cover for them and their horses.

After killing the driver and shotgun rider, they'd kill whatever passengers were inside, then leaving the bodies in the coach, they'd drive it about eight hundred yards off the road where it couldn't be seen by any traffic. They'd quickly strip the coach and unhitch the harnessed team. The timing of the robbery was important as it was scheduled to arrive in Virginia City late in the evening. By the time they noticed it was long overdue, they wouldn't be able to send out a posse.

They'd trail the team behind their own nine horses to make a heavy trail on the dark and presumably empty road. One by one, the gang members would peel off from the heavy parade until only one led the team of six horses from the coach another mile or so down the road. He'd send the team on its way and join the others at a location they would choose on the way to setting up for the robbery.

The stagecoach team may not keep going along the road for very long, but it didn't matter much. After they broke open the strongbox and emptied its contents into their saddlebags, they'd continue to go deeper into the wild country and then after one night's cold camp, they'd continue riding through the rugged landscape until they reached their canyon.

Cash had already told them that after this job, they'd return to the ranch and pack up their gear to move closer to Helena where there was more money ripe for the picking.

It was so perfect that none of them could see how it could go wrong. It didn't go horribly wrong, but it surely didn't work as well as Cash had expected.

When they'd spotted the oncoming stage, Jack Epperson was supposed to shoot the driver and Harry Brown's job was to plug the shotgun driver while Jimmy Parsons and Snake O'Hara eliminated the passengers. The boss and Max Johnson would cover their backs before they pulled the lifeless coach from the roadway.

Jack did his job and sent his .44 into the driver's chest but Harry's shot from less than forty yards had buzzed past the shotgun rider and slammed into the driver's chest at the almost at the same instant that Jack's bullet arrived. Either of them would have been fatal, but that left a very alive shotgun rider.

As Jack and Harry were cycling their Winchesters' levers to make a second shot that neither had thought would be necessary, the shotgun rider cocked both hammers to the scattergun. Even as the coach began to rock and twist when the driver slumped over and released the team's reins, he yanked the shotgun's trigger sending dozens of lead pellets at the two riders.

Harry took two of them which made him miss his second shot much more badly than he'd missed his first, but Jack's second .44 found the shotgun rider in the right side of his neck, ripping though his carotid artery before pulverizing his fourth cervical vertebra. His head began bouncing back and forth as blood spurted from the open artery.

Harry had screamed when he felt the shotgun pellets slam into his right side, but there was so much noise that no one noticed that he'd been hit.

Jimmy and Snake did their job and emptied their Colts into the coach's cabin, killing the three passengers. One was an elderly woman, but it didn't matter to either of them. They would leave no one to identify them but were wrong in their belief that there no witnesses.

Less than a mile north of the robbery, John McInnis was returning to his small ranch another six miles past the ambush site. He was driving a buckboard with his twelve-year-old son, Coby, after doing some shopping in town. One of his purchases was a new Winchester carbine for his firstborn.

He and Coby had spotted the stagecoach heading their way and were stunned when they witnessed the sudden attack. John pulled the buckboard to a stop and pulled his own Winchester from the scabbard on the side of the driver's seat. Coby's new carbine had never left his grip since leaving Homer Richfield's gun shop, but it was empty. Not that it made any difference to his father who had no intention of going anywhere near that robbery.

When he began to turn the buckboard around, Coby exclaimed, "Pa, we gotta help!"

John didn't even look at his son when he loudly replied, "We can't help those folks, Coby. We need to get back to town and tell the sheriff. I need you to look at those robbers with your young eyes and tell me all you can see before we're too far away."

Coby may have been disappointed for being unable to shoot outlaws with his bullet-less Winchester but did as his father had asked. At that distance, all he was able to do was count their number but could still make out the colors of their horses. He also noticed that one of them had two white stockings on its forelegs.

He told his father what he could see as the buckboard finished the turn and began racing back to Virginia City without being spotted by any of the outlaws as they were concentrating on the stagecoach.

As soon as Coby finished talking, John said, "It sounds like that gang that killed half that posse from Watson last month. I reckon that Sheriff Wolfson won't be chasing after them with less than twenty men."

"Can we go with him, Pa?" Coby asked excitedly.

"We're gonna have a bad enough time explaining to your mother why we're so late. I'm not about to have to tell her that we joined a posse with our buckboard."

Coby snickered but still wished he could have put his new repeater to good use.

————

Before they moved the stagecoach off the road Cash and the others finally noticed that Harry had been hit. Neither wound was that serious, but his right arm wasn't working at all and he was still bleeding.

Cash had Jack tend to Harry's wounds as they led the stage from the road and after five minutes they dismounted. Cash and Max opened the boot and unloaded the passengers' luggage before removing the strongbox. Jimmy and Snake were inside the cabin going through the passengers' pockets and the bags they carried with them.

Jack had wrapped Harry's wounds in bandages made from the contents of one of the travel bags before he began to unharness the team while Harry just sat on a rock watching.

Cash had brought a hand sledge to open the strongbox and with one long arcing blow, shattered the hasp's lock. Max was standing beside him watching eagerly as Cash lifted the cover and was still grinning when the boss began lifting bundles of cash from the strongbox.

"Damn! These are all singles and five-dollar notes!" he exclaimed as he pulled the last stack from the box.

Max lost his grin as he asked, "How much do you reckon is in there?"

"Not more'n six hundred or thereabouts. It's okay, but sure ain't the big killing we expected."

He grunted then kicked the empty strongbox before carrying the bundles of bills to his horse and dropping them into his saddlebags.

They still followed the original plan, but the disappointment of the less spectacular haul hung over them as they rode south leading the stagecoach team. They thought they had plenty of time before anyone even began to worry about the delay in the stagecoach's arrival, but even as they took the road, the enormous posse was being formed in Virginia City. Their salvation was only due to the late hour of the day.

They had barely reached the spot where they had agreed to meet after releasing the team when they were stunned as they heard the pounding hooves of a large posse pass by on the road just a couple of hundred yards away in the waning light.

Between the posse's surprising early appearance and Harry's wound, Cash decided that they couldn't afford to wait, so they rode across the rough terrain by the light of the moon heading for the ranch.

What they hadn't realized that as large as the posse was that had passed by, half of it was back where they had driven the stagecoach off the road. After discovering the carnage left by the outlaws, Deputy Sheriff Trudeau had sent two men back to Virginia City for supplies and a packhorse while the others followed the outlaw's trail but had to stop when they lost their light. They may not have been able to continue to track the outlaws, but the deputy sent the rest of the men with him back to Virginia City. He told one of them to let the sheriff know that he would stay put until he was joined by a fresh posse in the morning. He expected it to be much smaller, but hopefully a lot smarter than the one from Watson that had been chewed to pieces by the same outlaw gang who had just killed all of the folks on the stage.

By the time it was well after midnight, Cash had everyone dismount and they set up the cold camp. None of them was sure how far away the ranch was, but the horses were too tired and even the five men who hadn't been shot were ready to fall from their saddles. They didn't realize that just six miles back, a lone deputy sheriff lay on his bedroll waiting for reinforcements.

Within thirty minutes of stepping to the ground, the men were in their bedrolls.

TABBY HAYES

Tabby was having a much more difficult time falling asleep, which annoyed him. He was beyond tired after the long and trying day. It wasn't just knowing that Rena was sleeping next door that kept him awake. It was his overwhelming worries about the whirlwind that suddenly had engulfed him.

When he had started the day, his only concern had been finding another job. Now he had to avoid having six killers or a posse chasing after him and he had to do it while driving a buckboard with a woman. It was as if a mischievous God was tossing one problem after another at him and giggling when the poor human squirmed. He changed the perpetrator to the devil after a moment's thought rather than tempt fate.

But beyond those worries was another thread of thought. Rena's temptation aside, he'd found that he'd enjoyed just talking to her. His experience with women since he'd been on his own had been limited to hour-long stints that were spent mostly in the woman's bed after paying for her services. Yet when he'd talked to Rena, he found listening to her to be a revealing experience, and not just about her. He didn't want to admit it, but he finally realized what had really made him decline her offer. He didn't want her to see him as just another customer and he didn't want to treat her as one of those women he'd paid to spend time with him.

By the time he drifted into a troubled sleep, there were only four hours before the predawn began lightening the sky.

CHAPTER 2

Even though he only had a few hours of rest, Tabby still awakened early, but not with the predawn. Twenty minutes before he opened his eyes, the sun had risen but none of its direct rays made it to the ranch house.

He quickly rose, pulled on some clean socks, yanked his boots on then donned his shirt. He was soon dressed, complete with his gunbelt and hat before he walked out of the room and into the kitchen. He wasn't being quiet as he hoped his loud footsteps would wake Rena.

He was just going to wash his face before leaving the house but took a few minutes to start a fire in the cookstove. Five minutes later, he was leaving the house but still hadn't heard Rena stirring.

When he stepped outside, he swore when he realized that it was well after sunrise, but quickly headed for the barn.

After he'd slammed the kitchen door behind him, Rena's eyes popped open before she quickly slid out of bed. She began to make the bed out of habit before laughing and leaving it unkempt. She hurriedly changed into the same dress she'd worn yesterday and before Tabby had finished putting Philly in the buckboard's harness, she had exited the door and trotted to the privy.

As she jogged along, she spotted Tabby in front of the barn, but he wasn't looking her way, so she just kept going.

Tabby had found a bucket of grease and was going to hang it beneath the buckboard but when he peered beneath the bed, he didn't see a jack, so there was no reason to take the grease anyway. But when he was in the barn, he did find a double-bladed axe and a spade that he thought might be handy to have along. He carried them out to the buckboard and laid them on the bed. They wouldn't take up that much room anyway. He then stored his tack on the buckboard which still left plenty of room for Rena's four bags and anything else she might add that was within reason.

Rena had returned to the house while Tabby was in the barn. Before he returned, she washed and then filled the coffeepot. She was about to put the skillet on the hotplate when she looked across the room and spotted his Winchester leaning against the wall.

She took four steps to the open doorway and took a peek at the barn before quickly walking to his repeater and moving it to the space between the cookstove and the sink. It was only noticeable from a very narrow angle. If Tabby searched and found it before they left, she'd tell him that she had to move it because she was worried about knocking it over and having it go off. She knew that wouldn't happen, but she thought that because she was a woman, he'd expect her to be ignorant about guns. She may not be a seasoned shooter, but after spending so much time with men and listening to them brag about their prowess with their weapons, both natural and manufactured, she understood how they worked.

Tabby climbed into the driver's seat and snapped the reins. He could have just led Philly to the back of the house, but he wanted to see how he behaved when pulling the rig.

Philly may never have been in harness before, but he didn't have any problems as he quickly towed the buckboard to the back of the house.

He pulled the handbrake then clambered down before walking to the back door.

Rena heard him enter and smiled at him as she flipped the strips of bacon.

"Do we have time for breakfast?" she asked.

"Yes, ma'am. I'll load your bags onto the buckboard while you cook. Do you have anything else you need to load?"

"No, just what's in the bags. You'll find the food bag to be a bit heavy."

He nodded, then hefted two of the bags and found them both fairly light which meant they only had her clothes. He carried them outside and set them on the buckboard's bed before returning for the heavier ones.

Rena watched him make the trips and even as she set the cooked strips of bacon on their plates, she thought about changing her mind. He really hadn't done anything to deserve what she was planning to do, but she was operating under the mistaken belief that he would only be in danger if he was with her. She was convinced that once she was gone, Tabby would be angry, but he wouldn't have to face Cash and his five bastards. So, she left his Winchester where it was.

Tabby returned to the kitchen then smiled at Rena before walking to the room he'd used last night. He hung his saddlebags over his shoulder, picked up his bedroll bundle then grabbed her empty shotgun before leaving the room.

Rena smiled again and asked, "You aren't taking any of their clothes?"

"No, ma'am. I have enough to keep me warm."

He quickly stepped outside and loaded his things beside her burlap bags before returning to the house.

As soon as he entered, Rena asked, "Are scrambled eggs okay?"

"That's fine, Rena. It's quicker, too."

She nodded as she began cracking eggs and dropping them into the popping and spitting bacon grease.

———

As they were preparing to leave the ranch, the tired and unhappy outlaw band was heading their way. They'd awakened even earlier than Tabby had and by the time he was putting Philly in harness, they were already two miles from the site of their cold camp.

They were riding as quickly as the rough terrain allowed and Harry wasn't doing well even after Jack had removed the two pellets. He hadn't lost that much blood, so Cash was more irritated with him than sympathetic.

"How far out are we, do you reckon?" Max asked the boss.

"I'd guess about another hour or two," Cash answered loudly.

"I'm sure gettin' hungry," Jimmy complained.

Cash just glared at him. This job had put him into a sour mood and as his horse headed west, he was already planning on spending just a day at the ranch before they pulled up stakes and headed for Helena. He hadn't even given one thought of what they would do about Rena because it wasn't necessary. Each of them, including Jimmy, knew that they couldn't take her with them and couldn't leave her behind, either.

———

70

After polishing off their breakfast, Rena simply dumped the dirty plates into the sink as Tabby finished his third cup of coffee.

She was standing in front of the gap between the sink and the cookstove when he stood.

"I guess we'd better hurry," she said, "It's funny. I know that they won't be returning until much later, but I feel as if they're almost here already."

Tabby grinned before saying, "I've been that way since you told me that they were staying here. Let's get out of here, Rena."

She smiled and took his hand as they exited the kitchen without closing the door. She was already feeling guilty before they even reached the buckboard, but still climbed into the driver's seat as Tabby took the reins. He released the handbrake, snapped the leather straps and Philly stepped away.

As the buckboard passed the front of the house, Rena sharply asked, "Where's your rifle?"

Tabby yanked back on the reins before quickly checking the bed and then snapped, "I can't believe I forgot my Winchester."

He handed her the reins and said, "I'll be right back."

She watched him climb down then as soon as he entered the front door, she quietly popped the reins and Philly set off at a medium trot. She glanced back then pulled his saddlebags from the bed and dropped them to the ground before snapping the reins again making Philly pick up his pace.

Rena already had the buckboard two hundred yards away from the house when Tabby reached the kitchen and found an empty wall where he'd left his Winchester. He was confused by its absence and began to walk around the kitchen expecting to find it lying on the floor. It took him almost thirty seconds before he spotted it leaning against the wall in its semi-hidden location.

"Son of a bitch!" he exclaimed as he snatched his repeater then turned and raced back down the hallway.

When he shot out of the front doorway, he spotted the buckboard four hundred yards away and moving quickly.

He didn't swear again but took off at a dead run to try to catch her. He knew that he didn't have a prayer and could lob a few .44s in her direction to try to get her to stop but knew it would probably just make her drive even faster.

Rena didn't look behind her as she was sure that Tabby was running in pursuit and she knew if she saw him, she'd probably turn around and that would be bad for both of them.

Tabby only glanced at his saddlebags lying on the ground as he shot past and was already breathing heavily.

Rena was almost at the mouth of the canyon where the shadows gave way to the brilliant light of the morning sun. She brought Philly to a walk because there was no longer any reason to tire him.

Tabby had slowed to a jog but hadn't given up the chase yet. Even his volcanic anger was surpassed by his embarrassment of being so easily fooled. *What could he expect from a woman who'd lived that kind of life?* She only cared about herself. She probably made up that whole story about her life and was probably just the gang leader's girlfriend. The only argument he had against his new theory was that she'd left him his Winchester and dropped his saddlebags on the ground. All she had that belonged to him was Philly and his saddle.

But having his horse also meant that he was in bad shape, especially if that gang showed up. He was feeling the stab of pains on his sides as his legs began to stiffen, so he finally slowed to a walk and bent at the waist as he sucked in oxygen. He was done.

Rena drove the buckboard into the bright sun and turned east to follow the trail. If the trail had pointed directly into the path of the rising sun, she probably wouldn't have spotted the specks in the distance. But the bright sun was a few degrees to her left and she was able to see the six riders. The moment she saw them, she pulled on the right rein and Philly responded by beginning the U-turn to head back to the canyon.

When she turned the buckboard, it was just one of those quirks of timing that none of the six riders noticed her. Jimmy and Snake were talking about horses, Harry had his head down and Jack was watching him to make sure he didn't fall from the saddle. Max and Cash were arguing about how long they'd stay at the ranch.

Tabby still had his head down as he waited for his body to recover from the sprint, so he didn't see Rena drive the buckboard back into the canyon at a high rate of speed.

It was only when she was two hundred yards away that he heard the squeaking from that right rear wheel that still needed grease when he looked up and saw the buckboard heading for him.

He wasn't about to open fire with his Winchester, but slowly turned and began walking back to where his saddlebags lay on the ground. If she wanted to run him down, so be it. Why she was returning didn't even occur to him because he was so angry and still embarrassed.

Rena was surprised that he'd begun to walk away from her rather than toward her with at least his fist shaking at her. If he'd started sending some bullets in her direction, she'd understand.

He had almost reached his saddlebags when Rena pulled the buckboard to a stop fifty feet behind him. She stayed in the driver's seat and watched him grab his saddlebags from the ground, hang them over his shoulder then begin marching to the buckboard.

Without saying a word, he set his saddlebags where they had been before then slid his Winchester on top before climbing into the driver's seat and taking the reins from her hands.

He was seething as he snapped the reins and had Philly turn the buckboard around to head for the canyon's entrance.

After Rena hadn't said a word for twenty seconds, he looked at her and growled, "I should just push you off that seat and let you go back to your ranch."

"But you won't; will you?" she asked quietly.

"No, and I can't figure out why either."

She looked at him and quickly said, "They're coming. I saw them riding from the east."

"*What?*" he exclaimed, "*Why the hell didn't you tell me when I got on board?*"

"Because it doesn't matter now. They're going to be here soon and we'll both be killed."

"The hell you say! How far away were they?" he asked sharply as he popped the reins again to get Philly moving faster.

"I don't know. They were just specks, but we can't make it to where the trail turns north before they get here."

Tabby didn't answer as he tried to recall the landscape when he had found the canyon. He wasn't sure, but he remembered that when he was looking for the ranch house before he spotted the canyon, he had a decent view for almost a mile to the west. It was far from a trail, but he didn't need much. He just wanted to get far enough away to make it more difficult for them to get close.

The mouth of the canyon was getting close when he asked, "Do you know anything about the land heading west after the end of the canyon?"

"No. You aren't going to go that way; are you?"

"Do you have a better idea, ma'am?" he asked sharply.

She didn't reply but looked at the left edge of the canyon mouth almost expecting to see Cash and his band of bastards appear.

When they emerged into the bright sunlight, Tabby pulled back on the reins and looked to the east first. He spotted the riders who were about a mile away now and he knew that she was right that they'd never make it to the trail's northern turn. He was thinking about returning to the canyon and going past the house to the back of the canyon and wait for them, but he didn't like the idea of having only one way out.

He looked in the other direction and his eyes had barely reported what they saw to the west before he had the buckboard rolling in that direction. It was pretty much as he remembered. It was rough ground, but he thought they could drive at least a mile. After that, he had no idea of what to expect. He just had no other option.

————

When the buckboard emerged from the canyon for the second time, it was immediately spotted by four of the six riders.

"Who the hell is that?" shouted Max.

"It's Monique, but who is that feller with her?" Cash replied loudly.

"What do we do, boss?" Max asked.

"They can't go anywhere in that direction, so let's just keep goin' and figure it out as we go."

"I don't like this at all, Cash."

"After that worthless stage job, I don't like a damned thing."

They continued riding at a medium trot while watching the buckboard roll away into the rugged landscape to the west of the canyon.

————

Rena had been watching the riders as Tabby maneuvered the buckboard around the boulders, trees and other obstacles. He felt betrayed, embarrassed and naïve, and all of them were wrapped in intense anger. He didn't think of talking as his mind was a tornado of riotous arguments over what she had done and the horrible situation in which he now found himself.

After he followed the only path toward the southwest, he knew that the horrible situation had just gotten even worse. There was about another two hundred yards of reasonably clear ground, but the terrain after that was impassable for the buckboard.

He glanced behind him and spotted the riders who hadn't closed the gap between them. He didn't know why they hadn't raced after them, but it didn't matter. The only way out with the buckboard was back to the east.

Tabby kept the buckboard rolling toward the edge of a drop off that wasn't quite a ridge. There were trees on the left that would hide them from the outlaws, but that would put them into a natural pocket.

He was still fuming when the buckboard's left front wheel lifted onto a large flat rock. Tabby pulled the reins and just hopped down without bothering with the handbrake.

Rena had been staring backwards at the six riders and had kept her mind busy wondering what they would do. When the trees suddenly blocked her view, she whipped her head to the front and realized that they were trapped. She then looked at Tabby and was about to try to explain why she'd left him when the front of the buckboard rocked upward, and she had to grab the handrail to keep from being thrown to the ground. She didn't get a chance to say anything before Tabby hopped down from the driver's seat.

She stepped down from the buckboard and as she walked to the front where Tabby was going, she looked across the horse's back and asked, "Will you let me explain why I tried to run away?"

Tabby began to quickly unharness Philly when he angrily replied, "You don't need to make up some weak excuse, ma'am. You ran away because I gave you a horse. It's that simple. You left me there to deal with your friends and only came back because you needed my guns."

Rena looked across Philly's back as she exclaimed, "That's not true! I'll admit I came back because I was afraid, but that's not why I left you at the ranch."

Tabby had unharnessed Philly and led him around his side of the buckboard as Rena trotted down the other side.

When he reached the bed, he began removing his tack from the buckboard while Rena just stood with her arms folded and watched as he began to saddle his Morgan. She didn't blame him for leaving, but she wished that he would at least listen to her. He probably wouldn't believe her and think she was just trying to keep him here, but she didn't want him to leave still thinking badly of her. It was unusual for her as she hadn't cared what any man had thought of her since her father's death.

Tabby didn't even glance at her as he furiously added cloth and leather to his horse. It was when he was tightening the cinch that Rena finally spoke.

"Will you leave me a pistol?" she asked quietly as he lifted his saddlebags from the bed.

He lowered the heavy saddlebags then opened one and removed the gunbelt with his Colt Walker.

His volcanic rage had dropped to smoldering anger by the time he handed it to her and said, "You have five shots."

She looped the gunbelt around her waist and pushed it onto her hips as she waited for him to toss his saddlebags onto his horse, but he didn't.

He left them on the ground and after hanging his canteens on the saddle, he looked at the burlap bags and asked, "Which two bags do you want to bring with you?"

She gawked at him for a few seconds before asking, "What do you mean? I thought you were leaving."

"I'm not going anywhere. You can only take two bags with you and if there's time, you can move things around before I hang them over Philly."

She was still confused as she asked, "What are you saying? You're letting me take your horse?"

He finally looked at her with his angry eyes and said, "You were going to take him anyway. In case you haven't noticed, ma'am, the buckboard can't move another fifty yards from here unless it heads back to those killers. You can ride northwest and probably reach the road to Bannack in a few hours."

"You expect me to leave you here?" she exclaimed.

"Aside from the fact you were going to leave me back at the ranch, I reckon that once you're gone, I'd have a better chance of seeing another day. They might not even bother coming this way, but once you're gone, I might be able to talk my way out of this mess."

"How could you do that? They're soulless bastards who probably wouldn't give you the chance to say one word before they killed you."

"I don't matter to them, ma'am. If they don't see you, then I can tell them that I used you like they probably figured and then I just let you go. I can even pretend I want to join up with them. Once I have a horse, I can make my own escape."

"You don't think that they'll chase me down after killing you?"

Tabby snatched his Winchester from the bed then said, "Maybe. But you'll have a good head start unless you waste more time talking. But you said that they were going to move on soon anyway, so it's more likely that they'll just pull up roots now and leave. I'm going to head over there and keep an eye on

81

what they're doing after you tell me which bags you need to get loaded."

Rena glanced at the bags and then sighed before replying, "They'll chase me until doomsday and they're not going to let you talk them into anything. The moment they see that I'm gone, they'll shoot you and have to catch me."

He almost shouted as he asked, *"Why would they do that? Were you lying to me about them moving on? Just how much of what you've been telling me since I got here is the truth?"*

She glanced at the bed before she replied, "I haven't lied to you once, Tabby. They really did plan on leaving after they held up the stagecoach. It's just that, well, the reason they won't let me go is because I took Cash's saddlebag full of their money. It's in one of the burlap sacks."

"You took their loot?" he exclaimed in disbelief.

"I needed money to live on before we reached Bannack and I didn't want to take any of yours. I didn't think that they'd be back so soon. I thought I'd be gone and on the road to Bannack long before they returned."

"So, you left me on that ranch not even knowing that they would blame me for taking their money. That's even worse."

"I didn't think that way, Tabby! Really! I thought that you'd be so mad that you'd leave right away. I know you had enough money to buy another horse. That's why I dropped your saddlebags on the ground."

Tabby's anger was losing steam as he said, "You could have told me and not just run off that way. You really screwed things up now."

"I know. I felt really bad for doing it, but I thought it was better for you if you weren't seen with me. That's why I left you like I did. I thought that by the time they returned to the ranch house and found the missing money, they wouldn't even know that you'd been there. They'd hunt me down and nobody would be able to tell them you were with me. I was really thinking about you, Tabby."

He still wasn't convinced that she was being honest, but there wasn't time to talk anymore.

"I'm going to walk down to the edge of those trees to see how far out they are. If you want to come along, you can."

Before she could answer, he started to walk away at a fast pace. Rena hurried after him as she had much more to say.

As he stepped across the rocky ground, Tabby digested what she'd told him. It sounded plausible, but his residual anger didn't let him accept it as the truth. Not yet.

———

83

After having spotted the buckboard, Cash dropped back until he was riding beside Jimmy Parsons.

When he was close, he loudly asked, "Can they get out that way?"

"Nope. I was gonna tell ya that the only way out of here is using that trail. Are we gonna chase 'em down?"

"Not right now. I want to get to the ranch house and see what they took. We need to get Harry's bullet holes cleaned up, too. If we need to chase 'em down, we're not gonna go in there all willy-nilly. That's a good way to get killed."

"He's only one man, boss, and I reckon he ain't as good as we are with our Winchesters."

"It doesn't matter how good he is, Jimmy. He'd be set up and waitin' for us if we just rode in there like a bunch of targets. We need to check on our stash first and then figure out what to do about Monique and her new customer. If the money's there, then we might just let 'em go. We'll talk some more when we get to the ranch house. But once we enter the canyon, I want you to stay there and make sure they don't try to get to the trail."

"Okay, boss," Jimmy replied before Cash trotted to the front of the column to tell Max about his decision.

———

Rena still hadn't had a chance to continue her explanation before Tabby stopped when he was able to spot the distant riders.

He was staring at the six outlaws when she said, "I don't expect you to believe me, Tabby. But once you agreed to take me away from the ranch, I was so relieved that I only thought about me. The more we talked, the more I began to focus more on you. I soon realized that if you were with me, then you were in danger. I thought about just letting you go, but you wouldn't have left me after I told you how I'd gotten there; would you?"

Tabby still stared to the east as he replied, "No, I wouldn't."

"After I reached that same conclusion, I thought about just taking my bags and leaving in the night, but it was too late. I had already put their saddlebags full of money into one of my sacks and thought that the safest thing to do was what I did. It looks stupid now, but at the time, it seemed to be the only way out."

He glanced at her before saying, "You should have told me about the money before we reached the end of the canyon. I would have had you drop the saddlebags on the ground where they could find them."

"My mind was so full of worries about what would happen when we saw them that I forgot that the money was even there. You were pretty mad at me, too."

"I was and I'm still not very happy with you, ma'am. Let's just see what they're going to do now. They're approaching the canyon."

As they watched the six outlaws from a little more than a mile away, Tabby grip on his Winchester became vicelike with the thought of having to face six good shooters with his lone repeater.

Then he and Rena released a combined sigh when they saw the riders turn into the canyon and soon disappear.

"They're not coming!" Rena exclaimed.

"Not now, but I don't reckon that it'll be too long before they come out of that canyon in a bad mood. Let's get you on Philly and on your way."

He turned and began trotting back to the buckboard as Rena hurried after him but wasn't able to catch up.

Tabby figured they had less than forty minutes before the six outlaws reached them. Ten minutes to discover the missing stash, ten minutes to get ready to leave and another fifteen to reach them. Rena could be two miles away by the time they arrived. He wished he was as heartless as the men who would soon show up with their rifles, but he knew that only one of them could escape and it had to be her. He really couldn't see any other way to survive this mess. Either she left and lived, or they both died within an hour.

He stopped behind the buckboard, set his Winchester on the bed and began taking down her burlap bags when Rena arrived.

He'd just set the first pair on the ground when she picked them up and tossed them back onto the bed before saying, "I'm not leaving."

He turned and said, "You are leaving, ma'am. Even before you told me about the money, I already was planning on sending you away. It's the smart thing to do. I can't hold off those boys if they're intent on killing us both. The only difference the money makes is that it took away the chance that they'd let me talk to them, but that wasn't very likely. Even when I was ready to tan your backside, I wasn't going to let you get shot. The only choice we have now is whether one of us dies or both of us don't get to see the sun rise. If I leave, then they'd blow past you without even having to get off their horses. They'd run me down in a couple of hours."

"But not if you left the money with me. Pack your things and ride away, Tabby. It's what I should have let you do when you first showed up. I can generate some tears and convince them that it was all my idea."

"Now that's a lie, Rena, and not a very good one. I haven't seen you create a single tear even when you could have to make sure that I'd take you away with me. Besides, those bastards would just laugh before they made your days as a painted lady seem like a long vacation. You know that. I can throw enough lead at them to give you buy you at least two or three hours, maybe even until sunset. I'm not going to argue with you, ma'am. You need to leave."

"And what will I do after I reach Bannack? Even with the money, I'd still probably wind up in one of their whorehouses. Didn't you realize that?"

"I'm just a cowhand, ma'am. I'm not a gunfighter or even the kind of man a woman would want to marry because I've got no ambition to be anything else. I was going to leave you in Bannack after I was sure you were safe. I'd give you some of my money to last you a few months because that money in your bag belongs to other folks. I figured that as pretty as you are and as long as nobody knew what you did before, some decent man would ask to marry you and you'd settle down. I wasn't going to stick around town."

"I know," she said quietly, "it's just that I enjoyed talking to you last night and for a little time, I was hoping that you'd keep me with you even after Bannack. But no matter how pretty I am, it's hard for me to hide what I am, so no decent man would give me a second look. He'd hand me two dollars and then after a short visit, he'd leave. Then there's the other reason he wouldn't want to marry me, even if he thought I wasn't some cheap whore."

Tabby's anger was long gone as he looked at her and waited to hear the second reason. But no matter what she told him, he was determined to get her onto Philly's back and send her away. Even being a live prostitute was better than being dead.

Rena didn't sigh or even have sad eyes when she said, "I can't have any children. After that horrible experience when that woman took my baby, she must have damaged something inside me. I've never conceived again which made me perfect for my new profession."

"I'm sorry, Rena," Tabby said quietly, "But not being able to have babies shouldn't keep you from getting married. You're a smart lady and just having you around should be enough to make some feller happy."

"I'm honest enough with myself to know that can't happen."

Tabby still had a lot of questions about her fluid explanations that still left a lot of holes, but the clock was ticking.

"We don't have time to discuss what you'll do after you're gone, Rena. You can figure out something on the way, but you have to leave now."

She glared at him as she snapped, "I'm not going anywhere! You can't force me to get onto your horse, so you'd better just accept that and start getting ready for them to show up."

As much as he'd like to argue, Tabby knew that it was just a waste of time. He thought she was committing suicide by staying, but so was he. But even as that morbid realization reached his mind, another possibility occurred to him that should have been the first one to arrive. It should have been there when he first saw the impassable ground ahead, but he'd been too angry to think logically.

89

He looked at Rena who was still glaring at him and then looked at Philly.

"We're both leaving," he said quietly.

"But you said…" she replied then turned to look at his horse.

"I feel really foolish for not thinking about this earlier, but I figure I was too mad at you to think straight. Let's load up Philly like a packhorse and lead him out of here. If they follow, then they can't go much faster than we can because that ground between here and that road is pretty rough."

Rena was surprised that she hadn't come up with the solution herself but quickly replied, "We can do it! Let's start choosing things to take with us."

She was still wearing his Colt Walker as they began making their hurried selections.

———

While Tabby and Rena were lowering their choices to the ground, the five outlaws arrived at the ranch house and four quickly dismounted. Harry was slower to step down and by the time he was standing, the others had already blasted through the front door.

Jimmy Parsons was sitting in his saddle a hundred yards into the canyon watching the west for any signs of the buckboard's return. He wasn't happy with being given the job as he believed it showed a lack of respect. He'd been the one to tell Cash about the place and then suggest the bank robbery that had gone off so well and netted them more than three thousand dollars. The fiasco with the stagecoach heist had been Harry's fault and he thought that Harry should be the one Cash assigned to this unnecessary job. It didn't matter if Harry had been shot. They were just shotgun pellets, for God's sake!

After he'd seen them enter the house, he wondered if they were going to pretend that Monique had taken the money so he wouldn't get his cut. Then he expanded on that suspicion to the point where he began to think that he had become expendable. He'd only joined the gang a few months ago and he wasn't sure that he was trusted.

So, as he sat watching for the buckboard that he was sure wasn't coming back, he grew ever more nervous about what might happen when Cash and the others returned.

Inside the house, Cash was staring at the empty floor after flipping the bed onto its side.

"That bitch stole our money!" he snarled as he absent-mindedly gripped his Colt.

Max asked, "Do you reckon that feller she was with made her tell him about it? He might be a bounty hunter and tracked us here. When he found us gone, he coulda put a gun to her head and asked her where our stash was."

91

Cash continued to look at the dusty boards as he replied, "I don't care if he was the president of the country. Even if he is a bounty hunter and threatened to cut off her head, it don't matter. She told him and now our money's gone. We need to get after them before they get away. She's probably tellin' him everything about us. It's more likely she gave him a poke just so he'd take her along. She wasn't all that happy with us and probably figured out by now that her days were numbered."

"Okay, boss," said Snake, "How are we gonna do this? Even if he ain't a bounty hunter, we can't just ride fast into that bad ground."

Cash replied, "I already told you that. Let's all head into the kitchen and we'll talk," then he turned and asked, "How bad are you, Harry?"

"It ain't so bad, but I won't be able to shoot worth a damn. I can take some shots with my left hand, but those bullets ain't gonna be goin' where they're supposed to."

"I figured that. Let's go and set somethin' up real quick," Cash said before hurrying from the room.

The others followed in line but none of them were looking forward to chasing the stranger. If they'd known that he was just a cowhand, they might have been less concerned. But knowing that he would be waiting for them hidden behind any one of the dozens of ambush sites was still a risky situation.

———

Some of the things they would leave behind were simple: the pickaxe and spade were the first. All of Tabby's things were already on Philly in their usual locations so it was now just down to what Rena thought was necessary, but even that turned out not to be very difficult. The only debate came when she pulled out the saddlebags with the gang's stolen loot.

Tabby didn't bother counting it but asked, "If we left it on the buckboard, do you think that they'd still chase us?"

Rena had already given the question considerable thought and quickly replied, "I think so. Even if Cash isn't worried that I might tell the law where they are because they were already planning on moving, I think he'll want to kill me. He'll want to make me pay for taking the money in the first place and he probably knows that I heard where they would be going."

"Alright. I think we can put all four of your bags over the saddle seat, but that means we'll both have to walk. Can you walk that well in those shoes? The heels seem a bit tall."

"I'll be all right. If it gets too bad, you can cut off the heels with your knife."

Tabby glanced at the ruts they'd left behind them then looked at the buckboard.

"Take off your shoes, Rena," he said as he stepped over to the bed and picked up the axe.

She nodded then sat on a small boulder, unlaced her shoes and pulled them off.

Tabby took the shoes and set them on the almost empty buckboard bed. He didn't care about the buckboard or the axe but needed to make accurate strikes with the heavy blade. He didn't want to make her walk barefooted but didn't think she'd be able to move as quickly as necessary if she was wearing the two-inch tall heels.

Rena watched calmly as he raised the axe and slammed it into her shoes. She wasn't as concerned as he was because she'd taken several pairs of socks from the men's drawers to keep her feet warm. If necessary, she'd don three pairs of them instead of her shoes.

Tabby wasn't leaving much to guesswork as he lined up where he wanted to cut with a gap between two of the boards on the buckboard. When he made his first cut, the heel of the right shoe was split nicely just below the sole. He set it aside and moved the left shoe into position. After he arced the axe's head though the heel, the bottom part of the heel shot across the buckboard's bed and landed on the ground before Rena's feet.

She laughed as she picked it up and held it out to Tabby who had picked up her second shoe.

He tried to avoid smiling as he gave her back her modified shoes but couldn't. Why she could even laugh at a time like this seemed incredible to him, but at the same time, her reaction had a calming influence on his mood.

She pulled her shoes on while Tabby hung her bags over Philly's saddle. He took down one of the canteens and as she stood, he handed it to her.

"You're shorter than I realized, ma'am."

She was still smiling as she unscrewed the canteen but had to stop before taking three long swallows.

When she gave it back to him, she said, "I'm still almost as tall as you. What are you about eight inches over five feet?"

"A little taller, I reckon," he replied before taking two long swallows of water then screwing the cap back in place.

He hung the canteen and looked behind them before he said, "I don't think we should waste the time to go and look at the canyon. If they're close, then they'd have us trapped anyway. Let's go."

"Alright," she replied as Tabby took Philly's reins.

They soon entered the tortured ground that had made them leave the buckboard behind. Even though it was passable for a horse, that didn't mean it was easily traversed. But that difficulty wouldn't be any easier for the men who would soon be trying to kill them.

———

"Okay, that's the best we can do," Cash said which ended the discussion.

There were unenthusiastic nods around the table before he stood and said, "Let's get movin'. We got plenty of daylight left but I want this over before noon."

The five men stood and followed Cash down the hallway. Cash had made a mistake when he believed that the stranger would be waiting with his Winchester because he'd taken to heart the idea that Tabby was a bounty hunter. It was the only thing that made sense and Cash was now convinced that the man would want to claim the price on their heads.

That assumption also led him to believe that the man not only was a good shot but might have a longer-range rifle than a standard Winchester. They may not have had a Sharps or other buffalo gun, but he and Max each had one of the newer 1876 Model Winchesters that fired the more powerful .45-75 cartridge with its longer reach. Even if that bounty hunter had a Sharps, he couldn't reload very quickly and after that first shot, they would have the advantage.

Five minutes later, they were riding away from the ranch house.

Jimmy Parsons saw them leave and still wasn't very comfortable since he'd started imagining what they'd been talking about in the ranch house. He wasn't about to race away because if he tried, he knew that he wouldn't get fifty yards before he felt their first bullet punch into his back. He'd have to play it by ear. As he watched them getting closer, he wished that he had beaten Mark that day in the barn. It had been so close and he even after he'd lost, he should have shot his partner. He'd have been able to keep Monique and now he wouldn't be in fear of being backshot.

———

Tabby and Rena had lost sight of the buckboard ten minutes earlier as they followed their tortuous path.

Neither had said much since leaving, but now that they felt reasonably safe Tabby asked, "Do you know what kind of guns they had?"

"Not really. They all had rifles like yours, but two looked different."

"How were they different?"

"I'm not sure. They were longer and had a plate on the end."

"Did they say anything about them using different ammunition than the other Winchesters?"

"Not that I recall. But I do remember Jimmy Parsons asking Cash if he could get one like the one that he had. It was like it was better and he was jealous."

"That makes sense. I reckon it was one of the new Winchesters. It shoots a more powerful cartridge than the '66 or

97

the '73 like I have. They can hit targets further out and do more damage, too."

"If they're better, then why don't you have one?"

"I'm not a gunfighter or an outlaw, ma'am. Some of the folks with money will buy them to shoot big game and buffalo if they can find them anymore. My boss at the Slant 6 bought one and I got to use it once. It was pretty nice, but I had no use for it. I only bought my cartridge Colt before I left, and it's been around for years now. I just didn't have a need for new guns."

She smiled as she said, "Because you're just a cowhand."

He returned her smile before he replied, "Yes, ma'am."

They walked for another ten yards before she startled him when she asked, "Would you marry me?"

Tabby looked at her with wide eyes and asked, "Excuse me?"

"You heard me. When you were thinking of sending me on my own to Bannack, you said that I could find a decent man who would marry me even though I couldn't give him children. Would you do that?"

Tabby blinked before replying, "Like I told you, Rena. I'm not the kind of man any woman would even think of marrying. I'm too set in my ways and I couldn't provide for her anyway even when I was working, and I'm not even working now."

"Money isn't a problem now, Tabby. You know that. So, take the providing for your wife out of the picture and answer me. Would you marry me?"

"I can't do that to you, Rena. I'm just too fond of being on my own. I'd make a terrible husband."

"So, you'd be perfectly content to wave goodbye to me in Bannack or wherever else we part, knowing that I'd soon be satisfying more strange men."

Tabby felt just as trapped as he'd been earlier when she had refused to leave on Philly but knew that there wasn't an easy answer to this problem. He honestly believed what he had just told her.

"No, I wouldn't be happy knowing that you'd go back to that life. You'd have a lot of money, Rena. You could buy a business or something. Once you're a respectable businesswoman, everything would be better."

"You're lying to yourself, Tabby. You know better than that. If I showed up in a town with a saddlebag full of cash, the telegraph wires would be buzzing in just a couple of hours and they'd find out where the money came from. They'd know who and what I was, and I'd be in an even worse position than I was at Watson or even at the ranch."

"Do you think that I'd be able to take that money knowing where it came from?"

"No. I think you'd do exactly what I planned to do. You'd give the money to the sheriff and let him deal with it."

"Then how could I provide for you as a wife? You're arguing in circles and making me dizzy. I agree we should give the money to the law, providing the sheriff in Bannack lets me get to say a word before some angry mob lynches me from the church steeple. But then it puts us right back where we were when you asked your question about marrying you."

"I know that. When I asked, it was really just a much simpler question. Just forget about providing for me or how you want to be just a cowhand. I'm asking for a much different reason, so answer the question simply with a yes or no. Would you marry me?"

Tabby had never even given a thought to getting married and still didn't think that it was likely, so he decided to give her a truthful answer.

"Yes."

She didn't smile but asked, "Is that an honest answer, Tabby? You aren't just saying 'yes' to keep me from bothering you; are you?"

"No, ma'am. I figured if I ever did get married, which I never expected to happen, it would have to be a woman like you."

"You mean you wanted to marry a whore who couldn't burden you with children."

He rapidly shook his head before saying, "No, Rena. That's not what I meant at all. I'll admit that I think you're a very attractive lady, but that's not the main reason I gave you that answer. Before I showed up at the ranch yesterday, I never spent more than an hour with a lady and most of that time was spent in her bed. But yesterday, we talked for a few hours and I began to see you as more than just a pretty young woman. As you told me how you'd gotten to the ranch, I didn't even see you as a helpless woman who needed my help. I saw you as another person with problems that were worse than my temporary jobless situation.

"By the time you offered to let me join you in your bed, which I really wanted you to do by the way, I had to convince myself that I needed sleep more than the pleasure of being with you. It was only when I was lying on my bed later that night that I figured out that I didn't want you to think of me as just another one of your customers. I thought it was stupid, but it was there.

"I've been arguing with myself ever since and after you left me this morning, I felt like a bigger fool than I could have imagined. Here I was worried that you might not respect me and all the while, you'd been planning on taking my horse and running away. I was so hideously angry and ashamed for being hoodwinked that those thoughts of being more like a good man than your regular men disappeared."

"You are a good man, Tabby, whether you believe it or not. You're the best man I've ever met and that includes my father. You listened to me. You're also the first man I have ever invited into my bed because I wanted him to spend the night with me. I wanted you to make love to me, but I wanted you to stay and talk to me even more. I suppose I should tell you that I thought better of you because you turned me down, but I won't. I found myself disappointed and hurt. But I also knew that I had to leave you to keep you safe."

He looked at her before he asked, "That didn't work out as well as you expected; did it?"

She laughed lightly as she shook her head then said, "No, it didn't. So, if we really live through this; will you really marry me?"

"Now we've gone from 'would' to 'will'. Those are two different questions, ma'am. One is asking if it was possible and the other is asking if it will happen."

"I know, and now I'm asking if you will marry me if we survive."

"You sure are a persistent woman, Rena. I'll give you that."

She didn't say anything more but tilted her head slightly and just looked at him.

He understood the question was still out there and after just a few seconds, he replied, "I said I would, and I'm not going to worry about the difference between the words. So, if we get out of this alive, I'll marry you, but there are still a lot of problems we need to solve even if we don't get filled with their bullets. We won't have a lot of money and no place to live. I won't have a job either and I'm only good at working with cattle."

She then hooked her arm through has as they wound around the rocks before she said, "If we're still alive in a few days, then maybe we can go back to the ranch and live there. We could find some mustangs and start the herd again. Can you work with horses as well as cattle?"

"I was a wrangler at a couple of spreads, but how could we afford to buy the ranch? I have over six hundred dollars of my own, but that's nowhere near enough. Let's just think about staying alive until nightfall. We should find the road to Bannack by then."

"I hope so," she said as she glanced behind them then asked, "Do you think they've found the buckboard yet?"

"I don't know, but if they see it, they'll have to be careful and that'll give us more time."

"How long do you think we have to walk before we find the road?"

"To be honest, I have no idea. It took me more than an hour to reach the canyon and that was following a decent trail on Philly. We could be walking due west right now and getting no closer to the road. We have to go where the rocks, ridges, gullies and trees let us pass, so all we can do is keep moving."

"Thank you for not fibbing to make me feel better. It wasn't necessary anyway. Now that I'm not worried about what happens after we reach Bannack, I'm content."

Tabby felt her hand gripping his arm and he had to admit that he was feeling somewhat content himself. He still wasn't convinced that they were in the clear by any stretch of the imagination, but just having Rena with him was soothing. Since he'd arrived in Watson yesterday, so many strange things had happened, but the most unusual was his jolting revelation that maybe he wasn't going to continue his life as a wandering cowhand much longer.

"Do you think he's in one of them rocks, Cash?" Max asked as he sat on his horse beside the boss.

They were about less than three hundred yards away from the buckboard and each of them was scanning the location for possible ambush sites. None of them wanted to be the first to get any closer.

Cash replied, "Maybe. I'm gonna head into those trees and wind my way closer to that buckboard. I should be able to spot his horse before I see any sign of him. But if he's good enough to find us, then that bounty hunter would be able to hide his horse, too."

"Do you want me to come with you?"

"No, you stay here and take charge until I come back or call you in. If I don't see him, then I'll come out of those trees. He'll have to pop out of his hidey hole to take a shot and I'll drop to the ground. You bring in the other boys and start firing. I'll set up with my '76 and get a good shot when I can."

"Okay, Cash," Max replied.

The outlaw chieftain nodded then wheeled his horse to the left and soon entered the trees.

He kept his eyes focused on the buckboard as it appeared and then disappeared behind the passing pines. He was walking his horse slowly to give him more time to look at the surrounding boulders, trees and other rocky formations hopefully to find some sign of the man or his horse.

He still hadn't spotted anything when he figured he was as close as he was going to get. He could see the sharp drop-off before the buckboard and knew that it was too steep for him to have led his horse in that direction. So, after a careful examination of anyplace within Winchester range on the other side of the clearing, he pulled his '76 from its scabbard and cocked the hammer.

Cash took a deep breath, let it out and then nudged his gelding forward out of the trees. When the bright sunlight surrounded him, he felt incredibly vulnerable but let the horse continue walking closer to the buckboard as he kept his eyes dancing over the rocks ahead.

He didn't bother looking to his boys who were more than two hundred yards to his right as he approached the buckboard. The lack of gunfire didn't calm him but made him even twitchier. He began to suspect that this bounty hunter had ice water in his veins and was waiting for more targets to get within range of his repeater.

Still he slowly dismounted and walked to the buckboard. He stood with his back to the horseless buckboard and then waved his men in. He didn't bother checking for tracks or anything else as he continued to scan the rocks. He expected to see the man pop up suddenly when his boys were within Winchester range, and then he'd have to fire quickly. Once he had exposed himself, then Cash knew they'd have him.

He heard the hoofbeats of their horses as they approached and still waited for the bounty hunter to show himself.

It was only when his men began dismounting just a few feet away that he began to suspect that the man wasn't there at all.

When Max reached him, he bent over and picked up something and showed it to his boss.

"Will you lookit this," he said as he held it between his thumb and index finger.

Cash looked at the heel of a woman's shoe then said, "They ain't here. That feller cut off Monique's shoes so she could walk better."

"Are we gonna go after 'em, boss?" asked Snake.

"No, Snake. We're gonna let 'em leave and just hope they enjoy spendin' all of our money. Of course, we're goin' after that bitch and her new boyfriend! I don't care if he's the best damned bounty hunter in the territory."

He then looked at Jimmy Parsons and said, "Jimmy, you ride back to the ranch and load up a packhorse. We're going to follow them, but you should be able to follow our trail real easy. Alright?"

Jimmy nodded then said, "Okay, boss? How much food do you want me to bring along?"

"Enough to last us two days. It shouldn't take us that long because they're probably on foot. Even if they were ridin' double, they'd have to take it slow."

"I'll be back as soon as I can," Jimmy said before stepping into his saddle and turning his mare around.

He had only ridden a few yards when the others started mounting their horses. After they were moving, each of them pulled his Winchester from his scabbard because the boss's repeater had never left his hands.

They soon lost sight of the buckboard as they entered the harsh terrain.

CHAPTER 3

By the time Cash and his four men left the buckboard behind, Tabby and Rena had walked almost two miles. If they'd been on the Great Plains of Nebraska or Dakota, then they would have seen each other already. Of course, if they had been on the level ground of the plains, they would be driving the buckboard and be much further away.

But those two miles were much more difficult to travel and made discover much less likely. They may have walked two miles, but the twisting path was only about a mile and a half as the crow flies.

Since they'd come to an understanding of sorts, Tabby and Rena used the long and sometimes painful walk to talk about things that didn't involve death or what would happen if they did make it to Bannack. Tabby had also taken off his heavy coat and laid it across the top of his bedroll/blanket/slicker bundle. He knew he'd need it later after the sun went down, assuming they lived that long. Rena had followed suit and added her coat to the pile.

Rena continued the extended conversation when she asked, "How did you earn the nickname Tabby? I've been wanting to ask you since you first told me."

TABBY HAYES

"It was when I was working at the Jensen's spread north of Cheyenne. I was with the boys when we went into town to throw away some of our hard-earned pay. I may not drink much beyond a nice, cold beer and I sure as hell don't gamble because I'm not a good poker player and the house always wins those other games. My only real vice was visiting the ladies. Anyway, the boys were pretty greased up before the sun even set and they were heading for an all-out drunken stupor when I came down the stairs. I wasn't paying any attention because I was in a good mood for some reason.

"Well, just before I reached the barroom floor, Al Kendall yells something that I couldn't figure out because he was using drunk talk. I stopped and looked at him and figured he'd just yell it again, but he didn't. He suddenly yanked his Colt from his holster and pointed it at me. I figured he was going to put a .44 into my gut and began to drop when he fired. I felt a spray of splinters when his bullet crashed into a stair a good six feet over my head.

"Now Al was a better shot than I was, but he was pretty far gone, so I still thought he was aiming at me. But then he started laughing and Pappy Wilson pulled his six-shooter and shot even higher up the staircase then started hee-hawing like a drunk mule. Before Al shot again, I looked up the stairs and saw this orange cat with his puffy tail in the air and his big eyes wide as they could be. He wasn't even moving anymore he was so afraid.

"I suppose I should have run down to the floor to keep them from hitting me accidentally, but I figured the cat didn't deserve to be shot just for being there and some of those stray rounds might have hit one of the ladies. So, I raced up those stairs and even when Al fired his second round, I kept going. I snatched the cat into my arms and yelled for them to stop shooting."

"Did they?" she quickly asked.

"Yes, ma'am. They just kept laughing and pointing at me but holstered their pistols. Pretty soon every man in the place was laughing and yelling all sorts of things at me."

"At least the cat must have been grateful."

"You would think so; wouldn't you? But once I had rescued that feline, I found out soon enough that he must have blamed me for being one of those other boys that were trying to knock him down to just eight lives. Before I finished telling them to stop firing, his claws were already digging into my gut and arms. While I was the butt of all of that laughing and joshing from the floor, I let that cat drop and he skedaddled down the hall. I don't know where he went, and I really didn't care much. I wasn't about to go looking for him again. My shirt had blood stains all over it by the time I got to the bar and ordered a beer."

She smiled and asked, "So, that's when they began calling you Tabby."

"Well, not exactly yet, Rena. When we got back to the ranch then next morning, it wasn't too long before that story reached the rest of the boys and the family, too. The first nickname that the boys hung on me wasn't Tabby. It was a different name for a cat, and I wasn't all that happy about it which made the boys use it even more. They had three whole days of enjoying themselves with that nickname until the boss's daughter asked her daddy what they called me that name. He laid down the law to the boys rather than tell her the reason that they tried to give it to me. So, they settled on Tabby, and I kind of liked it."

"Why would you like it rather than Thom? It's a good name."

"It's okay, Rena, but most folks spelled it wrong anyway and using Tabby gives me a chance to tell the story. It's actually helped me land a couple of jobs, too."

"Well, it is a very good story, Tabby. I think I'll still call you Thom; if that's alright."

"It's fine. Just don't call me that other nickname."

Rena laughed and wished they weren't being chased. She had never felt so comfortable with a man before and even though he had agreed to marry her, she wasn't going to hold him to that promise if they reached Bannack. She didn't believe it had been fair for her to even pose the question.

After he'd told her the nickname story, he said, "You told me how you got to the ranch, but not how you wound up in Watson other than your uncle kicked you out of your father's house."

111

"It's not much worse than what happened after I was brought to the ranch, but at least maybe you'll understand how I got into the business."

She was already growing sore and tired from the walk but didn't say anything because she knew it was only early afternoon and they had hours more to go before they could stop.

"My father was doing well with his lumber business and I had a good life growing up. I should have been married by the time my father died, but he wanted me to be at least eighteen before I even began letting men visit me. I resented him for that even though I knew he had the best of intentions. I was his only living child by then and he was overly protective. When he died of pneumonia, I was devastated and alone. It got even worse when my uncle then moved into the house.

"After my uncle made a very disgusting suggestion, I basically offered myself to one of my father's foremen. I had saved almost six hundred dollars by then and asked him to take me away. He wasn't a particularly handsome or strong man, but I thought I knew him, and he was agreeable to the idea. I never even suggested that we get married. Of course, he never mentioned it either.

"We took the train west out of Minnesota and rode it across Dakota until we reached the end of track. I had no idea why he was headed that way and when we finally left the train, he said that he had a brother who was living in Virginia City and had discovered a rich vein of gold. I stupidly believed him, so we joined a wagon train to Virginia City. I still had four hundred dollars when we started out.

"By the time we reached Virginia City, I learned that he didn't have any brothers at all. He took all of my money and began prospecting for gold. He kept me around for over a year until he discovered that I was pregnant. Then when I began showing, he put me on the stage to Watson because it was the cheapest ticket he could buy. That was the last I saw of him."

"What was his name?" Tabby asked.

"Rolf Higgins. He was shorter than you and not nearly as good-looking."

'I'm hardly a handsome man, Rena."

"It gives you an idea just how badly I wanted to get away from my uncle; doesn't it?"

"Yes, ma'am."

"After I arrived in Watson, I had no money and a swelling belly. Even in that condition, I thought because there weren't many young, unattached women in town that some man would want to make an honest woman of me. When one did offer to marry me, I moved in with him and found he was worse than Rolf had been. I hadn't been in his house for a month before he brought in Mrs. Jones. At least that was the name she gave me at the time. I learned her real name, Ada Jefferson, later when I started working at Dilly's.

"She told me she was a midwife and after listening to my belly, told me that the baby had died, and she had to remove it, or I might die. I was so naïve about such things back then. I let her do what she did, and it almost killed me. I was bedridden for almost a month and my make-believe husband grew even angrier because he couldn't enjoy me as much as he had. He let me know that he wasn't happy with my inability to please him, too.

"I stayed with him for another year or so and even though I didn't get pregnant again, he became tired of me. By then, everyone in Watson knew me for what I was and there was no chance that I could ever marry anyone else. One day, he escorted me from his house and took me to Dilly's. Before we even crossed the street, I knew what he was doing. Dilly's wasn't exactly a big secret in town.

"I wasn't even upset once I realized where he was taking me. I knew that I was still pretty and that the whores who worked there were treated better than I had been since leaving Minnesota. I don't know if Dilly paid him for me or not, but I didn't care. I fit in easily with the other girls and never had a complaint. Would you be shocked if I told you that I began to enjoy what I did?"

"Yes, ma'am. I'll admit that I would be."

"I should amend that to say that I enjoyed being with some of the men who weren't as brutal as most or didn't smell like wild bears. There were quite a few who told me that they loved me, and even though I knew they told that to all of the girls, it made me feel better. When I was giving myself to one of those men, I felt almost like a real woman and not a whore. But before you start trying to think of me as some soft-hearted, lonely woman, I want to let you know that I enjoyed the act itself. Some men were much better than others, but it's not as if I was being assaulted three or four times a night."

Tabby looked at her and asked, "Three or four times each night? You never had a night off?"

"Not until I was brought to the ranch. I will admit that some of my customers were so violent that I was scared to see them come through the door, but there weren't as many as you might think."

"Is the man who brought you there still in Watson?"

"No. He was killed when he went on that posse to chase down the gang."

"How did you find out if you never went to town?"

"When Jimmy Parsons returned with the gang, he tried to make me proud of him for being one of the men who had killed him. It didn't matter to me because I put Jimmy into the same category."

Tabby then asked, "How are you holding up?"

"I'm sore and my legs are getting a bit wobbly, but I can make it."

"Philly's only carrying about eighty pounds, so I can set you on top of the burlap bags to give your legs a rest."

She glanced at his Morgan gelding before asking, "Are you sure?"

"It'll be fine. I'm used to walking and I have good boots. I can set you side saddle."

"I'm not worried about what you might see, Thom. I wanted you to sleep with me last night and I'm not ashamed to admit I hope you will tonight. Maybe seeing more of me will inspire you to do that."

"Maybe," he replied as he pulled Philly to a stop.

He placed his hands on her waist above the gunbelt and hoisted her onto the saddle facing him.

Rena was going to swing her legs onto the saddle, but soon realized it wasn't possible even if she was wearing britches. It wasn't as comfortable as if she'd been in the saddle seat, but it was much better than walking.

He looked up at her and asked, "Are you settled in, ma'am?"

"Yes, sir. I'm sorry I didn't get to expose my legs, though."

She was surprised when Tabby replied, "So, am I, Rena."

She started to laugh as he began walking again with Philly's reins in his hand.

———

None of the men trailing them were good at tracking, but they didn't need to have that particular skill to know where Tabby and Rena were going. They were all still mounted, but walking their horses was as fast as they could manage, or they'd risk having their mounts break an ankle.

Cash wished that he'd told Jimmy to bring some spare horses with him, but it was too late now. He didn't bother checking their backtrail to look for him because by the time Jimmy started following, they would be too far ahead to see him anyway.

But Jimmy hadn't even returned to the buckboard yet. After he'd reached the ranch house, he started a fire in the cookstove and set the coffeepot full of water on the hotplate.

He and Mark had paid to build this house and it was now his ranch. *If Cash didn't trust him enough to be included in their little conference while he waited at the end of his canyon, then why should he be loyal?* He didn't have any stallions on the ranch anymore, but when he'd sold the herd, he hadn't given all of the money to Cash. He'd kept four hundred dollars for himself and kept it in a hiding spot in the barn. As the water heated, he stepped out onto the small back porch and looked down the canyon at his property. There was a lot of good grass and water

117

down there and it was his now. He didn't have any partners and he began to imagine building up the herd again. He could hire someone to help him round up some mustangs and maybe even keep him around.

As he dreamt of restarting the ranch, he never gave a moment's thought about the wanted posters that had been nailed to every law enforcement office in the territory, and one of them had his name on it.

But even the pleasant thought of restarting the ranch didn't last as long as his cup of coffee. He tossed it aside and walked to the barn to start saddling one of the horses with a packsaddle. He decided that as long as he was taking one, he may as well take a couple of more as spares because it was the way they operated.

It took him more than a half an hour to get the horses ready to travel, but shortly after tying them to the long trail rope, he headed out of the canyon.

———

The reformed posse had been delayed by an extended argument in Virginia City about who would be going. Sheriff Wolfson was close to drawing his pistol to get some of the wannabe posse members to stay in town. Last night, he needed to find the gang, but today he needed to catch them. He only wanted good shots and men he could trust. He didn't want hotheads or men with shaky constitutions. So, by the time they reached Deputy Trudeau, it was already midmorning.

Nonetheless, the trail was easily tracked by the deputy, whose father had been a trapper and had trained him well in the skill of finding where game or men had gone.

When the posse of twelve dependable men had reached the trail that Tabby had used to find the ranch, they had to stop to let the sheriff decide which direction to go because there were tracks in both directions. It was Deputy Trudeau's skills that made that decision easier. He told the sheriff that all of the recent tracks were heading west. But the sheriff did send two of the members of his posse to follow the trail to the north. He told them to ride to Watson and tell Sheriff Smith that he was following the gang who had robbed his town's bank. What Tex Smith did with the information was up to him.

———

Jimmy Parsons had already passed the abandoned buckboard and was well into the rough terrain long before Sheriff Wolfson sent the two men to Watson. He was moving as quickly as he could and was gaining on the rest of the gang who were concerned about an ambush by the assumed bounty hunter.

When the posse reached the canyon entrance, it was Deputy Trudeau who again saved his boss time by telling him that the number of tracks meant that the ranch house was probably empty. It was also then that even he was confused by the ruts left by the buckboard that seemed to be headed for impassable ground.

Sheriff Wolfson looked west before turning to his deputy and asking, "Well, Paul, what do you figure they're doing? If they know we're on their trail, why the hell would they even take that wagon? They can't get very far going that way."

"It's probably a buckboard, boss. The ruts are too close together, but even a buckboard isn't going to get very far, and it's not loaded with much, either. But there are some other odd things about those tracks even beyond the buckboard."

"What's that?"

"Well, the gang turned into the canyon, but the buckboard had come out of the canyon, then turned around before coming back out again and turning west into that hard ground. Then the gang came back out again to follow the buckboard. So, far that's almost normal. But then another lone rider came back, then left again just a little while ago leading three horses. I think one was either a packhorse or maybe a second rider."

"You got all that from just those prints?" asked an impressed Sheriff Wolfson.

"Yes, sir. But those last prints are pretty recent, too. I'd guess less than an hour old."

"Good work, Paul. Let's get going again, but I need everyone to be ready for an ambush. I don't want to have another disaster like Tex Smith had to deal with."

Deputy Trudeau nodded then said, "We already had ours, boss."

"You got that right."

The ten-man posse then left the mouth of the canyon following the broken ground left by all of the iron clad horse hooves and the one buckboard.

———

In her elevated sidesaddle seating position, Rena was able to easily keep an eye on their backtrail as they kept moving. She was hungry but didn't want to mention it as she was sure that Thom was as well. She was already thinking of him as Thom and felt more comfortable using his real name as opposed to the funny nickname.

Tabby may have been used to walking and his boots were more suited to hiking that Rena's, but that didn't mean he wasn't getting tired or sore. If he'd walked the same distance over a flat surface or even a road, it wouldn't be so bad. But he was constantly having to step over rocks and down and up narrow gouges in the earth. Each step added more strain to his muscles and ligaments. They'd also been climbing a steady, but unnoticeable uphill grade which added to the difficulty of the terrain.

121

He may not have been able to stop walking but didn't see any reason to avoid getting something into their stomachs, so he dropped Philly's reins and let him continue to walk as he opened his left saddlebag. He reached inside and pulled out a leather pouch. As Rena watched, he extracted a smoked sausage and handed it to her before taking out another one and sticking it in his mouth.

Rena was already devouring the sausage before he returned the pouch to the saddlebag, but he still finished his before she did.

As she tossed the last of her sausage into her mouth, she lifted one of the canteens from the saddle and handed it to him without opening the cap.

"Thank you, ma'am," he said as he smiled up at her.

After taking a long drink he handed the open canteen back to her. She quickly emptied the canteen and closed the cap before hanging it back on the saddle.

"We're going to need more water."

"That's not a problem, Rena. In fact, when we spot a stream, we'll be able to get an idea where to go. All of the creeks and streams in this area run north, so if we find one, we can follow it to the road. It'll be better ground, too."

"That sounds good," she said as she looked at their backtrail.

She didn't stop watching when she asked, "Did you tell any of the women you visited that you loved them?"

Tabby kept his eyes on the ground in front of them as he replied, "No, ma'am. We both knew why I was spending the time and money with them. Did you think I should have said it just to make them feel better?"

"No. It's just the opposite. I was curious if you were one of the types who would get all gushy as if they cared."

"Well, I might have liked some of them more than others, but I never wanted to lie to them, either."

"Have you ever told a woman that you loved her?"

"Well, maybe not a woman, but I did tell a girl once."

With her eyes glued to their backtrail, Rena smiled and asked, "Okay. I'm waiting, Thom."

"I figured as much. I was fifteen and filled with the blazing lust that dominates all teenaged boys. I was smitten with a serious case of puppy love centered on a girl named Maggie Murphy. She was almost a year older than me. She had red hair and was already prepared to feed a dozen babies, if you get my meaning."

"Strangely enough, I did."

Tabby snickered before continuing.

"Well, I managed to find a little private time with Maggie in a small forest on her parents' farm. She was the first girl I even got to kiss. and then she kind of took me by surprise by introducing me to her tall mountains. That's when I told her that I loved her and she continued my education and let's just say she gave me a lesson that I'll never forget.

"Well, that was the last time I ever got to climb those mountains because when she returned to her home, her mother noticed the pine needles on the back of her dress and then Maggie confessed what she had done and the name of the lovestruck boy who had benefitted from her charms. After her mother told her father, she was not only banned from seeing me again, her father told my father which created a double vault door."

"Was it like Romeo and Juliet and you both still tried to see each other despite your families' objections?" she asked before turning her eyes to their backtrail.

"Sorry, ma'am. It wasn't even close. After that first confession that created the furor in the families, Maggie had to confess a week later that I wasn't the first boy who had spent time with her in the trees. The reason she had to confess was that Eddie Chappell had been spotted by her brother leaving the forest with a big grin on his face. When I found out that I was just a source of amusement for Maggie, it deflated my puppy love and I felt like a fool."

"Like I made you feel when I left you at the ranch."

"I'm not going to lie to you, Rena. I felt like a much bigger fool this morning and more than simply angry. I'll tell you right now that if you weren't as pretty as you are, then it was still possible that I would have tossed you off the buckboard."

"You wouldn't have done it even if I was a gnarled old crone."

"You shouldn't be so sure, ma'am. By the time I climbed into that driver's seat, I had convinced myself that you were just the gang leader's girlfriend and were trying to lure me into their gunsights. I was so mad that my mind was imagining all sorts of outrageously stupid reasons to explain why you had gone."

"I can understand why you would think that, and I don't blame…"

She stopped talking and put her hand over her eyes to block out the late afternoon sun as she stared at their backtrail.

Tabby had turned to look up at her when she stopped in mid-sentence then saw her focused behind them. He shifted his eyes to that direction and didn't see anything. He knew she had a better view from Philly's back, so he still watched as he waited for her to tell him what had attracted her interest.

When she didn't say anything for thirty seconds, he asked, "What did you see?"

"I'm not sure. I thought I spotted something moving back there on the right near that big outcrop of rocks, but then I lost it again."

"What did it look like?"

"I don't know. It could have just been the shadows, a deer or some other animal. Do you think it could have been them?"

"It could be. They'd be moving faster than we could, so even if they had started out an hour after we did, they'd be less than a mile back and with the twisting path we've had to take, they could be a lot closer."

She continued to watch in vain as she asked, "What can we do if it is them?"

"I'll tell you. but I don't want to hear any arguments until I finish."

"You're going to try to send me away again; aren't you?"

"Not away, Rena. Not like I suggested before. But if we see them, I'll take my Winchester and my saddlebags because they have all of my spare ammunition. I'll want you to continue riding Philly to get far enough way, so you'll have a chance to escape if they get past me. It's already late afternoon, so I won't have to hold them off that long before the sun sets and I can catch up to you."

"That's not going to happen, Thom."

"It's the best way to stop them. It's not like before when we were trapped with the buckboard. I just get them on the ground, and I have enough ammunition to keep them there until the sun sets. Then I'll just sneak away. They can't risk coming after me for a while. By then I'll have reached you and we can keep going in the moonlight."

Rena was still looking at their backtrail when she said, "I don't like it, Thom, but I'm not going to argue with you now. I'll think of a better reason for you to keep me with you by the time I see them for real."

"Thank you, ma'am."

Tabby hadn't seen anything moving back there, so he let Rena continue her observation while he picked up the pace as fast as he could. He wished the sun would move faster. Every second that they didn't see the gang, the closer they were to the protective shroud of the night.

―――――

It was Snake who thought he saw a momentary flash of movement ahead but wasn't sure enough to tell Cash. He just strained his eyes to see if he could pick it up again, but after another couple of minutes, he dismissed it as a four-footed creature of the wild.

Max was riding beside Cash and after looking behind them, he asked loudly, "Where the hell is Parsons with that packhorse? My belly needs fillin'."

Cash quickly answered, "He can't catch up to us, Max. Even if he galloped back to the ranch house and got that packhorse loaded and raced back to the buckboard, he'd still be a good two hours behind us. He'll only catch up to us if we have to stop. If we do, it'll only because we spotted that bounty hunter and Monique and opened fire on 'em."

"How close do you think we are?"

"Pretty damned close, I reckon. If this ground were any better, we woulda seen 'em by now."

Max grunted before taking his canteen from his saddle and taking a long swallow. This was already taking too long.

––––––––

Jimmy Parsons was just a couple of miles back and was still gaining ground. Unlike his partners, he wasn't hungry at all and except for his concerns about a possible conspiracy, he was in a decent mood.

What should have been his greatest concern was the large posse that had almost reached the buckboard. He simply had no idea that they were there.

––––––––

Rena was still focused behind them when they crossed the highest point of their difficult journey and began a gradual decline. It was just five minutes after they started the descent that Tabby spotted a small stream.

"There's our stream, Rena!" he exclaimed.

She quickly looked to the front and saw the narrow creek as it bubbled and splashed its way down the slope.

She grinned and excitedly said, "That's a beautiful sight!"

"Yes, ma'am. We'll let Philly get his water and we'll fill the canteens and drink all we can. We can get something to eat quickly, but we can't stay long."

"I won't complain."

The sight of the stream and the gentle downslope boosted their speed as they headed for the water.

Even Rena didn't bother looking behind them as she stared at the welcoming sight. If she had been watching their backtrail, she might have had her second glimpse of the five men who were determined to kill her and Tabby.

———

This time, it was Max who spotted a flash of movement ahead before Rena's head disappeared as they started on the downslope.

But just as Snake had done earlier, he didn't say anything. He just stared at the distant ground and waited to spot it again. The moment he saw a second hint of movement, he'd tell Cash. For now, he just rested his right hand on the brass butt of his Winchester '76.

———

Jimmy was closer than even Cash had estimated. Once he'd committed to taking the horses to the gang, he had kept a quick pace. He knew that if they had found the bounty hunter and Monique, he'd hear gunfire, so he could afford to move faster than they could.

The same couldn't be said of the posse that was following everyone. The recent ambush of the posse from Watson was a strong incentive to keep a slower, but safer pace, especially when they were in a more ambush-rich environment. Of course, the entire landscape was cluttered with good hiding places just like the location where the outlaw gang had almost wiped out Sheriff Smith's posse.

As the sun dropped closer to the mountains, Tabby and Rena reached the stream and after letting Philly's reins drop so the tired gelding could drink, Tabby helped Rena to the ground.

"Do you want to keep wearing that gunbelt?" he asked as he took the two canteens from the saddle.

"If you don't mind. I may need it to convince you to let me stay with you."

"I may not be a gunfighter, ma'am, but I'm pretty sure I could pull my new Colt before you could get that big old Walker out of its holster."

She laughed and tried to pull the heavy pistol free, but it wouldn't move.

Tabby saw the whole holster jerk upward and said, "If you want to shoot me, you'll have to release the hammer loop first. That's what's holding it in the holster."

"Oh," she said as she looked down at the pistol and saw the thin leather strip over the gun's hammer.

Tabby stepped to the creek's bank, dropped to his heels and pushed both canteens below the surface of the icy cold water. As the bubbles from the empty canteens popped into the air, Rena began scooping the water with her cupped hands.

She slurped the water from her natural cup and then wiped her hands on her dress before she asked, "How long are we going to stay here?"

"Not as long as we need to. The sun is almost below the tops of the mountains, so that'll give us some shadows, but not enough to disappear. We'll push on in a few minutes and hopefully, the night will fall before they can see us."

She glanced at their backtrail as she asked, "How far away do you think they are?"

Tabby capped both canteens and set them on the bank before he answered, "Honestly? I'm surprised they haven't caught up to us yet."

"Do you think that they might have given up or maybe they never followed us at all? I mean, we never saw them leave the canyon."

"You don't really believe that they'd let you take their money and just wish us well; do you?"

"No, I guess not. But why aren't they here yet?"

"I'm guessing that they're worried about an ambush. I know I would be and I'm just a cowhand."

She turned to look at him as she laughed and then said, "So, you keep telling me."

"It's what I am, Rena. It's all I've ever really known. Until I rode up to your ranch house, I expected to end my days out on a range."

"That's sad, Thom. That's all you wanted out of life?"

"Maybe not all that I wanted, but I told you before that I wasn't ambitious. I was content with my life because I had no real responsibilities. Now, I have responsibilities that I couldn't have dreamed of. And you, Rena, are the last person I would expect to call my life sad."

"I guess so," she said before standing and walking to Philly to get some food.

She had just flipped open the saddlebag's flap and pulled back the front to look for the leather satchel with the sausages when Tabby turned and spotted the hats of the first two outlaws.

He exclaimed, "There they are! Let's go!"

Rena whipped her head around and by the time she looked, she saw more than just the hats. They were around a thousand yards away, but seeing the gang made her freeze.

Tabby quickly hung the canteens over his saddle and grabbed Rena's elbow.

She snapped out of her momentary shock and quickly said, "I'll walk, Thom."

He didn't reply but grabbed Philly's reins and started quickly walking alongside the stream's bank with Rena close beside him.

———

Max and Cash spotted Tabby and Rena at the same moment but it was Max who shouted, "We got 'em!"

With the threat of ambush gone, they picked up the pace as fast as the terrain would allow and quickly began to close the gap.

Even though they had been spotted, Tabby and Rena soon lost sight of the outlaws when the stream made a turn to the northeast and they trotted behind a wall of rock.

"What will we do?" Rena asked as they jogged along the rocky ground.

"We're going to have to find a place to set up a defense."

"I'm not leaving."

"I know. That option is gone now anyway. Just keep an eye out behind us while I try to find some place where we can hide Philly."

"Okay. Maybe one of these days you can tell me how you came to give him that name."

Despite the incredible danger in which they found themselves, Tabby laughed and replied, "It's related to the Maggie Murphy story."

Rena was smiling as she kept glancing behind her but knew they were in trouble.

Tabby legs felt like rubber and he hadn't told Rena that there was now a large hole in the sole of his right boot. He knew it was the least of their problems.

When they started out again, they were still more than six miles from the road as they had been traveling close to a parallel course until they reached the stream.

———

But after they disappeared from view, Cash had everyone slow down as the threat of ambush returned. Not only that, but the shadows were getting more extensive and darker, which made those ambush sites more difficult to find.

They weren't losing ground on their prey, but they stopped gaining it as well.

Jimmy Parsons wasn't slowing down at all as he followed their trail. He was still on the incline as he led the packhorse and two spares and was less than a mile behind them. He was the only person of all those involved who wasn't concerned about being shot.

The posse was losing ground to Jimmy and the rest of the gang as they followed, and the increasing shadows had the same effect on them as it had on Cash's bunch. Sheriff Wolfson was convinced that they wouldn't catch up to the gang of killers before sundown. They'd have to set up a cold camp and resume the chase tomorrow.

———

Even as Sheriff Wolfson realized the likelihood that his posse wouldn't catch up with the gang, a smaller posse led by Sheriff Tex Smith was ten miles out of Watson hoping to catch sight of the gang as they reached the road. He'd sent a telegram to Sheriff Kuchen in Bannack before they'd gone, so he'd be on the lookout for the gang if they headed away from Watson.

As he rode away from his town, Sheriff Smith hoped that his posse would be the one to bring justice to the men that Cash and his outlaw gang had killed. He wasn't concerned about the lost cash, although the bank was in bad shape after the loss. He wanted revenge. He and his men had one advantage the others didn't. They were more familiar with the area and each of them knew that the gang had no path to escape now. They had Sheriff Wolfson's big posse behind them and his smaller one blocking the most likely exits from that hard country that they'd entered. Neither the posse chasing nor the one waiting knew why Cash had left their hideout and chosen such an unusual path to make their escape.

————

Rena hadn't spotted the gang again and didn't realize that Tabby was doing all he could to keep that from happening. He had shifted their path away from the stream and followed a more torturous path to put as many tall obstacles between them and the outlaws. He knew he couldn't keep going at this pace and suspected that even after riding for most of the day, Rena wouldn't last much longer either.

As he stepped over the small rocks and climbed and dropped over the taller ones, he was scanning the jumbled terrain for someplace to set up a defense. It wasn't as easy to find as he'd expected once he set his criteria. There had to have a clear line of sight for at least sixty yards and have no or at least hard paths around the flanks. He needed to keep them in front of him. After the sun set, they could sneak away if they were still alive.

It was the best tactical decision, even if he had no idea what tactics were. After all, he was just a cowhand. But even that one had problems beyond the difficulty in finding the perfect site. All of the possible choices were almost due east. The ground that the stream used to head toward the road was by nature, the best path. That meant the terrain that the water found unsuitable for passage was covered in boulders and sharp outcrops of granite and laced with gullies. In the few boulder-free areas, tall pines had taken root which removed Tabby's desired clear firing zone. The path before him looked almost like a wall with narrow gaps to allow passage into a maze.

It was his only option as he led Philly to the east, their new path again almost parallel to the roadway. The forbidding terrain before them also presented one other problem that was literally unseen. Neither of them had any idea if there was a path through that wilderness. They could find themselves in a prison of their own if they found themselves completely blocked by the edge of the mountains or stopped by a sharp and deep cliff.

Rena finally noticed the change in direction when she lost sight of the stream and glanced to the front.

"I thought we were going to follow the stream?"

"That was before we saw them. We can't move as fast as they can and if they can keep us in sight, they'd run us down in a few minutes. If we followed the stream, there wouldn't be any place to hide."

"Oh. If the stream was heading for the road, then we aren't anymore; are we?"

"No, ma'am. If we can hold out a few more hours, we can lose them in the dark. Then we can use the moon to figure out a rough direction and head north to get to the road."

She nodded then glanced behind them and still didn't see anyone.

"They aren't there yet. Did they slow down again?"

"I reckon so. Once we disappeared again, they have to watch out for an ambush. That's why I went this way. They're still gaining on us, though. We need to get into those trees ahead. Between them and the rocks, they'll be really worried about being drygulched."

Rena laughed lightly and said, "I didn't know that we were so terrifying."

"It's the unknown, Rena. We know that they're after us but if they can't see us, then they don't know if a bullet will find them before they see the shooter. If they knew I was an average shot at best, then they probably wouldn't worry about an ambush."

"Are you really just an average shot?"

"At best. I keep telling you that I'm just a cowhand and the only reason we carry guns is to keep from getting gored by a nasty-tempered bull or to keep a stampede from trampling us into dust. Some of the boys practiced a lot just because they enjoyed it and I reckon some of them were still kids who wanted to be a gunfighter. I liked my guns and took care of them, but I didn't practice all that much. I didn't want to waste my pay on ammunition when all I'd be shooting is a big old bull from just a few feet away."

"You said that you did some hunting when you were out in the line shack. You can't be a bad shot and expect to kill game; can you?"

"No, ma'am. I'm not that bad. I had to take my time, though. Trust me, those bastards who want to kill us are all much better with their Winchesters than I am and two of them are carrying more powerful ones than I have."

She took his hand as they neared the first pine and said, "Well, Mister Hayes, even if you're not as good with your rifle as they are, you're the best man I've ever met."

He glanced at her and replied, "I reckon I'm the only man you've met for a while that spent this much time with you just talking."

"That's true, but you're also the only man who spent any time at all listening."

Tabby took a look behind them, didn't see the gang in the shadows, then as they passed between two tall pines, he said, "When we find someplace to set up ahead, then we can talk some more until the sun goes down."

"I hope we can have more conversation tomorrow."

"So, do I, ma'am."

After passing those two pines, it wasn't even a three minutes before they exited the stand of trees and Tabby discovered as ideal a defensive location as he could have hoped to find. There was only about a hundred yards of relatively clear ground, but the right side of the clearing was almost a wall of granite. The left side was less formidable, but the tall sharp rocks and scattered smaller pines would make it a very difficult approach.

Directly ahead of him, the ground started a noticeable climb and at the end of the clearing, the rocks on the left and the wall on the right converged like a funnel leaving a narrow path.

"There's where we'll stop, Rena," he said loudly as he pointed at the pass over the rise.

"What's on the other side?"

"I don't know, but it doesn't matter right now. Let's get up there and then we can set up and wait for them."

"Alright."

———

While Tabby and Rena headed for their path to safety, the five outlaws had reached the stream and stopped to water their horses. They had each dismounted and filled their canteens as their mounts drank.

Cash was on his heels next to Max as he said, "They're headed into that rough country. He's settin' us up, Max."

"I figured that out, Cash. We can't let 'em go. Besides, Jimmy should be gettin' close with some grub."

"I'm not worried about gettin' food into my belly, Max. I'm just not pleased with the idea of gettin' a .44 into my gut."

Max glanced at Harry Brown and Jack Epperson before quietly saying, "We can have Jack and Harry take the lead and if that bounty hunter takes a shot at 'em, we'll know where he is and then we've got him."

Cash peeked around Max at the unsuspecting cannon fodder named Jack and Harry, then nodded before standing. He and Max hung their newly filled canteens on their saddles and mounted. When the boss left the stream, the others followed suit and soon they were headed east at a walk.

Before they'd gone twenty yards, Cash didn't try to disguise his intent when he loudly said, "Everybody pull your Winchesters, but don't cock the hammers yet. Jack, I want you and Harry out front. Let's spread out as far as we can, too."

Jack stared at the boss for just a couple of seconds before he nudged his mare to take the lead as Harry matched him. Cash may have told them to spread as much as possible, but those gaps were dictated by the terrain so most of the time, the furthest any man was from another was just four or five yards. Despite understanding why Cash had them sent out front, both

Jack and Harry rode toward the pines with their Winchesters in their hands. They may not have been happy about it, but that bounty hunter and Monique had their money, too.

———

After reaching the pass, Tabby and Rena had the first look of the landscape beyond the summit and it was a disheartening sight.

"How can we get through that, especially at night?" Rena asked as she stared.

"We'll worry about that later. Let's get set up. We don't have much time."

"Okay"

Tabby led Philly into a small clearing on the north side of the pass where there was a decent crop of grass and after his gelding began grazing, Tabby pulled his Winchester and then opened the right side of his voluminous saddlebags and pulled out a box of .44-40 cartridges for his repeater. He didn't bother with the box of .45s for his Colt because he knew it would never reach pistol-firing range.

"What can I do?" Rena asked.

"Grab a canteen. I'm going to wait over there in that break in the rocks. You can be close, but once bullets start flying, I want you to duck down so you can't get hit."

She felt useless but knew this wasn't the time to argue, so she just answered with a quick, "Okay," before they walked to the narrow gap between the enormous jagged stones.

Once they were in a reasonably comfortable position where Tabby had as good a view as he could have hoped for, he took off his hat and set it on the ground. He was sitting on a small narrow ledge on one of the rocks as he stared at the hundred-yard long clearing.

Rena was tucked in close on his left side so she could sit and still see what he was seeing.

"Now that we have time, can you tell me how Philly got his name and why it's somehow tied into your heartbreaking discovery of the wiles of women?"

Tabby snickered as he continued to watch for the outlaws, then said, "After I learned that Maggie Murphy was giving herself to other boys, I was heartbroken and felt like an idiot. Then about a month later, I discovered that the first boy she'd honored with her gift was the most disliked boy in our school, at least by the other boys.

"His name was Phil Dickerson and he was a big boy, but not very manly, if you know what I mean. He was a bit flabby and what irritated all of us was that he was the teacher's pet, and not because he was smart. It was because he would flatter her and have a good belly laugh at all of her sad attempts at humor. If that wasn't enough to make the other boys dislike him, it was his even more irritating habit of always acting as if he was popular. I mean, if any of the other boys would tell him he was a fat slob, or that he smelled like a skunk, he'd just laugh and pound us on the shoulder with his fat hand as if we were just joshing him. We always said he was too stupid to figure it out, but we knew he really believed that he was so well-liked that we were his buddies.

"Anyway, before I had my interlude with Maggie Murphy, I finally got under Phil's skin when I called him a horse's ass. I don't know why that insult bothered him. He could have been having a bad day or maybe he was fond of the mare he rode. Whatever it was, when I called him that, he didn't laugh. He scowled at me and shouted for me to take it back. I never did figure out how anyone thought you could take back words that were already heard either. We got into one of those back and forth boy arguments and I finally said that when I had my own horse, I'd name him Phil and every day, I'd pat his behind and say, 'Howdy, Phil.'"

Rena was grinning as she asked, "That gets you to Phil, but not Philly."

"I did name my first horse Phil and he earned the moniker, too. He was fat and lazy. I got him cheap and I had him for three years. Every day, I'd do what I said I would, too. When I wasn't sure that I could trust him to go five miles, I just turned him out to pasture and bought Philly. He was a handsome boy and I wasn't about to insult him with that name, but I wanted to keep some part of that tradition alive, so I named him Philly. Most folks think it's because I came from Pennsylvania, so I usually don't tell them how I picked the name. Philly doesn't seem to care."

"And when you found out that the original Phil had been the one to deflower Maggie, I imagine that only added to your humiliation."

"Yes, ma'am. When I heard about it, I imagined the pair of them naked and that ruined any of those earlier fond memories of Maggie in her glorious natural state. It put me in my place."

She was about to comment again when Tabby shushed her, and she shifted her eyes to the open ground. The clearing was in deep shadows as the remaining sunlight was being blocked by the trees and surrounding tall rocks but there was no doubt that someone was emerging from the trees.

Tabby cocked his Winchester's hammer as he stood and took two steps closer to the front of the rocks and pressed his shoulder to the wall of granite on his left. He kept his repeater in his right hand as he continued to watch.

Harry and Jack were walking their horses about six yards apart as they saw the clearing ahead. The short journey through the trees seemed like hours as they imagined feeling a .44 slam into them with each step of their horses' hooves.

As they were about to enter open ground and without even looking at each other, they simultaneously let their reins drop to let their horses find their own way as they cocked their

Winchesters and began to scan the rocks ahead for that bounty hunter.

Jimmy Parsons had spotted the stream and couldn't see anyone, so he led the horses to the water while he remained in the saddle and studied the ground. He soon found their new direction and after the horses had drunk their fill, he turned them to the east. He knew he was close.

More than five miles north, after spreading out to cover almost a mile of ground, Sheriff Smith's posse patrolled the road on foot, expecting one of them to spot the outlaws at any moment. The sun was low in the sky and if they didn't show up soon, they'd return to Watson.

Sheriff Wolfson's much large posse had already dismounted and set up a cold camp about six miles south. They'd pick up the trail again in the morning.

———

Even before he spotted the two riders emerging from the shadows, Tabby knew what he was going to do. He couldn't risk getting into a full-blown gunfight with six killers. He needed to keep them at bay until the sun went down.

He let the first two riders enter the clearing but didn't see the others yet. He did notice their Winchesters in their hands, so he knew that they were expecting an ambush. What he didn't want was for them to see his muzzle flare in the shadows. He stepped back until he was next to Rena then lifted his Winchester to his shoulder.

He still settled his sights on the rider to his left after seeing the bandage on the arm of the other man. If he managed to actually score a hit, it would have been an unexpected bonus.

He squeezed his trigger and his carbine popped against his shoulder as the .44 caliber slug exploded from his muzzle.

Even though Harry and Jack were expecting an ambush, when the crack of Tabby's Winchester reached their ears, they were startled and both opened fire at different spots. Neither of their shots were even aimed where Tabby was still standing with his sights set on them, but it didn't matter.

Tabby held his second shot as Harry and Jack quickly began making good use of the repeating action of their Winchesters and peppered the distant rocks with .44s.

Behind them, the other three outlaws stopped their horses before leaving the trees and watched as Jack and Harry emptied their rifles.

A few hundred yards back, Jimmy heard the explosion of gunfire and stopped. He was torn between going into that firefight or returning to the ranch. He glanced at his backtrail and for the first time, he wondered if there was a posse behind him. The stagecoach must have been discovered soon after they left it, and it wouldn't take long for them to form a posse. He imagined after what had happened to the posse from Watson, it would be the size of a company of army cavalry.

He took a deep breath and nudged his horse forward.

———

After each of their hammer's fell on empty chambers, Harry and Jack backed into the trees to reload.

When they were close, Cash walked his horse between them and asked, "Did you see him?"

Jack quickly answered, "Yeah, boss, we did. He's really dug in good in those rocks. We had to empty our Winchesters to keep his head down. We were sittin' ducks out there."

Harry glanced at Jack but didn't put the lie to his claim that they'd seen the bounty hunter.

Cash then asked, "Is there a way we can get around him?"

"I don't think so, Cash. He's in there tighter than a tick on a hound dog."

Max then said, "Maybe we should rush him. He might get a hit on one or two of us, but if we come at him all at once and keep firin', then he probably won't even get a shot off."

Cash didn't immediately dismiss the idea but asked, "Jack, where was he when he fired?"

Jack hesitated for just a second before saying, "He's on the right side of that break in the rocks up ahead. There's about a hundred yards of open ground. We could get across it in just a few seconds."

Cash was still unsure that it was the best way to deal with the problem, but they had to get the bastard. If the bounty hunter didn't have their money, he wouldn't have bothered chasing them at all. Now turning around wasn't even on the table. The mad charge across open ground wasn't a brilliant idea, but the light would soon be gone and then it would be even less likely that they'd get their money back. He also knew that to work, he couldn't just use Jack and Harry as cannon fodder again. They'd all have to go at the same time.

"Alright, Max. You're probably right. All we can do is blast across that open ground. But I don't want to open fire until we know exactly where he is. We'll have to give him one shot and once we see that muzzle flare, we concentrate on that spot. Okay?"

"Okay, boss," Snake said as Harry and Jack began reloading their still hot Winchesters.

The others all waited as the two shoved .44s into their loading gates.

———

After Tabby's shot, Rena had plastered herself against the rock as .44s ricocheted off of the surrounding granite, but Tabby kept his eyes on the two shooters.

When they were empty and began to back into the trees, he said, "They're going back to the others who stayed out of sight. I was expecting them to race out of those trees with their rifles blazing, but I think those two were sent out to find out where we were."

Rena stepped away from the rock then asked, "They'll be back though; won't they?"

"I'm sure they will. They're not going to let us get away with their money."

"What if we just tossed the saddlebag with the money out to the ground? Do you think they'd let us go?"

"It's possible, but I don't reckon they would. I don't know those bastards at all, so you'd have a better idea of what they'd do. Some men get so mad and forget why they were doing something in the first place. If that Cash Locklear is one of those types, then we could give him his money and all I have, and he'd still want to shoot us."

"Cash isn't like that, but Max and Snake are. Jack and Harry, the two that were doing the shooting will do anything that Cash tells them to do. Jimmy is just a first-class bastard who only thinks about himself."

"That's what they all do, Rena, or they wouldn't be outlaws. I only thought about myself for all of my life too, you know."

"That was before you met me."

He grinned at her before saying, "That's true, I reckon."

Then after a short pause, he lost his grin and said, "A few hours ago, you made me madder than I've ever been in my life. Now I find myself agreeing with you that I'm thinking more about you than me. It's pretty surprising."

"I'm still afraid, Thom, but if I have to die today, I'm content that it'll be with you close by. I'm so very grateful that you arrived at the ranch house yesterday."

"I hope that doesn't happen, Rena. I'm just getting to know you better. I'd feel kind of cheated if we didn't make it out of here."

She just looked into his dark eyes then nodded before turning her attention to the clearing.

Tabby set his eyes in that direction and wished those foul men turned around but knew they weren't about to give up the chase even if they got their money.

———

Cash was about to get everyone in position to make their attack when he heard hoofbeats behind him and turned with his Winchester ready to fire. The others all quickly twisted in their

151

saddles and just before their rioting nerves made them pull their triggers, Jimmy announced his arrival.

"Howdy, boys! I heard the shootin'. Did you get that bastard?"

"Jesus, Jimmy! You startled the hell out of me!" Cash exclaimed as he lowered his rifle.

"Sorry, boss. But did you get him?"

"Would we still be here with our Winchesters cocked if we'd gotten him, Jimmy?" Cash asked sarcastically.

"No, I reckon not. Where is he?"

"About a hundred yards on the other side of that clearing. We were just getting ready to go after him. We don't have much time before we lose the light, so tie off those horses and pull your Winchester. When you're ready, get in line next to Snake. Hold your fire until you see his muzzle flash. We're not going to gallop across that open ground, but don't ride straight either. Keep movin' your horses side to side as you fire. Jack said he's buried in the rocks of the right side so as soon as he fires, we're going to fill the air with bullets. Okay?"

"Okay, boss," Jimmy said as he walked his horse to the nearest pine.

The other five outlaws watched as he tied off the trail rope then slid his Winchester from its scabbard. He then walked his horse to the far-left side of the line beside Snake and cocked his hammer.

Cash was on Snake's other side and Max was to his right. Now that they were all together again, Cash expected to have his money within ten minutes.

Cash's unwarranted respect for the man's marksmanship had been the reason for telling his men to keep a fast pace and to zigzag. It would more than triple the time they would have taken with a straight charge. If he'd known they were just facing an inexperienced shooter, the results would have been much different.

———

Tabby's lone spent cartridge had been replaced, so he had sixteen shots available and the open box of .44s sitting on a nearby rock. He'd thought about having Rena hand them to him if it became necessary but wanted her out of the path of any incoming rounds. He planned on firing a few shots and adding fresh cartridges when he had a chance...if he had a chance.

He didn't believe that he'd be alive much longer and wished he could have convinced Rena to leave. But even now, he understood that she had been right all along. Even if she made it to Bannack safely with the saddlebag full of cash, her life would probably return to the same sorry existence she'd experienced since leaving her father's house. It was the only reason he really was worried about dying. He had to give Rena a chance for a better life, even if he had no idea of how he could do it.

Tabby had his Winchester cocked and held loosely in both hands when the six men exploded out of the trees. He wasn't stunned or even surprised, but knew he had to start firing as they'd be across that clearing in just seconds. But he wasn't about to trust his marksmanship. He may have hated the idea, but he had to aim at the bigger targets: the horses underneath the outlaws' saddles.

None of the men who left the cover of those trees even imagined that the bounty hunter, or any other man would intentionally shoot horses. But they weren't facing a bounty hunter or a man who was accustomed to gunfights. Tabby had never shot a man before, but he had shot quite a few horses when they'd been injured or diseased.

So, just as they exited the trees, it was Snake who was the first to get a hint of the difference when Tabby's first shot plowed into his dark gelding's chest. The horse didn't even scream as it twisted and crashed to the ground, throwing Snake to the rocky surface. It may have been a clearing, but it wasn't a soft, grassy pasture. It was just devoid of boulders and trees.

Snake landed awkwardly, bounced the back of his head off of a foot-tall jagged piece of stone then tumbled across other rocks before coming to a stop. His hat and Winchester left him shortly after he left his horse, but it didn't matter to Snake anymore. He lay on his back with blood pooling beneath his head as the other five began firing.

Jimmy Parsons had started firing just as Snake's horse crashed beside him and after taking his one shot, he looked back to see what had happened.

Cash thought the bounty hunter had missed but didn't bother giving Snake a glance as he aimed at Tabby's muzzle flash.

Harry, Jack and Max missed a shot as they took a second to change their sights from the right side where they'd expected the bounty hunter to be to the left, but all of them soon resumed firing.

Tabby didn't take time to watch Snake's horse fall but had fired at Cash's horse and missed as their bullets began to arrive. He had to ignore them but kept his sights on Cash's handsome gelding and fired again.

Cash was firing when Tabby's third shot cracked into his horse's forehead. The thick bone deflected the bullet, but the horse reared in pain, throwing the gang leader from the saddle. He was more fortunate than Snake and landed on flat ground, but almost as awkwardly as Snake had. He blew out his breath as he struck the hard earth and his Winchester flew from his hand. He laid flat for a few seconds while his horse bucked nearby. Then he realized that the greatest threat to him now wasn't the bounty hunter, but his own horse's hooves. He rolled onto his stomach, then grabbed his Winchester and began running as fast as he could toward the trees.

The other four outlaws were closing the gap to Tabby and Rena and not one of them had yet realized that their horses were the targets.

It was just fifteen seconds after starting the charge when Tabby's fourth shot missed Jack's horse entirely but drilled into the right side of Jack's chest, splintering a rib and lodging in the middle lobe of his right lung. Jack grunted and dropped his Winchester before leaning over his horse's neck and starting to turn him back to safety. But when he made that sudden turn, his still healthy mare rammed into Harry's gelding and Harry was sent flying out of the saddle

Jack didn't pay any attention but righted his mare and sent her racing back to the trees. He saw Cash scrambling ahead of him and Snake lying unmoving on the shadowed ground, but his biggest concern was making it to those trees. He was bleeding profusely from his chest wound and he had difficulty breathing but thought he could make it if someone stopped the bleeding.

Max was almost at the end of the clearing when his horse took a .44 in the left side of his neck. The gelding screamed and began to buck, but Max stayed in the saddle for another twelve seconds. It would have been a good time for a bronco rider in a rodeo, but it didn't count for much as Max fought to keep from being tossed. He did lose his grip on his Winchester '76 almost immediately and because he was able to stay on his horse's back for so long, he was more than thirty feet from where his Winchester landed when he finally flew into the air.

He landed on a rock just as Snake had, but it was his left upper arm that struck the hard chuck of granite. He screamed in pain as the arm bounced off the unforgiving surface. Once he stopped moving, he quickly scanned the ground for his repeater but couldn't find it in the dust raised by his gelding who was still bucking wildly nearby.

Max didn't waste too much more time looking as he began to race to the trees in a crouch with his injured left arm dangling by his side.

That left only Jimmy Parsons on his horse and he hadn't even fired his second shot yet. He saw the disaster spread out in the small clearing in front of him and even as Harry was trying to climb back into his saddle, he knew that if he continued, he'd be as dead as Snake. He quickly fired once more before whipping his horse around and heading back to the safety of the nearby trees.

Tabby didn't fire at Harry as he mounted and raced away staying low over his horse's neck. He kept an eye on them until all of them were out of sight.

He didn't turn but asked, "How are you, Rena?"

"I'm all right. How bad is it?"

He replied, "One is probably dead because he's lying in the middle of the clearing, but I don't know about the other five."

"No," she said as she stepped closer, "how bad is your wound?"

"Wound?" he asked with wide eyes as she pulled at his shirt sleeve.

He looked at his left forearm, saw a hole in the flannel and some blood and only then did he feel the pain. He didn't want to stop watching the trees because there was so little time for them to make another attempt that he expected them to ride back out at any moment.

So, he held out his arm and asked, "Can you look at it? I have to stay focused on the clearing. I don't even remember getting hit."

"Alright," she said as she unbuttoned his sleeve and pulled it up to above his elbow to inspect the wound.

When she found it, she said, "It's not bad at all. I think it was made by a piece of rock from a ricochet. I'll go get something to wrap around it."

"Thank you, ma'am," he said with a slight smile as he continued to stare at the tree line.

Behind the cover of the trees, the four outlaws who weren't bleeding stood around Jack who was laying on the pine needles. His earlier self-prognosis had changed after he found that his breathing was growing even more difficult.

"Can you patch me up, Cash?" he asked as he looked at the gang leader.

"I don't reckon there's much we can do for you, Jack. You're still losin' a lot of blood and if we throw somethin' over that hole, it's just gonna let you keep livin' in pain a little longer."

Jack nodded then said, "Get that bastard; will ya, boss?"

"Yeah, we'll get him. I'll make sure we get you buried proper, so the critters won't get ya."

"Thanks, Cash. I appreciate it."

Cash stood then looked at the other three and asked, "Max, how is that arm of yours?"

Max tried flexing his elbow and grimaced before replying, "It's pretty bad, but I don't reckon anything's broke. But I left my Winchester on the other side of that flat ground."

"Snake's rifle is closer than Jack's. We need to get that bastard, but I don't think we can risk another bull rush like that one. He's a better shot than we figured."

"Lucky, too," Harry said, "When he missed, he hit our horses."

"At least Jimmy was smart enough to bring us some spares. Okay. Now it's gonna be dark pretty soon, and that's when we'll

159

make our move. Let's take a little break to get something to eat. We're not gonna use the horses this time. After the sun is gone, we're gonna cross that open ground on foot, but not in the middle. We'll walk on both sides, so he won't hear us comin'."

Max then said, "I should be better before we go, Cash."

Cash nodded before saying, "Alright. Let's get something in our bellies and we can figure out how we'll get that damned bounty hunter."

Ironically, in their attempt to kill Tabby and Rena, they had effectively transformed Tabby from a cowhand to a bounty hunter, even if he didn't realize it.

———

Rena used one of the pairs of socks she had taken from the men's dressers to wrap around Tabby's wound as he continued to watch the trees.

When she finished, she pulled his sleeve back down before buttoning the cuff.

As he lowered his bandaged arm, Tabby said, "Thank you, Rena. I thought that they would have already come at us by now."

"Do you think that they might have gone?"

"They lost one and maybe some of the others were injured. They were being tossed off their horses like a bunch of cowhands trying to break a herd of mustangs."

"Did you try to shoot their horses?"

"I'm afraid so. I couldn't afford too many misses, so I had to aim at the bigger targets. I wasn't happy about it, but I had to do it."

"I know. It did stop them, too. How much longer are we going to stay here?"

"I'm not sure yet. I would have thought that they'd have to make another charge before they lost the light, but we're losing light pretty fast and they're still in those trees."

Before Rena could say anything, a shot echoed from the trees and she whipped her eyes in that direction expecting to see them making their second attack.

When the clearing remained empty of riders, she asked, "What was that?"

"They were either finishing off an injured horse or one of their own," he answered as he released his Winchester's hammer.

He looked at the clearing where one dead horse, a dead outlaw and two still living horses but one was still struggling.

"I'm going to do something that sounds stupid because it is."

She nervously asked, "What is it?"

He didn't reply but strode past her and rounded the edge of the rock near the pass then took a few steps down the decline toward the open ground before stopping.

Tabby looked at the trees then spotted Max's Winchester '76 on the ground just a few feet away. He didn't have any ammunition for the new repeater but having a second rifle would be a real bonus. There were two other Winchesters on the ground as well, and he was pretty sure they were both '73s. He had already decided to run down to the flat ground and shoot both injured horses. Snatching the '76 would be easy but having another '73 would be even better.

He still hadn't answered Rena's question as he slowly leaned his Winchester against the rock.

"I'm going to run down there and grab two of those Winchesters. I'll shoot both horses and then I'll get back here as fast as I can."

Rena quickly exclaimed, "You can't do that! They'll shoot you!"

"I don't think so, Rena. If I see any movement, I'll get back here faster than a jackrabbit."

As Rena prepared to deliver her second objection, Tabby shot down the pass and headed for the first Winchester, the '76. He didn't even look at the trees and only slowed as he reached down and snatched it from the ground before heading for the closer '73. He finally took a look at the trees just before he neared the fallen repeater and thanked his lucky stars when he felt the steel and wood in his grasp.

He turned to his right and trotted toward Max's horse. By then, Cash's wounded animal had already gone into the trees. Max's gelding had already slowed as blood dripped from his neck and was just tossing his head as he tried to stop the pain.

Tabby felt like a criminal as he approached the wounded animal.

"I'm sorry, sir. I wish I was a better shot or the man who was riding you was a better man. You didn't deserve this."

He leaned the '76 against his leg and raised the '73. He didn't have to cock the hammer, so he just aimed it at the horse's head and squeezed the trigger. The gelding crumpled to the ground and just as Tabby was preparing to sprint back to Rena, he stopped and quickly untied the saddlebags from the dead horse. He tossed them over his right shoulder then took a Winchester in each hand before he raced back to the pass.

In the forest, each of the four outlaws flinched at the shot as they prepared to dig into their cans of cold beans.

"What is he doin'?" asked Jimmy as he grabbed his nearby Winchester.

Cash just paused and replied, "I reckon he was killin' Max's horse. It was the only thing still breathin' out there. He sure ain't comin' in here."

They resumed their quick dinner as the sun disappeared behind the mountain leaving a deep red sky in its wake.

————

As soon as Tabby reached the top of the pass, he trotted behind the rock on the left and bent over at the waist as he gasped for breath.

Rena walked beside him and snapped, "That was stupid, Thom! You're lucky you got back here in one piece."

He nodded but grinned as he said between breaths, "I told you that before I left, ma'am."

"Don't ever do anything that stupid again!" she exclaimed as she stood before him with her hands firmly on her hips.

"I can't make that promise, Rena," he said as he straightened.

He walked to the side of the boulder where he left his Winchester, took a long look at the clearing then said, "They're going to try to sneak up on us after dark."

She stopped glaring at him and turned to look toward the trees.

"What are we going to do?"

"Leave before they get here. I can't be lucky enough to stop them again."

They both turned to the east and their only escape route. They hadn't really paid much attention to the area since they'd arrived and now that they were able to study the ground more thoroughly, another problem was easily apparent.

"We can't go that way," Rena said with more than a hint of dejection.

"Sure, we can. We just can't bring Philly. We have to leave him here and go on foot."

"You're serious about that?" she asked sharply.

"We can't go back and it's the only way out of here short of climbing mountains. We'll have to do some climbing if we go in that direction, but not more than a few feet now and then. I don't see any mountains behind it, so we really don't have a choice."

"What will we take with us?"

"Let's start packing what we can before they get here."

"Alright."

Tabby felt bad about leaving Philly, but it was better than shooting him. He now had three Winchesters, but the '76 used a different cartridge and he thought about leaving it behind but put off that decision until after they'd done an inventory.

After each of them pulled on their warm coats, he unsaddled Philly quickly and set his bedroll/blanket/slicker bundle aside. That would be coming along. It was well past chilly already and they needed something to keep warm because they surely couldn't build a fire. He'd hang his big saddlebags over one shoulder and the money saddlebags over the other. The Winchesters all had lanyards for attaching straps, so he could use Philly's reins to sling them over his shoulders. He'd stuff the two sets of saddlebags with food and other necessities until they were bulging.

He then looked at the set of saddlebags he'd taken from the horse he'd shot and opened the first flap. Most of the things he found weren't worth taking along, but when he found two boxes of the .45-75 Express Winchester cartridges for the '76, his thoughts about leaving the new rifle behind vanished.

As he sorted the saddlebags' contents, Rena had taken the money saddlebags from the burlap bag and set it aside, knowing that Tabby would want to return the money.

Before she started on her clothing bags, she asked, "What will you be carrying, Thom?"

"I figure I'll carry a set of saddlebags over each shoulder including that one with their stolen money, all three Winchesters and a heavy bag with some food and maybe a couple of plates and tin cups."

"You're overloading yourself. I can carry some of that. You're not much bigger than I am"

"You'll be carrying your clothing bags and both canteens. If you want to have a Winchester over your shoulder, I'm making straps for them in a minute."

"Okay. We'd better get moving."

Tabby nodded before they started their hasty repacking of items that they would take along.

He made the three Winchester straps quickly but knew that they might become a problem if he needed them quickly.

It took them almost twenty minutes before Tabby hung the first set of bulging saddlebags over his left shoulder and then slid the second even heavier set over his right. They were more cumbersome than he'd expected, but he didn't say anything. Before they left, he cut a large piece of thick leather from his saddle skirt now that he didn't need it anymore. He slipped it into his heavy jacket pocket before hanging the '76 over his left shoulder and just gripping his '73 in his right hand. Rena already had the second '73 hanging over her back.

His suggestion that he carry a burlap bag of food and tinware was ignored when Rena simply hung her two clothing bags over her left shoulder and then added the food and tinware bags over her right.

"We're regular pack-people," Rena with a grin said as she looked at him.

"We're going to be dead pack-people if we don't start moving."

She took his free hand then they both took one last look at the dark clearing before they headed east.

CHAPTER 4

An hour after Tabby and Rena had made their escape, the four outlaws stealthily left the cover of the trees and walked along both sides of the into the dark clearing. By then, their prey was already more than eight hundred yards away. The first sixty yards of Tabby and Rena's trek was no different than it had been since they left the buckboard. But then they reached the daunting large, sharp rocks and rounded boulders that had made it necessary to leave Philly behind.

Each climb over a granite obstacle took energy and time. Tabby would climb first and then assist Rena to his new perch. Some of the rock formations were so tall that it would take three or four climb and assist steps to cross the obstacle. The longest they were able to walk without a climb was less than a hundred yards. Big round boulders and tall rocks weren't the only impediment to their progress. There were gullies and small cliffs that made their journey longer and more treacherous. Some of the gullies were deeper than others, but what they most feared was finding a cliff that would stop them from moving at all.

Their heavy loads made those difficult climbs and slides even harder and more dangerous, but they had to keep going.

When the moon rose, they shifted their direction to the north, but the terrain didn't improve. They tried to keep their passage as quiet as possible, but they still knocked over loose stones. Tabby's grunts and an occasional subdued yelp from Rena when she slipped or banged a knee only added to their concerns of being heard.

But their decision to leave so quickly gave them enough of a cushion that even if they had been heard, it would be impossible for the outlaws to catch them.

Cash and Max were on the left side of the clearing and Jimmy and Harry were on the other side as they snuck closer to the pass with their Winchesters in their hands. When the moon rose, they felt exposed and just as Cash was preparing to dash the last few yards, they were all startled when Philly suddenly trotted down the incline.

Max was startled by the gelding's sudden appearance and screamed an obscenity. His cry was so loud that Tabby and Rena heard it over a thousand yards away.

Cash knew that any chance of surprise was gone, so he raced up the inline and when he passed the blocking boulders, he whipped his Winchester in a wide arc searching for the bounty hunter and Monique.

"They're gone!" he shouted.

When they heard Max's scream echoing off of the rocks, Tabby and Rena froze as they were preparing to mount an eight-foot tall jagged chunk of stone. Their lack of movement allowed them to clearly hear Cash's shout of discovery.

Tabby then said, "I don't know what spooked them, but now they know we're not there anymore."

They were at the end of their endurance, so Rena asked, "How much longer do you think we have to go before we rest?"

"Let's climb over this one and then we'll rest on the other side. I don't think that they can find us now even if they could find our footprints."

"Okay. Let's get over this one before I collapse."

As they climbed with their heavy, swinging loads that threatened to pull them to the rocky ground, their four pursuers were trotting back to the trees.

When they reached their horses, Cash snapped, "They figure they're safe now, but I ain't givin' up! I'm gonna shoot that bastard and then take every stitch of cloth off Monique and leave her to face the bears and wolves. If any of you wanna head back to that ranch house, go ahead. You can have the money from the coach heist in my saddlebags, but you ain't gonna get a penny of the big stash."

Max quickly said, "I'm comin'."

"Me, too," Harry added.

Jimmy hesitated before he said, "You can't take the horses in there, boss."

"I know that, you moron! We're gonna take our saddlebags with some food and canteens and we'll run those two down. They been walkin' all day and she's slowin' that bounty hunter down. They can't go very far. With the moonlight we should catch up with 'em in a couple of hours."

Without waiting for any more discussion, Cash began to rummage through the packs that Jimmy had brought with him and soon had the ground littered with tins and bags of jerky.

He pulled his saddlebags from his wounded horse's back and began adding food while Harry did the same. Max's saddlebags were still out in the clearing on his dead horse, so he just stuffed some jerky and two tins of beans into his jacket pockets.

Jimmy hadn't picked up anything as he stood with his horse's reins in his hand.

When Cash hung his saddlebags over his shoulder, he noticed that Jimmy wasn't moving and asked, "You comin', Jimmy?"

Jimmy summoned his last bit of courage and calmly replied, "I reckon not, Cash. I've got my ranch now and I don't figure we'll catch that bounty hunter."

Cash stared at him in the darkness that hid the disgust in his eyes as he said, "Okay, Jimmy. Just leave us three good horses. Take mine back with you and see if you can fix him up."

"I'll do that, boss," Jimmy said in relief.

As he turned to walk to Cash's wounded animal, the outlaw boss's right hand snapped down to his Colt, and in one smooth, practiced motion, flipped off the hammer loop, took hold of the grips, and lifted it from its holster. As he brought it level, his thumb pulled back the hammer and with his trigger already pulled back, he released the hammer with his muzzle just four feet behind Jimmy's back.

The flame from the Colt briefly illuminated the nearby tree trunks before Jimmy screamed and arched his back as the .45 drilled through his back, liver and then his diaphragm before exiting the lower part of his chest.

Jimmy didn't die as quickly as Max and Harry hoped as he continued to wail and thrash on the ground and blood poured from both the entrance and exit wounds. Jack's unburied body lay just four feet beside him.

Cash didn't waste another bullet as Jimmy's screaming became sobs but just quietly half-cocked his pistol, then opened the loading gate and removed the spent shell before filling the empty cylinder with a new cartridge.

"Let's get movin'," Cash said, "Those horses will be here when we get back."

"Okay, Cash," Max said as they started back toward the clearing.

Jimmy was silently praying as they left and took another minute and a half to die.

———

Rena had just stepped to the ground and she and Tabby were in the process of shedding their baggage when the Colt's distant report reached them.

They both stopped, but after a few seconds of silence, they resumed ridding themselves of their burdens which was an incredible relief.

Tabby was second to be free of encumbrances when he lowered his two Winchesters onto the burlap bags. Once his hands were free, he and Rena collapsed into each other's arms to keep from dropping to the ground in exhaustion.

"What were they shooting?" Rena asked as she held onto him tightly.

"I have no idea, but it wasn't that close. I'm not all that sure 'cause it's night, but I'd guess it was about a mile away."

"How far are we from the road?"

"I wish I could tell you, Rena, but your guess is as good as mine. At least I'm pretty sure that we're headed in the right direction now because we've been going downhill."

"We have? You could have fooled me. How long are we going to rest?"

"I think we can stay here all night, or at least long enough to get some sleep."

"Thank God! I thought you were going to say fifteen minutes."

"I'm just as tired as you are and I need to fix my right boot, too. I've got a hole in the bottom, so I'll cut a piece of leather and stuff it in there."

"We've been working so hard, we didn't feel the cold, but it's going to get colder and we'll feel every bit of it."

"Yes, ma'am. But we'll be able to keep each other warm."

She laughed before saying, "You're keeping me pretty warm right now, Mister Hayes."

"I'm just trying to stay on my feet, Rena. Let's get something to eat and set up our camp."

"Alright."

After they separated, the first thing they did was to find a little privacy to hurriedly empty their overfull bladders.

Setting up the camp itself took all of five minutes as Tabby untied the cords holding his bedroll/blanket/slicker bundle and spread the bedroll across a patch of clear ground. He set his blanket over the top and then the slicker to keep out the frost that was sure to arrive before the predawn. He just hoped that it would only be frost and not snow. The snow might be useful for covering their tracks, but it would be a real problem climbing those stony obstacles in their path.

After opening a tin of beans and cutting off large pieces of a small ham, Tabby and Rena sat on the slicker to share their sumptuous feast.

_____

After climbing to the top of the pass, Cash and his last two partners stared at the forbidding rocks in front of them. In the moonlight, they looked even more impassable.

"How are we gonna find 'em in that mess?" Max asked.

"Let's see if we can pick up their trail. It's gonna be hard, but they couldn't have gone too far."

Harry grunted before they started toward the rocks. Cash could see the footprints in the low light but suspected that once they climbed over those first few boulders, it would be more difficult. He was still firmly convinced that even without their horses, they could catch them within a couple of hours. He knew that they had to be even more tired than they were and were carrying more weight.

_____

Rena was snuggled in close to Tabby with her head resting on his bicep and her back pressed against him. They were staying warm under the slicker and blanket but using the bedroll as a mattress. There were two reasons for their choice in sleeping accommodations: they might need to make a sudden escape and the bedroll would be a tight fit for both of them. As it turned out, sharing their body heat was a much better way to stay warm than one sleeping in the bedroll and the other using just the blanket. Besides, each of them was still wearing a heavy coat.

Rena had been so exhausted when Tabby pulled the blanket over them that she expected to fall asleep in just seconds, but she'd been awake for more than five minutes already. She knew that Tabby was still awake and not just because he wasn't snoring.

"Do you know what's strange, Thom?" she asked softly.

"I think it would be easier to list the things that weren't strange about all of this, Rena."

She laughed lightly before saying, "No, it's about me. I'm nothing more than a common whore, but when we were about to lay down on the bedroll, I felt like a girl about to go to her first social. I didn't even feel that way when I was a schoolgirl. I don't know why I felt that way, but it was more than just a surprise, it was wonderful."

"Rena, you may have been a prostitute, but I haven't found anything common about you yet. Maybe I will tomorrow, but we'll just have to wait and see. Now when I pulled up that blanket, do you know what I felt like?"

"What did you feel like?"

"A tired cowhand who needs some sleep."

Rena laughed and pulled his hand over her shoulder.

This may have been the first time that Tabby had ever slept with a woman, but even having her warm backside pressed against his hips didn't hold back the overwhelming need to sleep.

Rena tried to recall if she had ever spent the night with a man when all they did was sleep.

Less than a minute after the last word had passed between them, they were both in deep slumber.

———

Cash, Max and Harry were about eight hundred yards south of the sleeping pair when they had to stop themselves. They may have been able to move faster, but they still had to climb and descend the same rocks and boulders. Having to find their tracks in the moonlit shadows cancelled the gains they would have made with their faster pace.

When they decided to get some sleep, they rued leaving their bedrolls on their horses because they believed that they would have caught the bounty hunter and Monique already.

So, using their hats as pillows the three outlaws lay on their backs and were soon sleeping uncomfortably, expecting to resume the chase in the predawn which was just a few hours after they'd stopped for some rest. Unlike Rena and Tabby, they didn't share each other's body warmth because it wasn't manly.

As they slept, the frost began to form across the cold ground.

———

The earlies to awaken were the three who were least comfortable. Harry was the first to stir when he rolled over in his sleep and a sharp stone reminded him that he wasn't on a soft mattress.

"Damn!" he groused loudly as he popped into a sitting position.

His expletive awakened the other two and the grousing continued as the three men stood in the soft light of the predawn.

"It's cold!" snapped Max as he wrapped his arms around his heavy coat.

Cash looked around him and said, "That's not our biggest problem, Max. Look at that frost."

Max and Harry scanned the white landscape and understood the issue. Climbing over those rocks, even in the night, was hard, but trying to climb over them when they were covered in a thick layer of icy frost was almost impossible.

"What do we do, boss?" Harry asked as his breath formed white clouds.

"We ain't goin' back, but they can't move either. I reckon they mighta even heard you when you woke us up with that yell. They can't be that far away."

"Sorry, but I was asleep."

"It don't matter. They know we're here, so let's get somethin' into our bellies and we'll see if we can find a way around those damned rocks."

———

Neither Tabby nor Rena had heard Harry's shout as they slept. They were still pressed close under the blanket and slicker and their shared body heat kept them relatively comfortable.

They were only around two miles south of the road but much closer to the men who were trying to kill them and were already awake.

They were only awakened by an odd lesson in Newton's laws. Rena's long sandy hair had looped around Tabby's left ear, so when she moved her head just a couple of inches away from him, the strands yanked against his ear and startled him. He jerked back slightly, pulling Rena's hair back and they almost banged heads.

Their eyes popped open and when they realized what had caused them to harshly end their slumber, they both began to laugh.

But their amusement didn't last long when they remembered why they were there. Tabby quickly tossed aside the blanket and slicker then stood. He was sore and stiff and imagined that Rena was in worse shape, so he offered her his hand.

Rena took his hand and was grateful for his assistance as she slowly got to her feet.

"Look at the frost!" she exclaimed in a muted voice.

"I know. We've got to get moving. We can chew on some jerky while we walk. How are you doing?"

"I've felt better but I think I can make it after I start moving around."

"Okay, let's start packing things, but I don't want to take everything. We have to be close to the road and we can move faster if we're carrying less of a load."

"I agree with you, so I'll let you decide what to leave behind."

He nodded before just taking two steps and turning away from Rena to answer nature's call. Rena took his cue and stepped behind some bushes. As she lifted her dress, she acknowledged that she normally didn't care what men saw. But after her schoolgirl reaction when she was about to share their bedroll mattress, she wasn't surprised.

Tabby began sorting what they would take. He didn't take any extra clothes or any tins of food. He only packed the jerky.

181

Ammunition was heavy, so he only took a box of .44s. As he looked at the box of .45 Long Colts, he shook his head and thought he should have bought one of those Remingtons. He had eight spare cartridges in his gunbelt, so that should be enough. He then looked at the .45-75s for the Winchester '76. He was going to leave it and the cartridges behind, but then took the box slid it into his right coat pocket. He'd leave the outlaw's '73 and keep the newer '76.

As the box of cartridges dropped into his pocket, he remembered the piece of leather he'd taken from his saddle to fix his shoe. He knew they were rushed for time and he wasn't sure it really mattered, so he just left it there and hoped it wouldn't become a problem.

He left Rena's clothing bags on the ground. Even though they weren't that heavy, he wanted her to carry as little as possible. The two canteens were necessary and so were the saddlebags with the outlaws' stolen cash.

As Rena approached, she looked at the two piles and asked, "What will I be carrying?"

"The canteens. I'll carry my Winchester, the '76 and the two saddlebags. The rest will all stay behind."

"Even the ammunition and the other rifle?"

"It doesn't matter, Rena. They have enough firepower already and if they take the one I'm leaving behind, then they'll have to put up with the weight. We won't be spending another night out in the cold, so the blanket and bedroll aren't necessary."

"Are you sure I can't carry more? I can carry one of the rifles."

"I know you can, but I want to stay balanced."

"Liar."

Tabby grinned and said, "Maybe. Let's load up and see if we can find some way to get out of here without climbing any of those slick rocks."

She nodded and as she hooked the two canteens over her shoulders, she scanned the surrounding terrain in the growing light. She looked back at the last rock they'd surmounted knowing that was where the outlaws would be and then examined the other directions.

As she was looking and Tabby was hanging the rifles over his shoulders, she thought she heard something, but it was faint and indistinguishable. It wasn't the outlaws or even a deer or coyote. It was constant almost like the wind, but there wasn't any breeze at all or there wouldn't be so much frost.

She was still standing still and just listening when a fully laden Tabby approached her and asked, "Are you ready to get out of here, ma'am?"

She surprised him when she replied, "Shush! Do you hear that?"

Tabby thought she might have heard the outlaws approaching, so he stared at the boulder behind her as he held his breath and attuned his ears to the slightest sound. But instead of footsteps or a stone being kicked, he finally heard the almost delicate and constant noise that she must have noticed.

He slowly shifted his eyes to his right and then stopped when he was facing almost ninety degrees from where he'd been looking.

Rena finally asked, "What is that?"

"That, ma'am, is water. I think it's that stream we found yesterday. It must have curved to the east as it headed downstream."

"Can we follow it to the road like we were planning on doing yesterday?"

Tabby turned and grinned at her before he took her arm and said, "Yes, we most assuredly can. The ground it passes will be clear and even if we have to walk in the water, we won't have to climb again. We could be on the road in a couple of hours. We might even be having lunch in Watson."

"I don't care where we have lunch as long as we're safe," she said as she grasped his arm and they began walking toward the sound.

They were walking due west and parallel to the road, but even if they'd known their direction, it wouldn't have mattered. If

184

they found the stream, they wouldn't have to make any more tortuous climbs.

———

As they began to move, the posse chasing the gang was mounting their horses to continue the chase.

Joe Wolfson soon had them moving more quickly now that he was no longer concerned about an ambush.

———

After spending a few minutes exploring, it was Harry who discovered a narrow path around the rocks, but it was a good two hundred yards west of the rocks. Without realizing it, they were soon walking in the same direction as Tabby and Rena just seven hundred yards apart. It was those rocks and boulders that both were trying to avoid climbing that kept them from seeing each other.

The stream that had attracted Tabby and Rena had been curving to the northeast for miles and was two hundred yards further from the outlaws if they kept moving in the same direction.

The sun was rising as the posse rode north, the outlaws walked west, and Tabby and Rena made their way in the same direction.

Ten minutes later, Sheriff Smith's posse left Watson to resume their watch along the road. He hadn't heard anything from Bannack, so he told the men that if they didn't spot the outlaws before noon, they'd return to Watson. He had no idea where they could have gone, but with Sheriff Wolfson's posse behind them, there was no place else they could go.

———

"You didn't fix that hole in your boot; did you?" Rena asked as they trudged along.

"Not yet. If we have time to take a break, then I might. It's not too bad."

"Does your sock have a hole in it, too?"

"Yes, ma'am. Hopefully, we shouldn't have to climb any more rocks. If we find the stream, all we need to worry about is a waterfall."

"It's not like we're walking on a polished marble floor, Mister Hayes. Are you sure you don't want me to carry one of those rifles?"

"No, I'm fine."

She looked ahead to find the stream. The sound was a little louder, but she still couldn't see it.

Tabby was more concerned about that hole in his boot than he'd let on. He was trying to avoid limping and wished he'd taken the time to cut that piece of leather before they left. He wasn't worried about limping so much as he was concerned that he might start bleeding and leave a red path for the outlaws to find.

He was certain that they were still behind them because of the last two gunshots. He didn't believe that they would waste bullets on their injured horses. Besides, he'd only hit one of the other horses and he'd trotted back into the trees. He suspected that they had killed their wounded man or had an argument about returning to the ranch or getting their money back.

It came down to who had won the argument. After what Rena had told him about each of the outlaws, he was sure that the harder ones were the ones who had been the first to fire and they would be the ones who wanted their money back at all costs.

But what it also meant is that at least one of the men who had returned to the trees was now dead, and it might be two. So, they would have no more than four men chasing them and maybe only three. They still had the advantages of being better shots and having no hesitation to kill. He had felt badly for shooting their horses and still wasn't sure he'd be able to put a bullet into a man if he could see his face.

As they slowly headed west with the sun at their backs, he hoped they found that stream and followed it to the road before he had to face that issue.

He was still ruminating about the moral dilemma when they had to shift to the right to avoid a long outcrop of hideously sharp granite that looked like nature's sword and after passing by the point, they spotted the stream just twenty yards away.

In subdued excitement, Rena exclaimed, "There it is!"

They had to avoid racing to the rushing water but still picked up their pace.

They soon reached the stream, and after lowering the Winchesters and the saddlebags to the bank, Tabby dropped to his heels and joined Rena who was drinking from the ice-cold water. He was still slurping when Rena dropped their canteens to the smooth rocks alongside the flowing water and began unscrewing their caps.

Tabby's eyes followed the water's flow as the stream headed northeast and almost started giggling when he saw a clear path for more than a thousand yards.

Before he said anything, he looked upstream past Rena and then continued to scan the ground until he was staring behind them. Finding no one, he sat down and pulled off his right boot.

Rena was dipping the second canteen into the stream as she said, "I'm glad to see that you're going to fix that boot."

"It won't take long," he replied as he pulled the leather patch from his pocket.

He unbuttoned his coat and slid his big knife from its sheath then picked up the holey boot and laid the leather on the sole. After stabbing some holes in the leather along the outside of the boot, he set the boot down and began to slice the small sheet of leather.

It didn't take very long because he wasn't trying to make it perfect. He returned his knife to its sheath and then inserted the temporary sole into his boot and then pulled it back on. He didn't waste time changing his socks because they had left them behind anyway.

Rena had already hung the canteens around her shoulders and was standing nearby as Tabby hung the saddlebags over his shoulders then swung the '76 over his left shoulder and picked up his '73.

Before they began to follow the stream's bed, Tabby reached into the saddlebag on his left shoulder and pulled out the bag of beef jerky. He handed three large pieces to Rena then stuck three in his mouth before returning the bag to his saddlebags.

When he took the jerky from his mouth then ripped a piece of one of the strips with his teeth, Rena laughed and said, "I thought you were going to eat all three at once."

Tabby was chewing, so all he did was smile at her before she bit off a chuck of one of her pieces and they began to walk along the bank. Now they were walking almost directly into the rising sun and knew that it wouldn't be long before they spotted the road.

It had taken Tabby only three minutes to complete the hasty repair of his boots, but they were a costly three minutes. If he had postponed the job, then they might not have been spotted.

————

Cash, Max and Harry were behind that sharp outcrop of rock that had diverted Tabby and Rena when they spotted the stream. It was a welcome find as their canteens were dry.

They had just refilled the canteen when Max glanced downstream and said, "The ground around that creek is a lot better for walkin', Cash."

Cash was wiping his mouth with his sleeve as he replied, "I noticed that already, Max. If we follow that stream, we should be able to get ahead of 'em. Let's get movin' faster."

It was just ten minutes later as the three outlaws were walking at a brisk pace along the bank when they passed the end of the natural sword and Cash spotted two figures in the distance about six or seven hundred yards ahead. It was difficult to make them out with the sun in their faces, and it wasn't long before they disappeared again, but he was sure that he'd just spotted the bounty hunter and Monique.

"There they are," he said calmly so they wouldn't be heard.

Neither Max nor Harry had caught sight of them, so Max asked, "Are you sure, Cash? I didn't see a damned thing with the sun in my eyes."

"Yeah. I'm sure. Let's keep goin'. I don't figure they spotted us 'cause I only had a short look. We need to catch up to 'em quick, too. I figure we're less than a couple of miles from the road and we're headed that way. If we don't get 'em soon, we're in trouble."

Without waiting for an answer, Cash began to jog along the bank temporarily leaving Max and Harry behind. They soon matched his faster pace but had to stay in line to make use of the easier ground created by the rushing water.

————

Even though they had no idea that their pursuers were so close, Tabby and Rena were moving at a faster pace than they had earlier. The improved ground was only one of the reasons. It was their excited anticipation of finding the road that really drove them to increase their speed. They had finished their jerky and were looking forward to having a real lunch in Watson after giving the gang's money to the sheriff.

As they walked, Tabby asked, "I wonder if those folks will try to lynch me before I get a chance to give them their money back?"

Rena laughed and replied, "They'll have to lynch me first, but as much as I hate the thought of going into that town, at least

191

they know me. They may not like me very much, but they know who I am."

Tabby grinned as he said, "I'll bet a lot of the men like you."

Rena lost her smile and didn't reply. She had been looking hopefully toward a new future and it was almost as if her sordid past hadn't existed at all. She knew that Tabby hadn't tried to make her feel bad with what he'd said, but it still hurt. *How could she even think about returning to the ranch with Tabby if she couldn't go into town knowing that she had sold herself to so many of the men who lived there?* She had felt like a schoolgirl last night and now the realization of what she really was hit her hard.

When she hadn't laughed or even commented, he looked at her and knew that he said something he shouldn't have.

"I'm sorry, Rena. That was a stupid thing to say. I know that I keep telling you that I'm just a cowhand and I'm not very smart, but that was stupid and unkind."

"No. That's all right, Thom. I was liked by many of the men in Watson. Too many."

"Do you want to go to Bannack instead?"

"No. It's too far away. Can we stop talking about it? Please?"

"Yes, ma'am."

They were still walking along the stream bank when Tabby glanced behind him. The sunlight that blinded the outlaws now bathed them in its bright light for a few seconds.

Tabby tried to quell the panic that suddenly rose inside him. He needed to be calm or they'd never reach the road. He had to make sure that Rena didn't panic either.

He hooked his only free arm around her shoulders before he said, "They're about six hundred yards behind us, Rena. We need to move faster."

Rena whipped her head around but didn't see them, so she asked, "Are you sure?"

"Positive. They're blocked by those tall bushes right now, but they're coming."

"Okay," she replied before they began to jog.

———

Even though all three outlaws were looking for the couple, when Tabby had spotted them clearly, that same bright sunlight that had shone on the chasers had put Tabby and Rena into a shadow and none of the three men had seen them.

They were still moving at a brisk pace but if they had seen the man and woman, they would have moved even faster.

———

As they raced alongside the stream as quickly as they dared, Tabby and Rena had to avoid the larger rocks that still lay in their path. But even as they made their hurried escape, Tabby was glancing at the landscape to the east for someplace to use as protection. Ironically, after all of their climbing and near falls to reach safety, now that they needed one of those big boulders, the closest were a good two hundred yards away.

Tabby had his eyes slightly to his right when disaster struck. It may not have been such a momentous event under any other circumstances, but now it might prove to be fatal.

Rena had taken a quick glance behind them expecting to see the outlaws when her left foot came down on a wet, round rock that was no more than four inches in diameter. If the center of her shoe sole had landed on the top of the rock, then she wouldn't have had the problem. But when her foot contacted the rock slightly off center, the rock popped away and her foot slammed to the ground awkwardly, twisting her ankle badly.

She felt onto the rocky ground and screamed in pain. Tabby rocked to a stop and turned to Rena who was on her back grabbing at her painful ankle.

"I think I broke it!" she exclaimed as Tabby set his rifle on the ground and let the saddlebags slide from his shoulders.

He looked upstream before he began to feel her injured ankle with his thumbs.

"I don't think it's broken, Rena. It's probably just a bad sprain. Let me help you up."

"Okay," she replied as he lifted her to her feet.

When she put weight on the injured ankle, she grimaced and said, "I can't walk, Thom. I'm sorry."

He looked upstream again and even though he couldn't see the outlaws, he knew that they'd probably heard Rena's scream and they'd reach them shortly.

He picked up the two saddlebags and then hung his '73 over his other shoulder before scooping her into his arms.

"Keep an eye out for those outlaws. There are only three of them now."

"Okay."

He struggled to move now that he had Rena in his arms. She had mentioned often that she was almost as big as he was, and now he wished he was a lot bigger and stronger or that she was petite and much lighter.

As difficult as it was, he knew he had to find some protection from those three killers. Even if he did, he was unsure if he'd be able to stop them.

———

The outlaws had just slowed to catch their breath when they heard her scream and they all knew that they were close, so they picked up their pace again.

When they spotted them, Max loudly said, "He's carryin' her! Let's get him while his arms are full!"

Tabby had managed to carry Rena for just twenty yards when they were seen but didn't bother looking back as he focused on the nearest good-sized rock that seemed miles away as he struggled under Rena's weight.

Rena could feel his legs straining and wasn't worried about being dropped but that she was turning him into a target. She was watching behind them as best she could as he swerved and bounced along.

Suddenly, the three men appeared about four hundred yards away and she exclaimed, "They're closer, Thom! Put me down and find yourself someplace where you can defend yourself. They won't bother with me. They just want their money."

Between grunts and gasps, Tabby said, "I'm not going to do that, Rena. They'll just shoot you out of spite as they pass by."

"I don't care, Thom. Put me down!"

"Go to hell, Rena," he snapped as he lugged her toward that faraway boulder.

Rena continued to watch the outlaws as Tabby's grip seemed to get even tighter. She knew he was right, but she thought at least he'd have a better chance to survive if he wasn't burdened with her. They were gaining quickly now and even she understood that they'd soon be within Winchester range.

"They're getting closer, Thom. I think they're going to start shooting."

Tabby knew he didn't have a chance of making it to that boulder before they could reach him with Winchesters, so he looked for anyplace at all that would at least serve as some form of protection for Rena.

He shifted his direction slightly to his right and quickly pulled to a stop beside a small cluster of rocks that weren't even a foot high.

He lowered her to the ground behind the rocks, then slid both Winchesters from his shoulders. He looked at the rapidly approaching outlaws who were around two hundred yards away then dropped both saddlebags to the ground and shrugged off his heavy coat. The air's temperature didn't matter now.

Tabby stretched out his coat on the ground near the rocks, tossed his Stetson to the side then quickly lay in the prone position and grabbed the '76. He assumed there was a cartridge in the chamber, so he just cocked the hammer and rested the wooden forearm on one of the rocks. He didn't bother using the ladder rear sight because he wasn't that good of a shot anyway.

Once he had the rifle ready to fire, Rena snatched his '73 and cocked the hammer before matching his position and setting the repeater on a rock just as he had.

Tabby didn't comment when he saw his Winchester's barrel suddenly appear to his left, but it did make him smile.

————

The three outlaws who had just moments before thought they'd have no problem with the bounty hunter had been surprised when he had stopped in what appeared to be open ground and then quickly set up.

They had already stopped before Rena had aimed a second Winchester in their direction.

Harry looked at Cash and asked, "What are we gonna do now, boss?"

Before Cash could answer, Max quickly said, "That bounty hunter can pick us off a lot easier than we can 'cause he's set up and we'll have to be movin'."

"I know that, but I have a '76 and I can lob bullets into him from two hundred yards easy."

Max nodded as he stared at the bounty hunter. None of the three had noticed that Max's '76 hadn't been left behind. After picking up the lone '73 still left on the ground in the dark, they'd chased after the couple and hadn't gone back to look for the newer model repeater. The advantage that Cash believed that they had simply didn't exist. The one advantage they did have with their greater shooting skills could have won the day for the outlaws, but they all still were firmly convinced that they were facing an experienced bounty hunter. If they had only known that the man behind that Winchester was just a cowhand then they would probably have taken a different approach.

Cash finally said, "He's got the sun at his back, too. We need to stay out of range. I'll stay here and start sending .45s into them while you circle around both sides. Once you're in position, I'll reload and then we'll all start walking at the same time as we keep firing. Even if I don't get lucky with one of my shots, we'll still get him."

"Okay, Cash," Max said, "I'll go around the right side and Harry will take the left."

"Just make sure you stay out of range."

Max snickered then said, "I ain't stupid, Cash."

He and Harry then separated and began walking.

Rena said, "It looks like they're going to surround us."

"Yes, ma'am. I reckon that they don't think you can shoot that Winchester."

"I can shoot it, but I'm not sure I can hit anything."

"That makes two of us, Rena."

As they watched the outlaws separate, Rena said, "Thom, I wish that you would have just run to that boulder and left me."

"Then how could I marry you? I'm not going to wheel a coffin into the courthouse and ask the judge to pronounce us man and dead lady."

Rena turned to him and smiled as she asked, "You really are going to marry me? I thought you were just saying that to shut me up."

"Maybe, but I figure that any woman who can put up with my snoring is worth keeping around."

She laughed, then as soon as she said, "You don't snore," Cash fired his first shot.

Rena's eyes whipped back to the west as the .45 slammed into the ground eight feet behind Tabby's repaired boot.

"*He can shoot that far?*" she exclaimed.

"Yes, ma'am."

"Aren't you going to shoot back?"

"I want to see if he's going to start walking this way, but I figure he's going to wait until those other two are ready before he does. If he takes another shot, then I'll start returning fire."

Tabby had the front sights on Cash when he saw the outlaw chief's muzzle bloom with smoke then heard the crack of his second shot a fraction of a second later. The second .45 ricocheted off a small rock to Tabby's right, so he decided that he may as well make use of the ladder sight after all. He quickly pulled it upright and set the range to two hundred yards. He knew a good marksman would adjust for the altitude and temperature, but he didn't have a clue how to make those calculations.

But when he set his sights back on the shooter, he found that he did have to lift the muzzle slightly to bring the front sights in line with the adjusted rear sights.

When Cash fired his third shot, the ground just in front of Rena exploded showering her with dirt and small rocks.

"Are you okay?" he asked quickly without taking his eyes off his sights.

"I'm alright," she replied as she blinked her eyes and then used her dirty dress sleeve to clear the dust from her face.

Tabby was watching the outlaw chief cycling in a new cartridge when he pulled the trigger. The pop into his shoulder was more noticeable than his '73, but he didn't pay any attention as he reached for the lever to bring in a fresh cartridge believing that his first shot would only serve to make the shooter duck or move.

Cash was bringing his Winchester to bear when Tabby fired, and he didn't even flinch. He knew that the '73 could send a .44

this far, but it lost accuracy at the range and the bullet would have much less power even if it did hit.

So, when the .45 slammed into the right side of his gut, just below his ribs, he grunted and dropped his repeater. He pulled his jacket aside then stared down at the large hole in his belly that was already gushing blood as his hand pressed against his shirt.

"Son of a bitch!" he cursed as his hot blood flowed through his fingers and dripped onto the ground.

He knew that he wasn't going to live much longer and shifted his eyes to the distant bounty hunter.

"You bastard!" he screamed as he reached down and picked up his Winchester with his blood-soaked fingers.

Tabby was stunned when he realized that he'd hit the man, but even as Cash's scream reached them, he knew he had two other problems.

Harry and Max had both heard Cash's shout and looked back to their boss. They saw the blood under his open jacket and even though he was still walking with his Winchester, they knew that he wasn't going to last long.

They hadn't been able to make it to the sides of the bounty hunter's position, but with Cash out of action, they both knew that they couldn't wait much longer.

Max shouted, "Let's get him, Harry!"

Harry didn't yell back but began to walk quickly toward Tabby and Rena as Max started forward from the other side.

Max was the first to open fire at around a hundred and sixty yards, and Harry soon began unleashing a hurried series of shots.

Tabby knew he'd been lucky with that first shot, but quickly rolled his Winchester's sights to his left and let them settle on Harry as their bullets began slamming into the ground all around them.

He fired quickly at Harry but missed and recycled the lever as he cursed himself for jerking the trigger.

Tabby had just fired his second round at Harry when a .44 from Max's rifle drilled into the left side of his back just two inches from his spine. He grunted loudly but knew he had to keep shooting.

Even as he felt the pain from the bullet, Harry felt the powerful .45 ram into his chest, just below his left shoulder. It shattered a rib and then tumbled through his lung's left upper lobe, ripping tissue and blood vessels before it cracked into the back of his ribs and stayed there. His Winchester fell from his hands, then he dropped to his knees, but his left knee struck a ham-sized rock and he screamed in added pain before rolling onto his side.

Rena had fired three shots at Max, but knew she was just wasting ammunition as he continued to fire as he walked closer. He was still beyond the range of her Winchester despite Max's lucky shot that had put a .44 into Tabby.

After watching Harry fall, Tabby spotted Max and knowing that it was only a matter of time before one of his .44s hit Rena, he crawled on top of her, pressing her to the hard ground.

She exclaimed, "*What are you doing?*"

Tabby snapped, "Shut up and play dead!"

She quickly understood what he was doing but didn't know that he'd been shot. She believed he just believed that he might be killed and hoped the last outlaw would think she was dead too. She didn't like it but closed her eyes.

Tabby tried to set his sights on Max. With a moving Rena beneath him, his previous stable shooting position was gone, and his muzzle was dancing, but he knew he wasn't going to last much longer. His sharp reply to Rena had been in the hope that the last one would just grab the money and run after finding him dead on top of her.

Even as he tried to take a shot at Max, he forgot about a still-moving Cash Locklear who had his Winchester level and was preparing to fire.

Max was still firing and sending .44 into the ground around them just as Tabby thought he had the last outlaw in his sights.

Then a .45 from Cash's rifle slammed into his repaired right boot's heel and made him jerk his trigger backward.

The Winchester fired what Tabby knew was an errant shot, but he had to ignore the man who'd sent that bullet through his boot heel and quickly cycled the lever.

He was right that his last shot was a miss, but it was a good miss. It ripped the hat from Max's head as he was ready to fire again. Just as Tabby had yanked his last shot, the shock of having his hat shot off his head startled Max into almost ripping his trigger back sending the bullet almost fifty feet over Tabby's head.

After Max settled his sights on Tabby, he made sure that he was more controlled when he squeezed his trigger. He may have been steadier, but when his hammer fell, it landed on an empty chamber.

Tabby didn't realize that he was facing a man holding a useless rifle when he had Max in his sights.

Max knew he couldn't take the time to reload even a few cartridges and as he looked at the bounty hunter ninety yards away preparing to end his life, he dropped to the ground.

Tabby fired just after Max had dropped and as he worked the lever to bring a fresh cartridge into his chamber, Max popped to his feet and raced away. He left his holed hat on the ground as he zigzagged his way to safety.

Tabby knew that there was no point in trying to hit the difficult target, even if he could shoot him in the back, so he quickly changed his sights to the man who had just ruined his already patched boot.

When he looked in that direction, he didn't find the man standing. He saw him lying on the ground just fifty yards away with his eyes open.

After making sure the one to the north was still on the ground, he rolled off of Rena and kept his eyes on the surviving outlaw who soon disappeared behind some rocks.

Rena surprised him when she snapped, *"You told me to shut up?"*

"I'm sorry, Rena. I needed you to play dead and I didn't have the time to ask nice."

"Are they all dead?"

"No. One of them ran into those rocks up there, but I don't know if he'll be back. He'd have to come at us in the open and he's alone now. I figure it's more likely that he'll just sneak off."

"Are you all right?" she asked as she looked at him.

"Um. No, I don't think so. I think one of those two fellers ruined my nice shirt. I'm glad I didn't have my coat on."

Rena quickly knelt and looked at his back where she saw the bloody patch surrounding a hole.

"My God! Why didn't you tell me?" she demanded as she began ripping away the shirt.

"It doesn't matter, Rena. I can't get move very far. I know your ankle is hurt, but I think you ought to start following that stream again. You could make it to the road before noon and you'll be safe."

"You really believe that I'm going to leave you here to die?"

He rolled onto his side and looked up at her as he said, "He might come back, Rena. If you're still here, he'll kill you. I'm not going to die. You can get to the road and send help. I just can't come with you."

She didn't get weepy but quietly said, "You know you can't last long enough for me to find someone and send them back here to find you. Admit it."

"I'm not going to admit to any such thing. It's the only way, Rena. Take the money with you and start walking. Oh, and before I forget, I have a pocket on the inside of my coat. I have around six hundred dollars inside. Take my coat with you because you won't have any money after you give the bank their money back."

"Now I know you're lying. I'm not leaving, Thom. I'm going to stay with you no matter what happens. If you don't make it, then I'm still not leaving you. I don't even care if that last bastard come back. If you die, then I hope he does because I don't have a life without you."

"Now you're just being silly, Rena. Even with just my money, you could get on a stage to Denver or Cheyenne where none of those men will find you. You can still have a good life. Don't throw it away. Take the money and my coat then start walking."

Rena stared at him, the slowly removed her coat and set it aside. Then she stood and ripped off the hem of her dress and knelt beside him again. She ripped open the wet shirt and looked at the hole that still leaked blood. After folding the wad of cotton, she pressed it onto the wound, then stood and looked down at him.

"I'll be back in a minute."

"Just follow the stream," Tabby said weakly as she walked away.

He closed his eyes and wished that she would listen to him. He had no idea how much longer he could hold on because he'd never had a bullet wound and before yesterday, he hadn't even seen anyone else who had been shot. He just knew he was losing blood and after watching Harry die and then seeing the other one lying with his eyes open, he was convinced that he wouldn't be alive by sunset.

Rena painfully limped on her badly sprained ankle to where Cash's body lay on the ground.

"You, murdering bastard!" she growled as she pulled his knife from his gunbelt and began to cut off pieces of his coat and then his britches. It wasn't ideal bandage material, but it was all that was available and the other body was further away.

She hobbled back to Tabby but kept glancing to her right where the healthy outlaw had gone. She really did hope that he didn't run because she shared Tabby's belief that he wasn't going to live much longer no matter what she did.

Rena soon sat next to Tabby and began to make a better bandage to keep his wound from bleeding. It was already beginning to clot, so she began to hope that his body would be able to heal itself well enough to let them walk to the road.

As she finished applying the new bandage, she knew that it was closer to a prayer than a hope, but she couldn't imagine a life without him. She'd only had that dream for a couple of days now, but it had driven its roots deeply into her heart, mind and soul. Her meaningless, empty life had been given substance by the cowhand who was now bleeding to death before her eyes.

Tabby had opened his eyes when she returned but didn't say anything as she treated his wound. He believed that nothing she could do would help but understood that he couldn't convince her to leave no matter how big the lie or how rude he became. He wished he could tell her other things, but he knew that they would only make the inevitable much worse for her. He just hoped that she would leave after he took his last breath.

When she saw his open eyes, she managed a smile before saying, "The bleeding is stopping, Thom. I'm going to wash the wound in a little while and see if it's stopped."

"Okay, but that bullet is still in there, Rena."

"I know."

She stood and picked up both coats and laid them on the ground in front of him before she asked, "Do you want to move onto your coat? It'll be more comfortable."

He smiled as he replied, "No, thank you, ma'am. I don't want to ruin my coat. I'm really fond of it."

She touched his face with her fingertips then folded her coat before she lifted his head and slid it underneath. She then took his coat and folded it lengthwise and stretched it on the ground facing him.

After she laid down just inches away, she asked, "Do you want some water?"

"I'm okay. At least we have plenty of it. You have enough jerky, too."

"Can you talk?"

"Isn't that what we're doing, ma'am?"

She smiled then replied, "You're still a smarty pants; aren't you?"

"I like to make you smile, Rena."

"You do. You make me smile and you make me laugh, but most of all, you make me happy and give me hope."

"That's amazing; isn't it? I didn't even know you existed three days ago and just when I finally figured out that you made me happy and gave me something to look forward to, I go and do something as stupid as getting shot."

"Part of me wishes you had never shown up at the ranch house or I hadn't returned after seeing the gang coming back to the canyon. But as selfish as it seems, I'm happy that you did find me and didn't kick me off the buckboard when I came back."

"I'm glad that I showed up too, and you really weren't that close to being shoved off the buckboard either."

She then paused before she quietly said, "I love you, Thom. Please don't die on me."

"I don't have any control over what happens to me, Rena. I just finished telling myself that I wouldn't tell you anything that might make you even more determined to stay or get you more upset if I didn't make it. I was even thinking about being a real heel and saying nasty things to you to make you leave. Now I'm unsure that it's not more important to tell you the truth."

"What were you going to tell me?"

211

"I wanted to tell you that that I love you, Rena. If we had made it to the road, I would have told you that I really did want to marry you. Where we went or what I did for a living didn't matter anymore. I just wanted to spend my life with you."

"We picked a bad time to tell each other that; didn't we?"

"We did," he replied, the took a deep breath and asked, "Rena, will you promise me something?"

"Not if you're going to ask me to leave you here."

"Not if I'm still alive, but will you at least promise me that you'll leave if I don't make it? I'm already getting sleepy and I want you to promise me that you will."

She slowly shook her head before saying, "No. I can't make that promise. I'm not leaving this spot and it's not because of my bad ankle. I'm going to hold you in my arms and even after I feel your heart stop beating, I'm staying here. I don't know how long I'll last if Max doesn't return, but I'm not leaving. I would rather die with you than live with anyone else."

"Rena...", Tabby whispered as he closed his eyes, "Please."

She didn't answer but leaned forward and kissed him.

Tabby felt her lips on his and did his best to kiss her back. He knew it was far from a passionate kiss but thought it was the first and last one he would ever have from Rena. At least it would be the last he would feel.

CHAPTER 5

The extended gunfire had alerted the posse that had discovered the three dead outlaws and their horses before they bumped into the impassable ground taken by Tabby and Rena then followed by the three outlaws.

Sheriff Wolfson led his posse back to the trees where they collected the bodies and horses, including Philly. Deputy Trudeau took the lead as they began riding along the stream that headed toward the sound of the distant gunfire. They still didn't move very quickly as they had to be concerned that the gang was still nearby with their rifles ready to shoot anyone they saw.

But it was the men from Watson who were much closer and didn't have such hard terrain to cover. Sheriff Smith was one of the two men who rode toward the source of the gunfire following the stream that flowed from the south. It was almost like a road into the wilderness. He should have moved even more slowly than Sheriff Wolfson's posse, but his intense need for revenge drove him to move as quickly as possible. He and Charlie had their Winchesters in their hands as they trotted along the stream to the site of the gun battle.

So, as Rena and Tabby lay on the ground waiting for Max to finish them off a large posse was about three miles away coming from the south and Sheriff Smith and one member of his posse was following the same stream from the north but was only a mile away.

———

Max was still shaken by his brush with near death. He'd reloaded his Winchester but wasn't about to challenge that bounty hunter again. He was just too good with that rifle. Max began making his way south to get to their horses and even if he didn't have the big stash that Monique had stolen, he'd get the six hundred dollars from the stagecoach job that was in Cash's saddlebags. He had to borrow some other saddlebags before they'd left and would pick up his '76 when he got returned to that clearing where Snake had died. He wished that he'd had it when they traded slugs with that bounty hunter. Things might have turned out differently if he had.

He was making good time on his own because once he was clear of the bounty hunter, he headed for the stream. He knew it was the same stream where they'd watered their horses. It probably would add a mile or so because it followed such a wide curve, but it was better than climbing those rocks again.

———

Rena was still lying with a sleeping Tabby in her arms. She hadn't washed his wound as she had planned to do because she didn't believe it made any difference now. Tabby's breathing was shallow but regular. Like Tabby, she had no idea of how long a man could live after being shot in the back. From listening to the talk among the gang, she believed that any shot in the chest or the stomach was fatal. There were two dead bodies within a hundred yards that reinforced that belief.

She hadn't spoken a word to him since he'd fallen asleep, nor had she kissed him again. She wanted that one kiss to be special. She knew if he died, she would never kiss another man. Despite all of her morbid thoughts, Rena felt amazingly content if not happy. For most of her life, men had told her that they loved her, but after they left her bed, they probably didn't remember her name. If they had, if would be Monique and not Rena. But Thom had told her that he loved her and had only kissed her because she kissed him. In her deepest fantasies, she never believed that she would meet a man who honestly loved her. Now he was in her arms and he was dying. What happened to her after he was gone no longer even entered her mind.

Her eyes were closed. and she was drifting off to sleep herself when she thought she heard something moving. She didn't open her eyes as she knew it had to be Max Johnson who was about to kill them both. He must have returned and seen them laying on the ground and knew there was no danger anymore.

As the noises grew louder, she whispered, "I love you, Thom. Soon we won't have to worry about anything anymore."

———

215

Sheriff Smith pulled up when he spotted a body on the ground and put up his hand to keep Charlie Nestor from moving or talking.

Once he was sure that it was a body and not someone playing possum, he shifted his eyes to his left, further away from the stream and let them rest on what looked like two more bodies. The sight made his stomach twist and aroused his curiosity when he realized that one of them was a woman.

He kept his gelding still as he renewed his inspection of the site of the gunfight and found another body lying about a hundred yards from the two bodies.

He finally turned to Charlie and said, "It looks like they're all dead. I reckon that gang musta caught up with that woman and the man and killed 'em. It cost 'em two of their gang, but that means that four more are still out there. If they're still alive, and they headed back south after getting whatever they wanted, then they're gonna run into Joe Wolfson's posse. Let's go and identify the two that he doesn't have to worry about anymore."

"Okay, Sheriff," Charlie replied as they nudged their horses toward the first body.

Sheriff Smith may have believed that at least two of the outlaws were dead, but the recent massacre of his last posse still made him leery about a possible ambush. So, as he rode toward Cash's body, he scanned the rocks and trees for any signs of movement. He had led six men to their deaths in that last ambush, so at least now all he could lose would be two.

———

Rena heard the approaching sounds and wondered where Max could have found a horse, but it was unimportant. She felt Thom's heart still beating and knew he was still breathing, so her hope now was that Max shot her first so she wouldn't know that Thom was dead.

She spent what she believed was the last few minutes of her life remembering that first night they'd shared at the ranch house and how she'd been almost offended when he'd turned down her offer. She was smiling as her mind replayed the story of how he had been given the Tabby nickname and the one the other cowhands had tried to pin on him. Each of the stories he had told her returned in his own voice which masked the sounds from the real world.

Sheriff Smith was still in the saddle as he looked down at Cash's body and said, "That's Cash Locklear, the gang leader. I wish we knew who killed the bastard. He'd get a nice reward and they'd probably elect him mayor."

Charlie snickered and replied, "Not if he was one of them other outlaws."

"You never know, Charlie," he said as he shifted his horse to the other lone body. He was delaying the identification of the dead woman for as long as possible.

Rena thought she might have heard voices, but thought it was just background to her imagined Thom's stories and ignored them.

After walking their horses to the second one, Sheriff Smith said, "I figure that one's Harry Brown 'cause he's a lefty."

"We gonna go look at the last two now?"

"I suppose," the sheriff replied as he turned his gelding toward the man and woman who were wrapped in each other's arms.

"Ain't that somethin'? You ever seen any bodies holdin' onto each other like that before?" Charlie said as he pointed.

"I've never seen a woman who'd been shot before, Charlie. They sure seem to have died happy, though."

"I didn't figure anybody could die happy."

Sheriff Smith didn't reply as they drew closer to the couple and he saw the blood stain on Tabby's back which confirmed his belief that they were both dead. Then as they walked their horses even nearer, he began to think that the woman looked like Monique Dubois, which at least made more sense to him.

He could imagine some whore providing services to the gang and maybe the man who was wrapped in her arms was another gang member who had taken her and the gang's money. That sudden theory answered a lot of the questions that had popped into his head when he had first seen the bodies.

Rena heard their horses getting nearer but still believed it was just one horse that Max had somehow found, so she didn't even open her eyes. Even if she had, she wouldn't have been able to see the sheriff past Tabby.

It was only when she heard the horses stop close by that she changed her focus to what was happening in the outside world. She expected the next sound she heard would be the crack of a Winchester, so what reached her ears was totally unexpected.

After they pulled to a stop just feet from the apparently dead couple, Charlie exclaimed, "Hey, Sheriff! Ain't that Monique who used to work over at Dilly's?"

Rena's eyes flew open, then she shocked them both when she lifted her head and shouted, "Sheriff, you have to help him!"

The two men on horseback were still staring in stunned silence as she scrambled to her feet and yelled, "He's been shot! He killed all those bastards but he's still alive! Please!"

Sheriff Smith was the first to recover and after ramming his Winchester into his scabbard, he quickly bounced out of his saddle and trotted over to Tabby where he took a knee.

As Rena hovered nervously nearby, he rolled Tabby onto his stomach, and put his hand on his back. She heard Tabby groan as he changed position and his eyelids flickered.

"His heartbeat is pretty strong, Monique," the sheriff said as he began pulling away her bandages, "I figure he's gonna make it."

Rena didn't care what name he used after hearing his quick prognosis.

When Charlie stepped close, he looked at Rena and asked, "What's his name, Monique?"

She looked at him and snapped, "My name is Rena. His name is Thom Hayes and he's my husband."

Rena hadn't been seen in Watson for two years and even though most folks had heard that she and Elena Cortez had been taken away by two horse ranchers, no one knew her real name.

Charlie just gawked at her when Sheriff Smith looked up at him and said, "Charlie, cut off an eight-foot long length of my rope."

Charlie nodded and was pulling his knife as he headed for the sheriff's horse.

Sheriff Smith then looked up at Rena and asked, "What happened, Mrs. Hayes?"

"Can we just get Thom to town? I'll tell you on the way. The gang's money is in that saddlebag over there. I don't know how much is in there. Thom and I were going to return it to you, but they caught us first. How can you move Thom?"

Tex stood, snatched the saddlebags from the ground and after hanging them over his shoulder, he replied, "That's why I had Charlie get the rope. After he's in the saddle, we'll get your husband in front of him and tie the rope around their chests to keep him upright. You can ride with me and tell me what happened."

"Thank you," she said as she looked down at Tabby.

"Are they all dead?"

"Max got away. They were coming at us from three directions and Thom shot Cash first, then he was hit in the back before he shot Harry. The bullets were still hitting all around us, so he slid on my back to protect me and told me to play dead. He thought he was going to die, Sheriff. But just when we thought Max would finish us off, I think he ran out of ammunition. Thom still fired at him and he ran south into those rocks before you got here."

The sheriff looked at the distant boulders and said, "I'll worry about him later, but Sheriff Wolfson has a large posse coming from the south, so he'll probably get picked up."

Charlie arrived with the rope, the sheriff took it, handed it to Rena then said, "Let's get him up, Charlie."

As they lifted him from the ground, Rena grabbed his coat and put it on rather than donning her own jacket. She remembered that his own money was inside, and she would need money to care for him. She just hoped that the sheriff was right, and that Tabby would be able to wear the coat again.

As Charlie and the sheriff got him to his feet and started carrying him to Charlie's horse, a groggy Tabby tried to open his eyes and move his feet. Rena noticed and felt a burst of hope that he would survive.

When she began to walk, she was reminded of her own injury when her twisted ankle almost gave way. She stumbled and then began limping behind the sheriff and Charlie.

They reached the gelding and without being asked, Rena took Charlie's place supporting Tabby allowing Charlie to climb into his saddle.

Once he was mounted, the sheriff said, "Charlie and I will get him up there, but you'll need to get his leg over the horse's neck. Okay?"

"Alright."

They lifted his hundred and sixty pounds easily and once he was high enough, Rena lifted his left leg and pushed it over her head before Charlie and the sheriff slid him onto the horse.

The sheriff took the rope and ran it under Charlie's armpits and around Tabby's chest before tying it off.

"Let's get out of here, ma'am. I'll send some boys back for the bodies and all the other stuff."

"I don't care about any of it. We need to help Thom."

He quickly mounted, hung the money saddlebags over his horse's neck, then helped Rena onto his saddle behind him. She held on as he started his gelding along the stream and watched as Charlie set off worried that Thom might fall and take Charlie with him.

Before she started telling the sheriff the full story, she asked, "How far are we from town?"

"We're about a mile from the road and then just another four miles or so to town. We should be there in about an hour."

"We were that close and almost died," she said softly.

"Can you tell me what happened now, ma'am?" he asked.

Rena began the story with a short review of how she'd come to live with the gang, but once she reached the part where Tabby arrived at the ranch house, she started adding more details.

They reached the road just a few minutes later and almost immediately met two other members of Sheriff Smith's posse. He quickly instructed them to follow the stream and collect everything but the two bodies. He also warned them that one of the outlaws was still alive and in the area before waving them off and starting toward Watson at a faster pace.

Rena had ignored the look that Charlie had given her because she didn't care anymore. As soon as they resumed their ride, she continued her verbal report to the sheriff, but her eyes were trained on Tabby. His eyes were still closed, and his head was rolling around, but she knew in her heart that he was still alive.

When she told him that Tabby had been mistaken for Snake O'Hara because of his similar horse and hat, the sheriff didn't interrupt her. But he did wonder how she could have married the man so quickly and without coming into town.

———

As they were heading toward Watson, Max had reached the creek after his wide, looping walk around the forbidding rocks. After satisfying his thirst and filling his canteen, he began walking upstream. He figured he'd find the horses and something to eat in less than an hour.

He had just stood when he thought he heard clad hooves clattering against rocks and whipped his head upstream. He didn't see anything yet but stopped and listened intently. The instant he realized that his ears hadn't lied, he turned and began racing to the east away from the stream. He didn't look behind him as he knew that the posse would soon arrive. The big rocks were too far away, but there was a long, flat slab of granite that was just a couple of feet high just fifteen or twenty yards away that would have to do.

He whipped around the slab's edge and slid feet first to the rocky ground and was stopped when his boots rammed into a long shelf on the back of the protective chunk of granite. He wasn't sure if he was completely behind the slab but rolled onto his side with his Winchester clutched to his chest. He was breathing heavily when he realized that his dark hat was sitting out in the open just a couple of feet past the edge of the rock.

Max quickly reached out and snatched his hat before rolling onto his back and taking in deep, nervous breaths. He wished he wasn't breathing so loudly as he tried to listen for the posse's approach. He wasn't sure if he'd been spotted but would know soon enough. If he was seen, the next question was whether he threw up his hands or tried shooting it out. It depended on the size of the posse.

Deputy Trudeau was around twenty yards ahead of the others and had seen a lot of footprints along the stream, but hadn't seen Max. He sat in the saddle and scanned the area as he waited for the rest of the posse.

When they arrived, he pointed at the ground and said, "Those are all pretty fresh, boss. I reckon we'll run into them pretty soon."

"Okay. I'll ride with you now, Paul."

The deputy nodded and they began moving north along the stream again. They were just a mile from the site of the gunfight now and even though every one of them scanned the terrain, not one spotted Max hiding behind the slab of granite less than a hundred yards away.

Max was almost ready to giggle as he craned his neck watching the posse ride away. While he may have dodged that bullet, he knew he still had a lot of problems. He'd seen three bodies draped over horses and a lot of horses without riders. He was alone without a horse and no food. He didn't dare hunt with so many lawmen around, so after he lost sight of the posse, he scrambled to his feet and pulled his hat on.

The fastest route would be to follow that stream south, but he was worried about being spotted, so he turned and began walking toward that nasty country. He'd have to make it to the ranch. There would be food there and at least a couple of horses.

———

Max was already more than a half a mile away when Sheriff Wolfson's posse spotted the two men Sheriff Smith had sent to clean up the site of the shootout.

The initially tense approach was soon converted into a rapid exchange of stories. With the added assistance of the large posse, they soon had the entire area clear. They followed the stream toward the road leading the extra horses which now carried five bodies. The only surviving outlaw was nowhere to be found, but Sheriff Wolfson had no doubt that he'd be tracked down soon after learning that he was on foot.

Before they reached the road, Tabby had already been taken from Charlie's horse and carried into the back rooms of Doc James' barbershop. He wasn't a licensed medical doctor but had served as a corpsman during the war and was the sole source of medical help in the town. He may not have been able to diagnose and treat some of the illnesses and other complaints of the townsfolk, but he was very familiar with how to handle gunshot wounds.

He pulled off the soggy bandages from a semi-conscious Tabby as he lay on his stomach while Rena stood nearby.

Once they were peeled away, he said, "He's lost a lotta blood, ma'am. I need to get that bullet outta there, so you might wanna leave."

"I'm not going anywhere. Do you need any help?"

"Well, if you're stayin', go fetch some water from the kitchen and grab that bottle of whiskey from the cabinet over there when you get back."

She didn't ask where the kitchen was or why he wanted the whiskey, but quickly left the room to get the water.

Sheriff Smith had taken the money saddlebags to the bank and Charlie was already at Dilly's enjoying free beers and his newfound celebrity. He was telling a crowd of fascinated men the story of his rescue of the man who had killed those outlaws and made it sound as if he'd had to fight off the entire gang in the process. The inclusion of Monique in his tale added a well-appreciated titillation factor.

When Rena returned with the water, Doc James had already cut off Tabby's shirt. As soon as she set the pot on the small table near Tabby's head, he dipped a towel into the water and began to wipe away the dried blood.

She stepped across the room, opened the glass door and took out the half-full bottle of whiskey then returned.

After he finished cleaning Tabby's back as well as he could, he set the towel aside and took the bottle from Rena's hand.

She suspected that he was going to take a swig before he started. She knew what he was going to do with the bottle because she had visited him once when she'd been cut by a drunk teamster. But his reputation as a heavy drinker made her believe he'd finish half of the contents before looking for the bullet.

She was about to ask him to save the whisky for Thom, but he didn't tip the bottle to his lips. He just splashed some of the liquor onto Tabby's back. When the whiskey ran onto the open wound, Tabby grunted and arched his back but didn't say anything.

Rena was looking at Tabby's face when Doc James stuck his finger into the entry wound making Tabby grunt and grimace, but he quickly yanked his finger out.

Without looking at her, he said, "The feller that put that bullet into him musta been pretty far out. It came it at an angle too, so it didn't hit anything serious. It's not that deep and I should be able to get it outta there easy."

She didn't say a word as he bent over Tabby's back and without any saying how he would extract the bullet, he took a razor from the table and began cutting the edges of the wound.

Tabby softly cried out in pain but didn't move much as he was still barely conscious. Will James set the razor aside and pulled the wider wound apart and using just his fingers, reached into Tabby's back and grabbed the slug of lead.

Tabby didn't make any more noise as he lapsed into full unconsciousness. For a moment, Rena thought he had died and was about to lose control of her emotions when she saw more blood start leaking from his wound after the bullet had been removed.

Doc James examined the bullet and said, "That's even better news, ma'am. The piece of cloth from his shirt is still stuck on the bullet's nose. I'm still gonna feel inside to be sure that there's nothin' left, though."

"Is he still okay?"

"I reckon he'll be talkin' to you in a few hours, ma'am," he said before reinserting his index finger into the hole.

Rena felt her eyes beginning to mist and wiped them with her fingers as Doc James removed his finger and then splashed more whiskey on his back. Tabby was still out, but the shock of the alcohol still made him flinch.

Rena then stepped around the table and pulled a chair to where she could sit and see Tabby's face. She took a seat as Doc James began closing the wound.

———

Charlie was on his sixth beer and the Watson Bank of Montana president was still dancing in his office when Sheriff Wolfson's large posse rode into town.

The sheriff and Deputy Trudeau led the five body-laden horses and two free of any burden to the jail as the rest of their posse descended on Dilly's to add their stories to Charlie's.

———

Max had slowed down after putting a wall of rock between him and that posse but wasn't sure if he was going in the right direction. He had been using the shadows to give him an idea of his correct path, but it was getting close to midday now and they weren't helping anymore.

Then he caught a break when he spotted footprints and began to follow them. He didn't know who had created them, but at least he knew that they would lead him away from the posse. He was sure that he'd eventually come to that small pass that led to the trees. He'd still have to go into those pines to avoid the difficult terrain, but once he swung south, he'd know how to get back to the ranch. All he had to do was to avoid being seen.

———

The two sheriffs had spent twenty minutes sharing, digesting and documented what they'd learned that morning. Deputy Trudeau and one of Sheriff Smith's deputies took the five bodies to the mortician and then returned to start making an inventory of everything that they'd collected.

"Well, Tex," Sheriff Wolfson said, "if that feller makes it, then he's got quite a bundle comin' his way."

"Did you know that two of my friendly townsfolk tried to shoot that man 'cause he was ridin' a horse that looked like one of gang?"

"You're kidding. Really? Anyway, all of his happened in your jurisdiction, so what you do with their horses and gear is up to you. I'll just need to return the six-hundred dollars that they stole from the stage. How much was in that saddlebag?"

"After I returned the money to Oliver Piedmont over at the bank, there's still almost two thousand in that saddlebag."

231

"Count out the six hundred and I'll sign a receipt. It's your call, but I'd just give anything left over to that feller that did what we couldn't, even with all of those boys."

"I'm thinkin' the same way, Joe. Monique, I mean Rena, told me that he's just a cowhand. How is that for a kicker? All of us tough lawmen can't get the better of those bastards and a lone cowboy takes 'em all down."

"Except for Max Johnson. Do you know where he could be headed?"

"Yep. I reckon he'll try to make his way to that ranch that they were usin' as a hideout when they hit my bank. I still kick myself for not checkin' on that place after we lost 'em. I was too spooked to find 'em, I guess."

"I can understand that, Tex. When I heard about that ambush, it gave me the willies. That's why I had such a big posse when we left Virginia City."

"Well, let's start writin' our reports. I'll send Bill over to Doc James' place and tell Rena to come over when she can. I don't reckon her hubby is gonna be talkin' anytime soon."

"I thought you said she used to be a whore over at Dilly's?"

"She was, but she told me that she was married to that cowhand. I can't figure out how she coulda done that so fast but it don't matter. She seems to be pretty stuck on him and she told me that even after he took that bullet in the back, he rolled on top of her to keep her from being hit. That sounds like a man who is mighty impressed with her, too."

"I reckon so. Let's put pencil to paper so I can round up those boys. I'll send a telegram to Virginia City and Bannack to let 'em know that the gang isn't a problem anymore. We'll stay the night and head back to Virginia City in the mornin'."

Sheriff Smith nodded then opened a drawer and pulled out a stack of blank paper. After handing Joe Wolfson a pencil, they began to write.

———

Tabby had a fresh bandage and after tossing the damaged shirt into his waste bin, Doc James asked, "Why are you gimpy, ma'am?"

"Oh," she replied as she looked down at her foot, "I twisted my ankle on a rock when we were trying to run from that gang. It's okay."

"Want me to look at it?"

"No. It's swollen, but Thom said it wasn't broken. I'm in a lot better shape than he is. Where will he recover?"

"I don't have any place in here for him to stay, but I reckon the sheriff will be by in a little while and you and him can figure that out. I don't think he'll be laid up for long. I've seen men with bigger holes from Minie balls take up their rifles after just a week or so. Of course, the officers wouldn't let 'em rest unless we had to cut off both legs, so it wasn't like they were all bushy-tailed either."

He snickered as he continued to clean his small surgery.

When she'd looked down at her torn dress, she remembered that they'd left her clothing bags and other things somewhere among those rocks and she needed to buy some new clothes. She still wore Thom's coat, but didn't search his inner pocket for the cash yet.

As she sat she continued looking at Thom's peaceful, yet dirty and stubbled face. With the improved prognosis, she began to think of what lay ahead of them now. Just a few hours ago, she had been content knowing that she was about to die in his arms. But now that death was no longer likely, the contentment had slipped away with the danger.

She was back in the town where she'd worked as a whore before being brought to that ranch house to become a private whore. She began to feel the expected shame of being stared at by the men she'd serviced and the women who hated and gossiped about her. Even though Thom represented a whole new world, she was now living in her old world.

She took his hand and wished they were somewhere else, anywhere else, even back out there on that killing ground.

Doc James left the room and she let her eyes trace down Thom until she reached his feet. Seeing his damaged boots allowed her to shift her mind to more mundane problems. When they moved him to where he would recover, she'd take his boots to Ernie Allison, the cobbler for repair. She might buy him a new set when she bought some more clothes, too.

She was making a list of what she would need when she heard footsteps behind her. She looked up and saw Deputy Bill Carroll which made her stomach flip. Deputy Carroll was not only one of her more violent customers, but also didn't pay for her services. She doubted if Sheriff Smith knew about his visits, or at least about his demand for unpaid visits that involved more than just a short stint on the bed.

He smiled as he looked down at her with his hat in his hands.

"Howdy, Monique. The sheriff said to stop by and let you know that you had to come to the jail to write a statement. He said that you're claimin' to be married to that feller. We both know that it's not true; don't we?"

When all she did was silently glare at him, he said, "I hear my boss is gonna give you whatever money is left over, too. Are you plannin' on openin' your own whore house with that money?"

Rena growled, "I'm leaving Watson with Thom and never coming back."

"I thought they called him Tabby. That sounds about right 'cause he sure is small and probably just likes to have you rub his belly."

She quickly shifted her eyes back to Thom and fumed.

Deputy Carroll chuckled then said, "Don't forget to visit the jail, Monique," before he turned and left.

Her concerns about coming to Watson were now reaching the level of panic. *How could she stay here while Thom recovered if she had to endure that kind of taunting?* She didn't think it would stop at salacious words, either. She knew without a doubt that the deputy and other men would assume she was still available and even if they raped her, she couldn't say a word. She was fair game in Watson.

She took Thom's hand again and closed her eyes. She felt as if the walls were closing in around her and there was no place for her to run.

———

Max had finally reached the pass and stood looking at the trees across the empty hundred-yard wide clearing where Snake had died. He felt no sense of loss in his death or any of the others. He was just frustrated by his lack of resources. He was hungry and tired, but he had to make it to the ranch soon. He probably wouldn't get there today but hoped to find an empty ranch house by sunset tomorrow.

He walked down the incline and crossed the open space before entering the trees. He didn't expect to find anything, but to his astonishment and relief, he found two full tins of beans that had rolled against the base of a pine that the posse must not have bothered to take with them.

Max quickly used his knife to cut off the lid of one of the tins then poured some of the beans and sauce into his mouth. He made short work of the entire contents of the can and tossed it away. His chin and the front of his jacket were covered in the brown sauce, so even as he started walking, he began using his fingers to wipe the tasty liquid from his skin and coat and sucked his fingers clean.

————

After Deputy Carroll left, Rena stayed with Tabby. She wouldn't go to the jail until after they'd moved him. She guessed that they would carry him to Mrs. Dinwiddie's boarding house and that would present a whole new set of problems for her. Ida Dinwiddie was one of the louder members of the church group that had made it their goal to drive the women out of Dilly's. Rena wasn't sure if the woman would allow her to set one toe inside her boarding house despite what Thom had done to save the bank's money and eliminate the threat that the gang posed to the town.

It seemed that no matter what topic popped into her mind now, they all seemed to end in a confrontation with either past customers or those who sought to rid the town of her like.

She pressed Thom's hand in hers and wished there was some way he could just mount his horse and take her away from this town and her memories.

Doc James returned and asked, "Has he opened his eyes yet, ma'am?"

"No. Did you expect him to awaken?"

"I was kinda hopin' he might, but don't worry if he stays like that for a while."

"Do you know where they'll take him yet?"

"No, ma'am, but after Bill Carroll left, I figured that it might be better if you were the one who decided where he should go."

"Does it have to be in town?"

He scratched his chin as he replied, "I suppose it would be okay if he wasn't in town, but he'd need to have somebody to take care of him."

"I could do that; couldn't I?"

"I'd have to tell you what to look for and how to keep him clean and all, but I reckon you could. It won't be for a day or two, though."

"That's alright. I'm just uncomfortable staying in Watson. I'm sure you know why."

238

"Yes, ma'am, I figured that out right off. It kinda rubs me wrong, too."

She looked up at him curiously and asked, "Why does it bother you?"

He leaned against the table near Tabby's knees as he replied, "You used to be called Monique and worked at Dilly's. Isn't that right?"

"Yes."

"Now a lot of folks figure what you were doin' was sinful and were quick to send you to perdition. Then you got men like Bill Carroll who treated you and the other ladies worse than they treated their horses. Neither one of those is right by me. You see, durin' the war when I was patching up the boys in blue just like I helped your man, we always had a group of what they called camp followers.

"Now 'cause I was always away from the battles we were usually real close to those ladies' tents. I paid 'em visits pretty often and got to know some of 'em. Well, one of those camp followers was a lady named Olivia Newsome. It's a real pretty name; ain't it?"

Rena nodded but didn't say anything as Will James continued.

"For a few weeks, I only visited Olivia and we got kinda close. I was even thinkin' of askin' her to leave that camp and marry

239

me. It was a crazy idea, so I didn't mention it. I just kept visitin' her and sometimes we just talked. I was kinda embarrassed the first time we just did that, but she seemed to like it.

"It went on that way for a couple of more months until one day when I went to visit her, I found out that she was gone. I asked the other women where she was and one of 'em told me that she had to leave to have a baby. It really hurt 'cause she didn't even say goodbye. What made me feel even worse was that I reckoned I mighta been that baby's father.

"I couldn't go lookin' for her or I'd be charged with desertion, so I kept doin' my job. I'd visit the ladies every few days but just to look for Olivia. The army kept headin' south and I figured the more we moved, it was gonna make it even harder to find her again."

Rena then quietly asked, "Did you ever find her or at least know where she went?"

"Nope. After I mustered out, I went back to where she left me and tried to find even a hint of where she went, but never did. I was sad for not findin' her, but what I did was to always picture her smilin' with her baby bouncin' on her knee while she rocked on the porch."

"Did you marry someone else?"

"No, ma'am. I never met another woman like my Olivia. After a while, I just gave up. I replaced her with a bottle and figured I was gonna just drink myself to death. Then I got here and reckoned that I might as well do it in Watson."

"What happened? You've been here longer than I have, and I heard of your reputation with the bottle."

"I was just about as low as a man could get when one of the ladies from Dilly's was cut up pretty bad by some cowhand. There wasn't anybody who could help her, and I was almost sober when they asked me to help 'cause they knew I used to be a corpsman in the war. If it had been just some feller who got into a fight or damned near anyone else, I woulda told 'em to leave me alone. But she was a workin' girl like my Olivia. I had to help her, and I did.

"After that I began helpin' other folks. I remember sewin' you up once. You impressed me as bein' a brave lady just like my Olivia, but you were sad, too. Olivia wasn't that way, you know. She was in that camp 'cause our army burned her place down and she was alone. But she was still a happy person, which was a big surprise at first.

"She told me that it was a waste of life to go through life payin' a mind to all the bad things that happened. Sometimes I'd be talkin' to her when I was in a bad way. You know one of those long days havin' to hear the screams while we cut off legs and arms and watch when the boys still died. I'd be all hang dog, but I remember how she would smile at me and say, 'You watch, Will. Soon everything will be better.'. I hope she could still say that after she had her baby."

241

"Why didn't you tell me that before when you fixed my cut?"

He shrugged his shoulders then answered, "'Cause there was no reason to tell ya."

"Why are you telling me now?"

He pointed at Tabby and said, "'Cause you have a reason to start feelin' happy now."

She smiled and said, "Thank you for telling me, Doc."

He smiled back then replied, "Call me Will. I'm not a real doctor."

"I'm Rena, Will, and to me, you're the best doctor I've ever met."

He grinned down at her before turning and leaving the room.

Rena watched him go and decided that she'd try to live up to his memories of the lost Olivia. If they wanted to hate her, let them. She had Thom now and to hell with all of them.

———

Max was getting tired already and it was still mid-afternoon. He had another four hours of daylight but knew he wouldn't even reach the abandoned buckboard. He looked around and spotted a cluster of rocks that would keep him out of anyone's sight. He'd have one more uncomfortable night and hopefully sleep in one of the ranch house's beds tomorrow.

TABBY HAYES

Bill Carroll returned to the jail and told Sheriff Smith that Monique would stop by after they moved the cowhand.

The sheriff asked, "Is he awake yet?"

"Nope."

"Tomorrow, I want you and John to head out to that horse ranch that Jimmy Parsons and Mark Tinker set up. I reckon that's here you'll find the last one of those bastards."

Newly hired deputy John Lee looked up at Bill expectantly. Since he'd been hired three weeks ago, all he'd done is sit behind the desk. He hadn't even been allowed to join the posse that had waited on the road. When he heard the sheriff tell Bill Carroll to take him along, it had been a welcome surprise.

Bill replied, "Okay, boss. We'll head out there tomorrow mornin'. I'm gonna head over to Dilly's and talk to Joe Wolfson's boys."

"Go ahead. We all should do some celebratin' and raise a glass to Mister Hayes."

Bill glanced at John Lee then turned and left the office.

After he'd gone, Ted looked at his young deputy and said, "Now you be careful tomorrow. There's only one of 'em, but Max Johnson is a mean son of a bitch, and he's desperate. I wasn't gonna send ya, but you gotta face trouble sooner or later. Just don't go shootin' anything that moves. Got it?"

"Yes, sir."

"I'm gonna head to the house and talk to the wife. Then I'm swinging by the doc's place on the way back."

"Okay, Sheriff," John replied trying to mask his excitement.

As he grabbed his hat, Tex Smith was still unsure if he was doing the right thing in sending John with Bill Carroll. He knew the kid was smart and pretty good with his Winchester and pistol, but he was so inexperienced. But he didn't really trust his senior deputy either. He'd even begun to suspect that the flesh wound he'd gotten on the day of the robbery and slaughter hadn't been self-inflicted.

After leaving the jail, he stepped along the boardwalk and was considering going to the ranch himself with John, but he knew he had to start giving Carroll more responsibility. He never admitted it to anyone other than Rosalie that he wished it had been Bill Carroll who had been with him when they rode into those Winchesters. Holt Archer was a better deputy and better man.

———

Rena was alone in the back of the barber shop still holding Thom's hand. She was hungry, tired, dirty and knew she smelled worse than she did on a Sunday morning after two nights of work at Dilly's.

She had a newfound respect for Doc James now that she understood him better. She'd barely known him even though she'd lived in Watson for years. They worked and slept just a few hundred yards apart, but the only time she'd ever talked to him was when he'd cleaned and sutured her knife cut. Even then, they had only passed a few shallow sentences.

But now she felt stronger and more determined to act like any of the 'respectable' women in town and not some strumpet who was expected to bow to the 'good' people. Men like Bill Carroll were no better than those six bastards who had kept her in the ranch house and deserved her anger not her fear.

She smiled at the face of the man who had earned her respect and love. She was wearing his coat and still had his Colt Walker at her hip. She'd never taken the gunbelt off and had become accustomed to the weight. She'd almost discarded it when they had lightened their load, but Thom had given it to her and that made it special.

"Thank you for my Colt, Thom," she said softly as she rubbed his hand.

For the last ten minutes, Tabby had been in the same semiconscious state that he'd been in when they carried him into the barbershop. He heard voices but not words. The throbbing pain in his back hadn't been as intense in his lessened cognizance, but now that pain was growing stronger. It still didn't seem as bad as he expected a gunshot wound would feel.

He heard a woman's voice, then as he grew more aware of the world around him, he felt pressure on his hands.

Before he opened his eyes, he remembered what had put him into this state and was running it through his mind when he heard the woman's voice again.

"I'm going to have your boots fixed, Thom. The doc said that you'll be on your feet pretty soon, so do you want me to buy you a new pair while they're being repaired?"

Thom still had his eyes closed as he quietly answered, "I need a new pair anyway."

His voice was just a whisper, and Rena was unsure if she'd really heard him say anything.

There was a ten second pause before she asked, "Thom, did you say something?"

He finally opened his eyes and smiled before he replied, "Yes, ma'am. I said I could use a new pair of boots."

She began to quietly laugh as tears slid from her eyes.

"How do you feel?"

"Like Philly kicked me in the back. How bad is it? Where am I?"

"Doc James took out the bullet and closed your wound. He said it didn't go in too far because it was from so far away and hit you at an angle. He said you'd probably be walking around in a couple of days."

"That's good news. How are you doing?"

"I just have my twisted ankle."

"What happened after I drifted off?"

"Before I tell you all of that, now that we're out of danger, can I ask you what you plan to do?"

"Do you think I'm going to run off and leave you, ma'am?"

"Well, I did kind of force you into making a lot of promises. I really didn't give you a choice."

"What I told you wasn't because you forced me to say those things. Well, maybe the first time when you asked me if I would marry you. But after that, I made those promises because I wanted to. I still don't know where we'll go or what we'll do, but we'll do it together. I do love you, Rena, and I want to marry you."

She wiped her eyes then said, "I wanted to hear you tell me again. I guess that it's a woman thing."

247

"Could I get a drink of water before you tell me what happened?"

"Oh. Yes, of course."

She poured a half a glass of water and then had to lift his head and managed to get most of the water into his mouth before setting the glass back down.

She then proceeded to tell him what had happened since he fell asleep in her arms. She didn't hesitate to reveal her belief that they would both soon die when Max returned or how content she was just by holding him close.

Tabby was surprised to learn that five of the six outlaws were dead and was more than willing to let the law handle Max. He was just a cowhand.

Rena told him that the sheriff would be giving him all of the outlaws' horses and gear, and he wondered if the posse had found Philly but didn't interrupt her.

As she talked, he watched her animated face as her hands slashed and rolled. He'd never seen her so alive before, but he'd only known her for a few days. Not only that, but all of that time had been spent under almost constant threat of imminent death.

She finished her narrative by saying, "They need to move you out of the barbershop today. I had thought about taking you to the ranch after a couple of days, but now I don't mind staying in town until you're recovered."

"Why the change?" he asked.

"I had an interesting talk with Doc James. I'm not going to worry about what anyone thinks or says anymore."

"You never should have, Rena. Where will they put me?"

She smiled then replied, "I was going to suggest a room at Dilly's."

"That would be interesting."

"I was just kidding, Mister Hayes. I'd probably spend all my time telling visitors that I wasn't working there anymore."

Before Tabby could suggest another location for his recovery, Sheriff Smith entered the room and stopped next to Rena.

"How are you doin', Mister Hayes?" he asked as he looked down at Tabby.

"Better than I figured I'd be by now, Sheriff. Rena tells me that you were the one who got us out of there, and I'm grateful."

"I'm the one who should be doin' the thankin', Mister Hayes. That gang really cost this town and a whole bunch of other folks, too. I'm really sorry for the two idiots who took those shots at you when you rode into town. I told 'em right off that you couldn't have been one of those outlaws, but you were already gone."

"I can understand why they did. By the way, did you find my horse? He's a dark brown Morgan with white stockings on his forelegs."

"Yes, sir. He's in Topper's Livery with your other horses. We're givin' you all of their horses, gear and the money that was left over after returning what they stole to the bank and the stagecoach folks. A bunch of rewards will be headin' your way, too. I haven't figured out the total yet, but I reckon it'll be almost two thousand dollars by the time I add 'em all up."

"I appreciate all that, Sheriff."

The sheriff then looked at Rena and said, "Mrs. Hayes, I talked to my wife and we'd be honored to have you and Mister Hayes stay with us 'til he's better. Our boy Richie is eight and would love to talk to him. That way you both could write out your statements without havin' to come to the jail."

Rena glanced at Tabby before quietly saying, "Sheriff, you know who I am. Are you sure your wife wouldn't be ashamed to let me in her house? What if your son finds out what I was?"

"He won't find out from me or my wife, but I reckon he'll get some teasin' at school. After he gets to talk to you, then he'll know that you're really not much different than his mama. Then he'll can tell those other boys that they're bein' stupid. It'll make help to make him a better man."

She smiled and said, "I think you and your wife are already doing that, Sheriff."

"Call me Tex, Mrs. Hayes."

"Thank you, Tex. Call me Rena and I'm sorry I told you that I was married to Thom. We plan to marry but haven't had the chance yet."

"I kinda figured that out, Rena, but it don't matter much around here. Ol' Bob Taylor and Lilly have been stayin' together for more'n eight years now and have two young'uns but haven't tied the knot as far as anyone knows."

She looked at Tabby and asked, "Is that alright with you, Thom?"

"If the sheriff doesn't mind my snoring. I can wake up the whole town when I get going."

She laughed then looked up at the sheriff and said, "He doesn't really snore. When will they move him?"

"I'll go set that up right now. Rosalie, that's my wife, is already roasting a chicken for you. Did you want to come with me to Jackson's to buy some things?"

She looked back at Tabby and asked, "Can I leave you alone for a little while, Thom?"

"I'll be alright, but can you ask the doc to see me on your way out?"

"Is something wrong?" she quickly asked.

"Not so much as wrong, but more like really necessary."

"Oh. I'll let him know."

She stood, leaned over and kissed him on the forehead before walking out of the room with the sheriff.

A few minutes later, Doc James entered with an old pickle jar to help Tabby with his urgent necessity.

————

The sheriff arranged to have Tabby brought to his house later that afternoon, then he escorted Rena to Jackson's Dry Goods. He intentionally strode to the store with their arms linked to forestall any snide comments.

While they shopped, Deputy Sheriff Bill Carroll was having a raucous time with the civilian members of Sheriff Wolfson's posse. He had embellished Charlie Nestor's tale with more spicy revelations about Monique. It was only when one of the men from Virginia City asked if he was the deputy who had received the flesh wound and couldn't join the ill-fated posse that things became less friendly.

Bill felt as if the man was implying that he was a coward and slammed his half-empty mug of beer onto the bar as he glared at the man.

"Are you sayin' I'm yellow, mister?" he snarled.

The man was well into his liquor and felt brave for having been on the posse that chased those outlaws even though they had never seen one of them alive.

"At least I went after those bastards!" he snapped back at Bill Carroll showering the deputy with spittle.

"I was shot, you idiot!"

"Who did the shootin'? Are you sure that you didn't pop a piece of lead through your leg, so you didn't hafta chase after those bad boys?"

Bill's temper ignited into an instant inferno then grabbed his beer mug and after tossing its contents into the man's face, he smashed the empty glass over his head. The Virginia City man crumpled to the floor, but Bill's anger wasn't going anywhere.

When another member of the posse grabbed his shoulder to pull him away from his friend, Bill whipped his right fist into the man's gut.

Then all hell broke loose as the members of the posse descended on Deputy Sheriff Bill Carroll, who was then defended by some of the local boys. They may not have been very fond of Bill, but he was one of their own and no big town boys were going to throw their weight around in Watson.

As the melee attracted more participants, Al Frobisher, the bartender, grabbed his scattergun from under the bar.

At the top of his lungs, he screamed, "All of you stop it, or I'll let you have both barrels!"

He knew he wouldn't do any such thing, but usually just the sight of the shotgun would quell any barfights. But this was becoming a massive brawl and a deputy sheriff was in the heart of it. Not one man stopped swinging or trying to hit someone if he was too inebriated to see the man he was trying to punch.

Al scanned the saloon floor, didn't see anyone just watching, but as he was preparing to find the sheriff, he spotted three of the working girls watching from the top of the stairs.

He shouted, "Marie, go and get the sheriff!"

Marie was hesitant to go anywhere near that brawl, but when Lola said, "I'll come with you," all three of them quickly stepped down the stairs and slid along the wall before rushing through the batwing doors.

They were dressed in their working clothes and attracted the attention of the men who saw them as they trotted toward Dilly's when they heard the ruckus. The women who saw them just looked away.

They passed Jackson's Dry Goods and soon reached the jail. Deputy Lee popped to his feet when they burst through the door and Marie exclaimed, "*Where's the sheriff?* There's a riot going on in Dilly's!"

"I ain't sure. He said he was gonna go home and then go see that feller at the doc's place."

"Well, then you've got to do something!" Marie shouted.

John was unsure how to handle the problem, but figured he'd need the shotgun, so he grabbed one of the twelve gauges from the rack then pulled on his hat before the three women turned and left. He chased after them and hoped he'd find the sheriff on the way.

Sheriff Smith was in the ladies clothing aisle as Rena selected some dresses and other garments she'd need. He'd been there with his wife more often than he could recall, so he wasn't embarrassed in the least to be holding women's clothing in his arms.

She had just laid two nightdresses over his forearms when he heard someone burst into the front of the store and exclaim, "It's an all-out war over there, Bob!"

He turned in time to watch Bob Jackson rush out from behind his counter and follow Jake Packer out the door leaving no one at the cash drawer.

Rena had heard him as well and said, "Give me the clothes, Tex. You'd better find out what is happening."

"You got that right," he quickly replied and dumped his load of clothes into her arms before racing for the door.

———

When Deputy Sheriff John Lee entered Dilly's, he stopped just past the batwing doors. There was shattered glass from bottles and glasses all over the floor, a few broken chairs and several groaning men. There was still a core of fighting and wrestling near the bar with smaller fights going on in three other places.

He didn't see Bill Carroll when he cocked both hammers and shouted, "Stop right now or I'll fire!"

His threat was ignored just as Al Frobisher's had been, so he released one of the hammers, then aimed just above the painting at behind the bar on the left side of the saloon and pulled the trigger.

The shotgun had been loaded with #4 buckshot and it had been shortened by four inches. If he'd aimed higher, it would have punched a large hole in the ceiling and probably the roof, but he has aimed for bottom of the ceiling near the back of the large room.

Before the mass of lead pellets reached the bar, they had already spread more than three feet. Most of them slammed into the wall and ceiling above the long mural of a roundup, but some hit the painting and one struck the forehead of one of the men still swinging.

Deputy Sheriff Bill Carroll was ready to deliver a haymaker when the heavy pellet still carrying an immense amount of energy slammed into his head just above the bridge of his nose.

He was beginning to swing his fist, so when the projectile drilled into his head, he barely had time to feel any pain as he continued his rotation and spun to the floor.

The shotgun's loud report had its intended effect and the fighting stopped almost instantly.

John hadn't seen Bill Carroll go down as he wasn't the only man who was still fighting or falling. Once the fighting stopped, he slowly entered with the shotgun now level.

Al Frobisher had ducked behind the bar the moment he'd seen John enter with the shotgun, so he slowly stood and saw the young deputy as he walked closer.

No one had yet realized that Deputy Carroll had been shot. There were eight other men on the floor, and two of them weren't moving either. There was blood everywhere so the blood that had flowed from Bill's forehead wasn't noticeable.

Sheriff Smith had heard the shotgun blast as he raced along the boardwalk and assumed that Al Frobisher had needed to unleash his scattergun to restore order. It wasn't a common event, but it wasn't unheard of either.

He was surprised when he saw three of the working girls huddled outside because they usually didn't get up this early.

Tex passed the women and then slowed as he walked through the doors and saw the damage. After that initial view, he spotted John Lee with a shotgun in his hand and wondered if he had been the one to fire.

It was only when he spotted the damage from a shotgun blast behind the bar that he knew that his deputy had fired. The holes left by the shotgun didn't bother him. He was just glad that John had stopped the fracas.

John had almost reached Bill Carroll's body when Tex shouted, "Alright, what happened in here?"

Deputy Lee whipped around as his boss walked toward him but was scanning the barroom.

It was only when the sheriff reached John that he spotted Bill Carroll lying on the floor facing the bar.

"Get up, Bill!" he exclaimed as he looked down.

He felt like kicking his deputy because he knew that he hadn't been in Dilly's to stop the fight. He wouldn't be surprised to hear that he'd been the instigator, either.

When his deputy didn't move, Sheriff Smith sighed then said, "John, help me pick Bill up off the floor."

"Yes, sir," John replied before setting the shotgun on the bar.

As the other bruised patrons looked on, Sheriff Smith and his deputy each grabbed one of Bill's arms and lifted him to his feet.

The blood on his forehead wasn't any cause for alarm, so Tex looked at the bartender and said, "Al, give me a pitcher of water."

Not one person in the saloon believed that Bill was anything other than either drunk or knocked unconscious as the sheriff took the pitcher of water and dumped it over the top of his deputy's head.

When he still didn't stir, Tex slapped him across the face and shouted, "Wake up, Bill!"

When Bill still didn't open his eyes, Tex suddenly realized he may be hurt worse than he had first believed. He and John were still holding him upright as the sheriff put his hand over Bill's chest and held it there for fifteen seconds.

"Son of a bitch," he mumbled before saying, "Let's get him on his back, John."

As the two lawmen lowered him to the barroom floor, the other brawlers began to crowd around.

Bill's hair and shirt were still soaked, so Tex just rubbed his hand over the top of Bill's head then wiped the blood away from his forehead.

When John saw the hole, he knew that he'd killed Bill.

"I…I didn't mean to do it, Sheriff! I was aimin' real high just to warn everybody."

259

Sheriff Smith stood and looked at his horrified deputy. He was no longer concerned what had happened to cause the riot but had to focus on John. Even barfights as bad as this one had been weren't worth investigating anyway.

He put his hand on Deputy Lee's shoulder and said, "It's all right, John. It was just an accident. It was more my fault anyway. I never told you it was a sawed-off shotgun, or it had buckshot loaded. Let's head back to the office."

John nodded and let himself be turned and guided across the barroom floor.

Tex glanced back at Al Frobisher and then tilted his head toward Bill's body to let him know that he could move it to the mortician.

They stepped onto the boardwalk, passed the three women and began walking to the jail.

Sheriff Smith worried that John would quit. After losing Holt in that massacre and now Bill Carroll, he couldn't afford to let the kid lose his confidence. As they passed the dry goods store, the sheriff glanced through the open door and saw Rena at the counter but kept walking.

He would ask Joe Wolfson if he could ride out to the ranch tomorrow to find Max Johnson because he was sure that John wasn't up to it and he'd have to stay in town now.

At least Bill's death didn't create another widow. Breaking the news to Mary Archer about Holt's death had been worse than hearing those .44s buzzing past his head. She had two small children to raise on her own until she found another husband. He thought she'd find another man soon enough but doubted that he would be as good as Holt.

They turned into the jail, and after he sat John down in the chair behind the desk, he realized that he'd left the shotgun on the bar. It was too late to go back and get it now, but he was sure it would be returned to him soon enough.

He sat on the desk and said, "John, I need you to be the strong man I hired last month. We have a job to do and I can't do it alone."

John looked up at his boss and nodded before taking off his hat and setting it on the desk.

"I was aiming really high, boss. I didn't even fire both barrels."

"I know, John. You did everything right, but I shoulda warned you about the short barrels. Do you know why there was buckshot in those tubes?"

"No, sir."

"It was because I was still nervous after that bank robbery and ambush. I pulled the birdshot out of the shotgun the next day 'cause I figured they might come back. Then I forgot about it. So, don't go blamin' yourself for it. Okay?"

"Okay. Are you comin' with me to the ranch tomorrow?"

"Nope. I'm gonna ask Joe Wolfson to take a look before he and his posse head back to Virginia City. We have a lot of paperwork to do and telegrams to send. That cowhand layin' on the doc's table saved the town, but he sure cost us a lot of writin'."

A weak smile formed on John's lips before the sheriff grinned and slapped him on the shoulder.

"Let's get started on the paperwork. You can make an inventory of all we have from those bastards. We'll be handin' 'em over to Mister Hayes when he's back on his feet. The doc says he should be walkin' around in just a couple of days."

Tex already had a list in his office but returning to a routine is exactly what Deputy Lee needed. As John pulled out some paper and a pencil to start making a second inventory, Tex walked back to his office to write up a report of the fight and death of Bill Carroll.

———

Rena had heard what happened when Bob Jackson returned to his store. She had already amassed a pile of replacement clothes for her and some britches, shirts, socks and underwear for Tabby. She had looked at the boots and even though she wasn't sure of the size, picked out a pair that were just a little bigger than average. She used her own foot as a guide knowing that his feet were still a good two inches longer than hers even though he was only about three inches taller.

Bob Jackson didn't behave any differently toward her than if she had been the president of the Women for Decency.

But as he was ready to total the order, he asked, "Are the boots for Mister Hayes?"

"Yes, they are. He already had a hole in the bottom of the right boot, but then one of the outlaws shot his heel off. I don't know if they can be repaired."

"Well, ma'am, I'll tell you what. You let Mister Hayes know that those boots are a gift from me. Okay?"

She smiled before thanking him and paying for the large order with Tabby's coat stash.

Her ankle was still stiff and sore, but she declined his offer to have her bags delivered to the barbershop. She tried not to limp too badly as she left the store with a heavy sack in each hand.

As she walked along the boardwalk, she saw a body being carried out of Dilly's and knew it was Bill Carroll's. Just a little while ago, he had been harassing and insulting her and now he was dead. She felt not a shred of remorse for the man and thought that he had been judged, found guilty and punished by fate for what he had done to her and the other girls.

She gimped across the street and soon entered the barbershop.

Doc James had reverted to his more common occupation and was trimming Luke Rostowski's hair as she walked past and entered the back rooms.

She found Tabby smiling at her from his uncomfortable hardwood bed as she set the bags on the floor then stepped closer.

"You should have had someone carry them for you, Rena. Your ankle is probably going to take longer to heel than the hole in my back if you keep that up."

She sat down in the chair at his head and replied, "It gets stiff if I stop walking on it."

"Did the doc look at it?"

"No, but I told him what you said, and he agreed with you."

"Did you use my hard-earned pay to buy your new clothes?"

"Yes, sir. I also bought you more clothes and some toiletries for both of us. Oh, and Mister Jackson didn't charge you for the boots I selected for you."

"Thank you, Mrs. Hayes. I heard the sheriff call you that and it almost made me giggle. I never expected to hear anyone say that after I left home."

"When they found us, Charlie Nestor called me Monique and I angrily told him my name was Rena Hayes and you were my husband. I probably should have just ignored him."

"I'm not complaining, ma'am. For a lonely cowhand who was just looking for someplace to spend the winter without freezing his toes off, I've gotten used the notion."

"I really don't even care if we get married as long as we stay together."

"How about if we just get me back on my feet before we start thinking about walking down the aisle or standing before some government official."

"I'll agree with that. When I was in the store, I heard about a big fight in Dilly's and one of the deputies was killed. It was an accident when another deputy fired a shotgun to stop the fight."

"Did you know the deputy who was killed?"

"He stopped by while you were sleeping to tell me that we had to write statements," she replied, "He...."

She had almost told him what Bill Carroll had said but decided it wasn't necessary now. All it would do was to make Thom angry when all he could do was just to lie there.

Tabby had a pretty good idea of what she was going to say and why she didn't. He may not have had a lot of experience with women, but he was getting to understand Rena more with each word she spoke.

They were interrupted when Doc James led two men into the room. They were carrying a makeshift stretcher which was really just an old sign with a faded, poorly printed 'And Sons' painted on the worn surface.

Doc helped Tabby onto the stretcher and he somehow avoided getting splinters rammed into his bare torso.

Rena picked up her two bags and followed them out of Doc's barbershop and she was pleased that Will James walked with her behind them.

Before they reached the sheriff's house, Doc trotted around the stretcher bearers and jogged up the steps to the porch and rapped on the door.

By the time Tabby's board reached the bottom of the steps, Rosalie Smith had opened the door.

"Take him to the first room on the left past the parlor," she said before she stepped back.

Doc preceded them into the house leaving Rena on the porch with the sheriff's wife. It was an awkward moment for Rena as she looked at Rosalie. She'd seen Mrs. Smith in town, but they had never shared a word.

Her uneasiness vanished when Rosalie smiled said, "Would you like a cup of coffee, Rena?"

Rena returned her smile then replied, "I'd love some. Thank you, Mrs. Smith."

Rosalie took one of Rena's bags before she closed the door and they walked into the parlor.

"Call me Ros. When I was a girl, my parents called me Rosie and I hated it. I'm not fond of Rose either. Is Rena short for Irene?"

"It is. I really don't care for my full name either."

"You need to change out of that dress, Rena. It looks as if it's ready for the trash bin. Tex told me that you bought some more clothes, so do you want to get changed first?"

"I'd rather take a bath before I do, if that's alright."

"We can put on some water. The cookstove is hot, so it won't take long."

They reached the kitchen and Rosalie set Rena's bag near the table, so Rena left the bag she carried next to it and took a seat.

Ros poured two cups of coffee and set them on the table. There was already a small pitcher of cream and a full sugar bowl on the table, but Rena drank her coffee black.

267

Rosalie took a sip of her black coffee before asking, "How is your Thom doing?"

"The doc says he's doing very well. Thank you for letting us stay here. I know that having me here might cause you some embarrassment, so Thom and I will move after a few days."

"I don't care what those other women think, Rena. Without my husband, this town would fall apart, and they all know it. Besides, what you and Thom did for Watson is immeasurable. By returning the bank's money, you kept it solvent and eliminating that gang made the town safer."

"Thom did all that, Ros. I was more of a burden to him than help. He wouldn't have been shot if I didn't ask him to take me away from that ranch. Do you know I even tricked him into going back into the house abandoning him to escape on my own? I took his horse and left him to face that gang on by himself. What kind of person does that?"

Ros hadn't heard that part of the story because Rena hadn't told it to her husband, so she replied, "But you obviously changed your mind, or you wouldn't be sitting here having coffee with me."

"I only turned around when I saw the gang coming and couldn't escape. He was ready to shoot me when he got back on the buckboard, but he saved me instead. He always tells me that he's just a cowhand, and I suppose that's how he sees himself, but to me he's nothing less than a hero."

"He must be very impressed with you, Rena. We can talk about all of those things later. Let me at least get the water on the stove for your bath."

Rena nodded, then when Ros stood, she rose and helped to fill three large pots with water.

As they worked, Rena asked, "Is your husband from Texas?"

Ros laughed then replied, "He was born in Ohio and has never been within eight hundred miles of the Texas border. His real name is Clarence and he began calling himself Tex when he was just a boy for obvious reasons."

"Can't he use his middle name?"

"I won't tell you what it is but suffice it to say that Clarence would be a better choice."

Rena lugged a heavy pot to the stove and after setting it on one of the hot plates, she said, "Thom goes by Tabby most of the time. He told me the story of how he got the nickname and it's really funny, but I think you should hear him tell it. I imagine your son would be giggling through most of it, too."

"Richie should be home for supper soon. He's at the pond with his friends trying to catch fish or frogs or anything else that spurs their interest."

While they talked, Tabby was resting on his side on a mattress that seemed softer than it probably was after spending a couple of hours on that hard table.

He could hear the sheriff's wife and Rena talking but not what they were saying. He was relieved to hear the chatter because it meant that Rena had gotten past her fear of returning to Watson. He was pretty sure that she wouldn't want to stay, but at least she wouldn't be so stressed just by being in town.

He ran his fingertips over his bandaged back and began adding some pressure when they found the site of the gunshot. It grew more painful as he exerted more pressure, but he wanted to see how much he could tolerate. He'd been hurt a number of times and had even had the tip of bull's horn rammed into his left thigh a few years ago, so he knew he could handle more than most men.

When he stopped his experiment, he had a better idea of how long he would have to be bedridden. He was grateful that the bullet hadn't been too deep and hadn't hit any organs that would make for a long recovery. He'd still have problems twisting for quite a while, but if it had been in the front of his gut, it would have been much worse. Of course, that slug could have missed him altogether, but that's always true for almost every minute of our lives. If he hadn't been wearing a hat or riding a horse that made those two men mistake him for Snake O'Hara, then he never would have found Rena. Life is full of 'what ifs' and it can make a man crazy if he starts thinking about them too much.

———

While Rena and Ros talked and Tabby played the 'what if' game, Max was sitting on the ground about two miles north of the abandoned buckboard.

It was early in the evening and he had just finished the second can of beans. He looked south and thought about continuing but didn't want to risk running into that posse. If they were still out looking for him, they'd probably be broken up into smaller groups, but he still couldn't risk being seen.

He stood and walked further to the east until he found a well-hidden spot in a cluster of trees. He entered the shadows and looked for a reasonably comfortable place to lay down.

It was early, but he was still sore and tired from all the walking and his constant worry about being spotted had worn him down.

He felt safe among the pines and soon stretched out on the ground with his hat under his head. He still had the Winchester '73 lying beside him, but wished he had his '76. He liked the newer model.

Max still had his gunbelt around his waist as he drifted off but wasn't planning on leaving too early in the morning no matter how hungry he was. He needed to give that posse enough time to give up the chase.

———

Before closing up the office and heading home, Sheriff Smith had asked Joe Wolfson if he could check out the ranch in the morning before heading back to Virginia City. He hadn't needed to track down his counterpart as the two sheriffs and their deputies had to deal with the aftermath of the fight and shooting in Dilly's.

Joe understood the reason for Tex's request and even though the ranch was in the opposite direction, he said that he and Deputy Trudeau would do a search of the ranch in the morning after sending their troublemaking posse back to Virginia City.

––––––

Tabby had a companion in his sickroom, but it wasn't Rena as he hadn't even seen her since being transferred to the bed. Richie Smith was sitting in a chair pulled close to the bed leaving just enough space for his skinny, eight-year old legs.

"Are you really just a cowboy?" he asked after hearing Tabby's answer to his twelfth question about the shooting.

"Yes, sir. That's just about all I've ever done since leaving home."

"How'd you get so good with your Winchester?"

"I'm not. Your father is probably a lot better than I am. I'm sure that those outlaws were all better, too. I was just lucky."

272

"I guess that Deputy Carroll wasn't so lucky."

"No, sir, I reckon not. When bullets start flying around, they're not smart enough to go anywhere but the where the barrel is pointed."

Before he could ask another question, his mother called out to him from the kitchen and told him to wash for dinner.

"I gotta go," he said as he popped from the chair and trotted out of the room.

Tabby was still smiling when he heard Rena enter. She closed the door before he shifted his eyes toward his feet and saw her in the shadows created by the low light coming through the window.

"I see that you've changed," he said as she walked past the end of the bed and sat down on the chair.

"I wanted to look nice when I saw you again. I don't think you've ever seen me when I wasn't clean and had my hair brushed."

"You always looked nice to me, Rena. But I'll admit that you look even prettier now."

"How are you feeling?"

"I'm okay. I did some testing on my wound and I think I'll be able to walk in a day or two. I just can't do much more than that."

"I wasn't planning to make you do anything strenuous, Mister Hayes."

Tabby snickered as he shook his head then said, "Believe it or not, I really wasn't thinking about that, Rena. I was thinking about saddling a horse. I could mount and it would be uncomfortable to ride but lifting that saddle onto Philly's back would be a bad idea."

Rena then laughed lightly before saying, "I guess all those years of a different kind of strenuous exercise put that at the front of my mind."

Then she said, "Doc is going to stop by tomorrow morning to show me how to be more of a nurse, but do you want me to get you changed out of those dirty britches? You need a good cleaning, too."

"I'll agree that I'm a bit ripe, so I guess that I'd rather have you help me than anyone else."

"You don't want me to shave that stubble off of your face; do you?"

"I'd rather not, ma'am. It's not that I don't trust you with a razor near my neck, but I figure I'll just let it grow until I can handle a razor myself."

"Doc can do it when he stops by in the morning. He is a barber, you know."

"We'll see."

"I'll get the water and your new clothes."

After she stood, she leaned across and kissed him in a manner that was more suggestive than the almost mournful one they'd shared on the killing ground when each of them believed it would be the only one that they would ever share.

Their lips parted and she smiled before turning and leaving the room.

Tabby watched as she limped away, opened the door then disappeared before he spent a few minutes chastising himself for not joining her in her bed on that first night. It had become a fairly regular admonishment.

———

The washing and changing of clothes weren't as stimulating as Tabby had expected as the pain from his wound prevented him from focusing on Rena.

After he was clean and wearing his new clothes, but not his new boots, they shared the chicken dinner in his room while the Smiths ate in the kitchen.

When Rena took the dishes away and helped Ros with the cleanup, Sheriff Smith and Richie visited Tabby.

275

The sheriff told him what had happened at Dilly's and the plans to find Max while Tabby provided a more detailed explanation of the last few days.

The lamps were burning when Rena and Ros joined them in the room. The first thing that Ros asked was, of course, how he'd gotten the Tabby moniker.

As Rena had predicted, Richie giggled through most of the story but was confused when Tabby said that the other cowboys had given him a different nickname first. He had a suspicion that he shouldn't ask his father about it later, though.

Richie was already yawning when the Smiths left the room.

Tabby knew that there was no room on the bed for Rena, which was probably a good thing and with no other place for her to sleep, he assumed she had her own room.

"Where are you sleeping, Rena?"

"I'll be in Richie's room. He's sleeping on the couch in the parlor and says it's like camping out, so he's happy with it."

"Rena," he asked, "Where do you want to stay after I can move around?"

"I thought we could move out to the ranch house. With all those horses, we can use one for a packhorse. Then when you're feeling up to it, we can go get the buckboard."

The idea of using the ranch house hadn't surprised him, but the idea of retrieving the buckboard did.

"Why do you want to get the buckboard if we're only staying there for a week or two?"

"I was talking to Ros about that, Thom. She told me that a far as the law was concerned, I was entitled to the ranch. She said she'd have her husband get it changed if we wanted to stay."

"Do you want to stay? You told me just earlier today that you hated the idea of living anywhere near Watson."

"I discovered that there are good people here that don't judge me as much as I expected. First it was talking to Doc James. I had only spoken to him when he had to suture a knife cut. But while you were sleeping, he told me a story that made me realize that I really didn't know him at all. Then after talking to the sheriff and Ros made me understand how I had put the entire town into one basket.

"I know that there are men who still will look at me like the whore that I was, and many women will continue to stick up their noses rather than talk to me. But I can handle them now. I have you and I know people who don't think badly of me. If you want to stay on the ranch, we can even buy some cattle. You'll have plenty of money after all those rewards come in. What do you think?"

Tabby stared at Rena for almost a minute without answering. Unlike almost every other cowhand he knew, he had never even thought of owning his own spread. He was content with a life of no responsibilities and now he was suddenly looking at the enormous change of being a ranch owner. He had barely had time to adjust to the idea of being married. Even though he understood he would have to provide for Rena, he'd been able to push that planning into the back of his mind. Now it stared him in the face, and he was shaken by the notion.

"Can I spend some time to think about it, Rena? It sounds like a good idea, but it took me by surprise."

"Of course, you can. It surprised me, too. But once Ros told me that we could have the ranch, it seemed right to me."

Tabby smiled as she stood, then gave him a quick goodnight kiss before blowing out the lamp and leaving the room.

He spent a few minutes trying to find a reasonably comfortable sleeping position and settled on lying on his stomach. Despite having spent much of the afternoon either sleeping or unconscious, he soon fell into a deep sleep.

———

Max was even more uncomfortable as he tried to get back to sleep. He'd awakened after a couple of hours and even after taking off his gunbelt, sleep still eluded him. By the time he did drift off again, the night was colder and predawn was just four hours away.

CHAPTER 6

Just after daybreak, Sheriff Wolfson and Deputy Trudeau had already eaten their breakfast were riding out of town to check on the abandoned ranch house. They knew where it was, but only had seen it from the canyon's mouth.

They were wearing their heavy coats and gloves as they trotted along the road and clouds were forming before their mouths as their warm, moist breath escaped into the chilly air.

"You reckon we're gonna find that bastard?" Paul asked loudly.

"Maybe. Where else could he go? Maybe we'll get lucky and see him on the road. There won't be any other folks walkin' around out there at this time of day."

Paul snickered before replying, "That's for sure. If we don't see him at the ranch, then are we gonna look anywhere else?"

"Nope. Tex just asked us to check that place out 'cause it's where he figured the last one would be hidin'. If he ain't there, we turn around and we'll probably still be on the road past Watson before those other boys get movin'."

"That was one helluva fight, boss. Tex didn't seem all that upset about losin' Bill Carroll, either."

"If you knew him as well as I did, you'd know why. He wasn't crooked or anything like that, but he wasn't exactly a model lawman either. He figured he deserved more for just wearin' the badge. Tex says that he was handy with his pistol and mostly did a good job, but there were a few times where he'd come close to takin' that badge from him."

"Really? I thought he was a pretty good sort."

"That's 'cause he didn't work for you, Paul. If a man's a pal, then you don't need to worry much about what he does."

"Do you worry about me, boss?" Paul asked with a grin.

"You're damned straight I worry about you."

"*You do?*" asked the astonished deputy.

"Yup," Sheriff Wolfson replied with a straight face, "I'm worried that you'll be takin' my job before I'm ready to give it up."

Paul laughed as they turned their horses onto the trail that led to the canyon ranch.

———

Rena had provided Tabby with a steel skillet for his use before taking it away to wash it out. She returned a little while later with a tray and they shared a good breakfast.

"When is the doc coming?" he asked before he bit into a biscuit.

"He didn't say, but I'm sure he'll be by this morning because he needs to show me what I need to do and what to look for."

"You're doing pretty well already, Rena."

She was about to ask about the ranch again when Tex entered the room.

"How are you doin', Tabby?" he asked.

"I'm a bit stiff and my wound is throbbing a little more, but I'm all right."

"I'm headin' off to my office. Can you and Rena write those statements for me while I'm gone?"

"Yes, sir. Don't expect to be able to read my hen scratching."

The sheriff grinned before replying, "It can't be any worse than mine. I have to make arrangements for Deputy Carroll's burial and a few other things, but I'll stop by around noon. I should hear from Joe Wolfson soon, too. I hope he catches that last one. He's one of the worst of those bad boys, too."

Rena said, "He was actually the very worst. There were times when I thought he was going to shoot Cash in the back and take over, but it was always when Cash had his back to him. When they talked, he was almost subservient. I think Cash bought it, too."

"I wonder why he didn't just reload his Winchester and come back."

Tabby said, "I reckon it was because he thought I was better than I was with that Winchester. I was shooting at their horses the first time and was lucky the second, but if he thought I was a sharpshooter, then he might not want to face me with that '76 in my hands."

"That makes sense. Well, I'd better get goin'."

Tex gave them a quick wave and left the room.

Rena watched him leave and wistfully said, "I hope that the other sheriff gets Max."

"Even if he doesn't, I don't figure he'll be sticking around here very long. He'll probably head for Bannack as soon as he can."

"On foot?" she asked.

Tabby just looked at her without answering. He hadn't really believed what he'd just said. He suspected that if Max wasn't caught today, he'd have to be close by until he at least found a horse.

———

Max had left the trees just after sunrise. He was stiff and still sore as he trudged along avoiding the rocks and trees. He still had enough water in his canteen to last until noon, and by then, he hoped to find the ranch.

He'd been walking for almost two hours when he spotted the buckboard and felt as if he'd been freed from prison. He was just a mile or so away from the canyon's mouth and then another short trip to the ranch house and food.

———

Sheriff Wolfson mounted his gelding and looked back at the canyon behind the ranch house. He could see about a thousand yards before trees blocked his view and the only movement that he could see was a small herd of white-tailed deer.

"Are we gonna head down there, boss?" Paul asked.

"I don't think so. We need to get back to Virginia City and if he was in this canyon, then he woulda been in the house. If he saw us comin', he'd run, and we'd see him. That house ain't been used in a few days, so we're not gonna find him. Let's head back, tell Tex he ain't here and then go home."

Paul took one more look at the back of the canyon before they started their horses toward its mouth.

———

Max had just cleared the last of the trees that hid the buckboard and spotted the two lawmen leaving the canyon. He froze and watched nervously hoping that he hadn't been seen. He was about a mile away, but he was standing in the bright sunlight and felt like a lighthouse on a dark night.

He only breathed more easily when the two riders turned east and began to take the trail back to Watson. He still didn't move until they made the northern turn and soon disappeared.

Max slowly walked to his left as he slid into the trees. He wasn't about to risk being spotted again if they suddenly returned.

He stayed hidden behind a thick pine despite the demands from his stomach that he provided it with nourishment immediately.

———

Sheriff Wolfson stopped at the jail forty minutes later and told Tex that the ranch was empty. He wished Sheriff Smith luck in finding the last outlaw before he and Deputy Trudeau set out for Virginia City.

After he'd gone, John Lee asked, "Are we gonna look for that Max feller, Sheriff?"

"Nope. If he shows up in town or somewhere else, we'll chase him down, but we're too short handed to go lookin'. I don't reckon I can ask for another posse so soon, either."

Deputy Lee nodded and didn't admit how relieved he was. It had been difficult for him to even show up this morning. He'd only managed a couple of hours of uneasy sleep as he tried to forget the sight of seeing Bill Carroll's lifeless body.

Sheriff Smith then said, "Why don't you make rounds, John? We can't neglect our normal duties."

"Oh. Okay, boss," he replied before taking his hat and exiting the jail.

Tex sighed then pulled out his report about the deaths of five of the six gang members. He had to add a less tasteful paragraph about Max Johnson still being on the loose.

————

Max had finally given in to his growling stomach and headed for the ranch house. He had his Winchester cocked and his hammer loop off as he walked alongside the ruts left by the buckboard.

He may have convinced himself that the two lawmen were gone, but he wasn't sure that they hadn't left more members of their posse in the ranch house to wait for him. If he'd been just a little earlier, he would have seen them go into the canyon and know how many there were in the posse. That posse that he'd seen pass by was at least eight men and that left a half dozen whose whereabouts were unknown.

He approached the mouth of the canyon warily and watched as more of the land inside revealed itself. He soon spotted the barn but didn't see any horses. As he continued to walk, the ranch house slid into view and he stopped. He didn't see any smoke from the chimney or the cookstove pipe, but that didn't mean that they weren't in there waiting for him.

But the lack of horses, even if he couldn't see inside the barn or behind the house gave him enough confidence to enter the canyon.

He constantly switched his focus between the barn and the house as he made that mile-long walk. Each step was nerve wracking, but he continued at the same pace.

Max was just a hundred yards out when he stopped again. This was the well-known effective range of the Winchester in his hand, and he took a minute staring at the house to look for any movement in the windows.

He took one last glance at the barn before he resumed his slow approach to the house.

When he finally stepped onto the porch, his need for patience vanished and he threw open the door and rushed inside with his Winchester's butt against his shoulder. He was swinging it from side to side but didn't see anyone.

He didn't lower his sights as he began walking through the house. He stopped at each open door and let his Winchester's muzzle precede him as he scanned the empty rooms.

It was only when he reached the kitchen that he lowered his repeater and almost collapsed onto a chair. He blew out his breath before standing again and heading for the back door.

Max opened it quickly and stepped onto the small back porch before hopping to the ground and walking quickly to the barn.

He no longer worried about the posse, but he hoped to find a horse, and if he was lucky, a saddle.

But as soon as he passed through the open doors, he knew his luck hadn't improved.

"Son of a bitch!" he snapped as he looked at the empty stalls.

Without a horse, he'd be trapped here until he could find a way to get one. At least he'd be able to eat even if the pantry was almost bare. He'd have to watch the mouth of the canyon, but after that recent visit by those two lawmen, he didn't think they'd be back soon.

He finally released his Winchester's hammer and trudged back to the house to make something to eat. He was debating about starting a fire in the cookstove as he entered the back door.

———

Doc James was pleased with Tabby's rapidly improving condition and took about an hour telling Rena and his patient what each of them needed to do. He also warned them about the signs of infection but said that the wound wasn't showing any signs of the feared complication.

He asked if Tabby would like a shave but wasn't offended when his offer was declined.

After his visit, Rena and Tabby wrote their statements and then compared their completed literary masterpieces. Tabby admitted that hers was much better, but thought she used far too many words praising him.

With their statements sitting on top of the dresser, Rena finally broached the subject of the ranch again.

"Did you decide about the ranch yet?"

"Yes, ma'am. After I thought about it, I reckon that it's a pretty good idea. I'll have to get used to being a boss of sorts, but I think it'll be okay. With cattle prices as low as they are, I reckon I can head over to the Slash 6 and buy a bull and a few cows to get started. We'd need a bunkhouse and some other things, but that's not for a while."

Rena smiled and took his hands as she said, "Thank you, Thom. I think you'll make a wonderful boss, but don't expect to boss me around."

He laughed before saying, "I didn't figure that was about to happen, Rena. I can't recall being able to tell you to do anything since we met."

Rena was smiling as she reviewed the time they'd spent together and tried to find a single example when she'd done as he'd asked.

"I did play dead after you climbed onto my back and told me to shut up."

"That, Mrs. Hayes, was because I was squeezing the breath out of you. I do apologize for telling you to shut up, though. I could have politely asked you to be quiet."

Rena laughed then said, "You're not heavy enough to squeeze the breath out of me, Mister Hayes, and I believe you didn't have time to be polite as you were trying to shoot your rifle."

"You know, Rena, when I did that, I never even thought of you as a woman. That sounds odd, but I only saw you as someone I needed to protect from those bullets."

"I know. I'll never forget why you did it, either."

Then after a short pause, she asked, "Does it bother you that you'll never have a son like Richie to hear those stories of his brave father?"

"Would you believe me if I told you it doesn't? You seem to forget that just a few days ago, I never even thought I'd ever get married."

"You're not just saying that because you know I can't have children?"

"No, I'm not. I'll be perfectly happy to live on our ranch and take care of the cattle. Are you sad that you can't have babies?"

"I don't know how I feel about it. Until the idea of being a real wife instead of what I was, the possibility of a pregnancy was a nightmare. I really haven't spent much time thinking about it. I mean, you only agreed to marry me three days ago and then said we could live on the ranch a few minutes ago."

"Then just focus on moving to the ranch. Okay?"

Rena nodded but now that her inability to have a baby was in her mind, she found it hard to focus on anything else.

———

Max had built a fire in the cookstove and made himself an enormous meal which he devoured much too quickly.

He paid the price when he felt a sudden kick in his stomach, and he bolted through the open back door and vomited onto the dry wood of the small porch.

"Damnation!" he snapped as he wiped his mouth.

He looked at the stinking mess he'd left on the porch and knew he had to clean it in case the posse came back looking for him. He'd already picked out a hiding place that would require a thorough search of the house, but if they saw that disaster, it would loudly announce his presence.

He walked back inside and after rinsing the foul taste from his mouth, filled a bucket with water and started cleaning up the disgusting mess. He didn't do a great job, but just enough to make it look just like a stain in the dry wood.

He had set up a chair in the front room near the window so he could watch the mouth of the canyon, and after topping off his coffee cup, he walked down the hallway and took his post.

Max still doubted if anyone would show up for at least another day or two, but he wasn't about to be surprised.

As he sat and sipped his coffee, he spent most of his time trying to figure out a way to get a horse. After that, he'd have to get a saddle and then the all-important need to put some money in his pocket. He had less than thirty dollars and that wouldn't buy enough to get him out of the area. He had no idea that Jimmy Parsons' four-hundred-dollar stash was hidden in the barn. Even though he was still concerned about the posse, he thought that he might be able to walk to Watson during the night and just liberate a horse and saddle outside of Dilly's.

After that idea popped into his mind, he began to expand on it to figure out a way to pick up some money at the same time. He knew that Dilly's would probably have a decent amount of cash behind the bar just before it closed. That would mean he'd have to time it just right. He'd make sure that there were just one or two horses outside before going into the place and grabbing whatever he could. If anyone tried to make noise, he'd shut them up the best way he knew how.

After settling on his plan, he picked up the Winchester. As soon as it was in his hands, another potential threat suddenly reached his thoughts…that bounty hunter.

He'd spent so much of his time worrying about the posse that he'd forgotten about the bastard who'd caused all the problems and put him in this position. *Where was he?*

Max closed his eyes and tried to picture the last time he'd seen him and Monique. The bounty hunter was lying atop the whore firing his Winchester at him and Monique was shooting as well. Suddenly, Max realized that the man had been firing a '76. He wondered if it was his gun. But whether it was or not wasn't important right now. That bounty hunter's location was all that mattered. He had probably raked in quite a haul by killing the others and might have already left town, assuming he'd made it to Watson in the first place. But that posse had come back, and he hadn't seen the bounty hunter or Monique with them.

Then there was Monique herself. Max wondered if the bounty hunter was going to keep her with him after they got to Watson. Max was curious if the bounty on the other five would be more than the money she stole. He doubted it, so maybe he'd just keep her with him and head to Bannack or Virginia City. But they were afoot when he left, and they'd have to walk into town to buy more horses. That would raise more questions and he knew that Monique was well known in Watson.

He finally opened his eyes, shook his head to clear his head of the jumbled thoughts and just returned to his concern about the bounty hunter.

He looked down at the Winchester. He was at a disadvantage with the '73 and that bounty hunter was a damned good shot. The posse might not be back for a couple of days, but that blasted bounty hunter could show up at any time.

Max stood then walked through the front door and stood on the porch almost willing the bounty hunter to show up at the canyon's mouth a mile away. He was already tired of feeling like the mouse in this game. He wanted to be the hunter again.

He took in a deep breath then turned and walked back into the house angrily slamming the door closed behind him.

———

Rena had just returned to Tabby's room after carrying their dirty dishes back to the kitchen.

After she sat down, she asked, "When do you think you can walk again?"

"Strangely enough, young lady, I was just thinking that same thing. After you left with the plates, I thought I'd slide out of bed and surprise you when you returned. You got back before I made up my mind."

"Do you want me to help you?"

"No, ma'am. I can do this."

293

She stood and pulled her chair away from the bed and watched as Tabby bent his knees then slid his feet off the side of the bed.

When he pushed himself into a sitting position, Tabby was surprised that it was less painful than lying on his side. He didn't know why it would be that way but was grateful for the respite.

He slowly stood and then stretched his arms wide and said, "Ta-da!"

"How bad is it?" she asked expecting him to fall over.

"It's better than lying down. I'm going to take a few steps to see how that works."

Rena had already given him enough space, so she just watched closely as Tabby began to slowly walk past the front of the bed then circle back around.

"This feels pretty good, Rena," he said as he made another circuit at a faster pace.

"Don't start running, Thom."

"I may be a man, but even I'm not that stupid, ma'am."

"I have to admit that I'm impressed. I didn't think you'd be out of that bed for another two days."

"Doc James said I might be able to walk after a day if I could deal with the pain, but I'll have to tell him that the pain wasn't that bad at all. I wouldn't want anyone to punch me in the back, but I think I could even saddle a horse if I took it slow."

"Don't even think about it, Mister Hayes!" she snapped.

"I was just commenting about how good I feel. I know that I'd probably rip those stitches apart if I tried to saddle Philly. But this does mean that we might be able to move to the ranch tomorrow."

Rena smiled broadly as she asked, "Do you really think so?"

"I don't see why not. I'll need you to do some things before we can leave town, but I think we can make it work."

He carefully sat on the edge of the bed while Rena pulled the chair back into position and sat down.

"What do you need done?"

"I know that I said I could ride, but I think a buggy would be a better idea. See about buying a used one and then buy whatever else you think we'll need. Don't worry about all of that official stuff like the rewards. You pick out a horse and saddle for yourself and I'll have Philly saddled. We'll use another horse for the buggy and a fourth for a packhorse."

"I'll talk to Tex about the horses and see if he knows where we can get the buggy. I'm already getting excited and I never would have believed that I'd ever want to go back to that ranch."

"Well, Mrs. Hayes, it's after noon already, so you have a lot to do and only a few hours to get it done. It's really not critical, though. We can wait until the next day if you feel too rushed."

"Oh, I'll get it done, Tabby," she said as she stood.

"I'm Tabby now?" he asked as he smiled up at her.

"Unless you want me to use the first nickname that your cowboy friends gave to you after you saved that cat."

"Tabby is fine," he quickly said before she laughed and scooted out of the room.

After she'd gone, he stood again and resumed his slow circuits. He was so pleased with his progress that he tried twisting at his waist and instantly realized that he hadn't made that much improvement.

———

Sheriff Smith was surprised when Rena entered the office and after she explained what Tabby wanted to do, he assigned Deputy Lee to help her with what she needed.

Finding a used buggy turned out to be easier than she had anticipated and after paying just forty dollars, they walked to Topper's Livery.

She thought that one of the men in the livery was one of her customers but ignored him. She picked out a tan gelding from the batch that were now owned by Tabby and told Lou Topper that she'd need Philly and the gelding saddled in the morning before she chose a stocky mare as the one to pull the buggy. She almost forgot about the packhorse until Lou pointed to the pack saddle and the almost full panniers. She thanked him for jogging her memory and realized that with the packs, she wouldn't have to buy as much as she had expected when she went to Jackson's.

With the horses and buggy arranged, she and John left the livery and after the deputy entered the jail, she continued to Jackson's to add the supplies they would need.

When she entered the store, she immediately recognized Abigail Woodridge, the wife of the Lutheran minister and one of the most vocal members of the Women for Decency.

She smiled and as she passed the counter, she cheerfully said, "Good afternoon, Abby," then continued down the first of the three food aisles.

Mrs. Woodridge would normally have given a severe tongue lashing to that whore, but it seemed that everyone in town now regarded her as some sort of heroine, so she withheld her well-rehearsed admonishment. She almost stomped out of the store in frustration and wished that those outlaws had won the gunfight.

Bob Jackson was snickering as he watched Rena collecting tins of food. This was better than watching a concert at the new hall. He couldn't wait to tell his wife about how Rena had used a polite greeting to humiliate Mrs. Woodridge.

Rena may have been pleasant to her, but her stomach was still tied in a knot. It had been a very difficult thing for her to do, but she was more than pleased with the results. She hadn't intended it as an insult to the woman but wanted to let her know that she was no longer going to tolerate being a pariah.

She began carrying her loads to the counter as she found more things that they'd need. Bob offered to help, but Rena explained that she wasn't really sure and would only know what she wanted when she found it.

When she brought her last armload to the front of the store and set it down, she said, "I think that's all of it, Mister Jackson. Can we pick this up in the morning?"

"Yes, ma'am. Are you and Mister Hayes leaving?"

"Yes. We're going out to the ranch. He's already walking, but he can't do much until the stitches come out. He just doesn't want to be a burden on the sheriff and his wife."

"I don't reckon Tex sees it that way, but I'll have this all packed up and ready to go."

"Thank you."

She paid the bill before leaving the store. When she reached the boardwalk, she suddenly realized that she was still wearing

Tabby's coat and she'd left her jacket behind. She wasn't sure if it was in one of the panniers, but she didn't want to risk not having it when they left in the morning. She was sure it would be chilly, and Thom would need his coat.

So, she wheeled about and reentered the store.

"I forgot to buy a new coat for myself," she said to Bob as she passed, "This one is Thom's."

He smiled as she hurried down the clothing aisle and after stopping before the rack of coats, found the one that looked the warmest. It wasn't the most stylish, but that wasn't her concern. She added a pair of gloves and then returned to the counter and paid another seven dollars for the coat and gloves before making her second exit.

As she walked back to the sheriff's house, she watched the traffic and the folks who called Watson home. She knew most of them at least by name and too many of the men. But after the talks with Doc James and the time with the Smiths followed by the encounter with Mrs. Woodridge, she now thought of herself as just another citizen. She was no longer angry at the whole town, nor was she ashamed of herself.

She crossed the street at an angle and had to avoid a pair of riders but soon reached the other side and continued walking west with her new jacket over her arm and the new gloves in Tabby's coat pocket.

Rena passed Doc's barbershop but didn't see him inside as she continued walking through her town. She still wore Tabby's Colt Walker at her hip even though she had to remember to put it on before leaving the house. It had become as much a part of her wardrobe as her shoes now.

She entered the house without knocking and waved to Ros who was walking toward her.

"I hear you're leaving us in the morning."

"Mister Hayes says that he's up to it and who am I to deny him anything?"

Ros laughed then stopped when she was in front of Rena and asked, "Do you need anything?"

"No, I've just returned from Jackson's and we'll pick up my order in the morning. I ran into Abigail Woodridge when I entered the store."

Ros' eyebrows arched as she asked, "And how did that go?"

"I just said good afternoon and began shopping."

"She didn't say anything?"

"Not a word, but I think she wanted to say a lot more than just one word and none of them would be very nice. I've heard them all before anyway."

Ros laughed then hooked her arm through Rena's and escorted her into Tabby's room before turning around and leaving.

Rena saw that he was lying on his side again and as she laid her new coat over the back of the chair, she asked, "Are you feeling bad again? Do you want to stay?"

"No, ma'am. I'm fine. I'm just saving up my energy. Did you get everything done already?"

"I did. We have a used buggy and we'll be trailing two saddled horses and a packhorse. The order from Jackson's will be ready in the morning and it should fit on the buggy's shelf," she replied as she shrugged off his heavy coat and laid it across his knees.

"You are an amazing woman, Rena. I noticed that you're still armed. You don't expect to use my old hogleg; do you?"

"No, sir. It's just that you gave it to me, and I feel comfortable wearing it."

"Maybe you should carry one of the pistols that were donated by those outlaws. Tex showed me a list of what they had, and I told him that we'd give him most of the guns, but I'd still keep a couple of the pistols and two Winchesters."

"No. This one is special. I know I'll never shoot it, but I want to keep it."

She sat down and said, "I bought a new coat and gloves, too. I'm not sure that they found my jacket."

"It's in the back room of the livery with my bedroll and slicker. I guess the only things we're missing are your two bags of clothes, the heavy one with tins of food and cookware, my saddle and one Winchester."

"We're not going looking for them; are we?"

"I have no idea where they are anyway. We will get the buckboard though. I believe you already made that suggestion."

She smiled then took his hands and said, "We're really going to be living together."

"We are and maybe I'll finally get to take you up on the offer you made to me on our first night together."

"That was such an odd night for me. Part of me was disappointed that you hadn't joined me, and another part was pleased that you slept next door. I guess that was because it was the first time, I began to see you as a good man who would treat me as I always hoped a man would."

"Would you think any less of me if I told you that I've been irritated with myself for making that decision almost every hour we've been together? At least after we left the buckboard behind."

"No. I could never think any less of you," she answered softly.

Then she surprised him when she stood then managed to squeeze onto the bed with her eyes just three inches from his.

He was about to kiss her when the front door opened, and Rena hurriedly left the bed and took her seat again.

Richie trotted into the room and asked, "Are you leavin' tomorrow, Tabby?"

"Yes, sir. How'd you hear that so soon?"

"Eddie Jackson's father told him, and he told me."

"Oh. It's not like we're moving to Colorado. We're just moving out to the ranch, so we'll stop by pretty often."

"That's good," he said before bouncing out of the room.

After hearing his footsteps disappear down the hallway, Tabby watched Rena's eyes as she looked at the door and wondered if she was thinking about the question that she'd asked him earlier about children. He'd answered it honestly but hoped that she didn't think that he was really disappointed, and it would somehow drive a wedge between them.

He'd been making one adjustment to his life after another since meeting Rena and hope he didn't have to make another even more difficult one if she suddenly changed her mind.

———

Max had settled into a routine after his stomach revolution earlier. He had a more reasonable amount of food and then patrolled the outside of the house more to keep from going stir crazy than looking for potential threats.

Ever since he and Cash had teamed up, they'd always either been working on a new job or enjoying the spoils from the last one. They rarely had two days in a row where they weren't busy. They added men and either lost them or got rid of them, usually with a .44 in the back.

Now he had been doing nothing but walking and hiding for two days and it was making him crazy. He'd do some target practice if he wasn't worried about it attracting unwanted attention.

It was getting late in the day when he returned to the house and started making his own plans for getting money and a horse from Watson tomorrow night. He'd have to start walking soon after sunset, but he expected to be in Bannack before dawn the next day.

———

After supper, Rena didn't repeat her short trip to Tabby's bed as they'd be sleeping together tomorrow night anyway.

Instead, they spent their last night in the Smith home just making plans for tomorrow's return to the ranch.

TABBY HAYES

It seemed as if no one in Watson even gave any more thought to Max Johnson. It was as if he'd fallen off the face of the earth.

When Tabby fell asleep that night, his last thoughts were of Rena and there was no place for the last outlaw.

Despite what Tabby thought, Rena hadn't been thinking about her inability to bear children at all when she'd seen Richie leave the room. She hadn't even spent a moment on the question since talking to Tabby. She had resolved to just be a good wife and do all she could to make him happy. It was much more than she could have hoped for just two weeks ago.

The only one in the area who thought about Max was Max himself. He had finished the last details of his plan to leave the ranch and Watson behind and had already moved on to finding more partners. This time, he'd be in charge.

———

It was midmorning when Tabby and Rena waved goodbye to Tex and Ros as they drove the buggy out of Watson. They were trailing Philly, Rena's new gelding and the packhorse. Her large order had been too much for the rack on the back of the buggy, so Bob Jackson had hung two sacks over Philly's saddle.

As they left the town behind, Rena was snuggled next to Tabby. It was the first time they'd been that close since he'd laid on her back to protect her. This was a much more pleasant experience for both of them.

"When we get to the ranch house, I'll do all of the unloading and taking care of the horses," Rena said.

"I'm doing pretty well, Rena, but I won't push it. I promise."

"I'm already familiar with those kinds of promises, Mister Hayes. So, if I see any blood on your back, I'll shoot you myself."

Tabby laughed and asked, "You're going to shoot me with my own gun?"

"You gave it to me and the only man I deem worthy of being shot with the pistol is its original owner."

"Then I guess I'd better behave myself."

"I just want to be able to remove those stitches and finally make you accept my original offer."

"You won't have to make me accept it, ma'am. I'm already more than willing to join you, but something is preventing me from ending our chaste relationship."

She laughed then kissed him before saying, "Such big words for a cowhand."

"That's just because those cows knew all the short words, ma'am."

They were both grinning as Tabby turned the buggy off the road and began bouncing along the rough trail.

———

Max had a hot breakfast of beans and the last of the smoked pork. He'd had a short debate with himself about starting a fire in the cookstove, but he wanted the heat as much as the hot food. The house was still more than just chilly.

After eating his breakfast, he walked to the front of the house and resumed his watch. He knew that the day would just drag on as he anxiously waited for sunset and his walk to town. He wanted to get away from this ranch and everything else in this cursed country.

He had cleaned and reloaded the Winchester three times in his boredom and was thinking about doing it again. He suddenly stood, leaned the repeater against the wall near the window then began to pace in a figure eight around the front room.

Max hadn't slept well last night even though he'd stayed up late as he kept revising what should have been a simple plan. He hadn't realized just how important Cash had been to the gang. He'd been the one who did the planning and the other preparations that the rest of them simply followed. Now he had to do the planning himself and found that it wasn't as easy as he'd thought.

He knew that he'd probably be up all night tonight after stealing the horses and robbing Dilly's, so he knew that he had to calm down and maybe take a nap in the afternoon. He was cursing under his breath as he paced.

He finally stopped, took in a deep breath and blew it out before looking out the window to the mouth of the canyon. Once he was sure that no one was coming, he headed back to the kitchen to have some coffee.

In an effort to settle his nerves, he began whistling as he walked down the hallway.

If he'd looked just two minutes later, he would have spotted a buggy and three trailed horses turn into the canyon. But instead of preparing for his guests' arrival, he was filling his mug with coffee before sitting at the table. He had just missed the opportunity of not only eliminating the man who had caused all of his grief, but of getting the horses, supplies and cash he needed to make his escape.

———

The smoke from the ranch house's cookstove was just a light vapor as Tabby drove the buggy deeper into the canyon.

"I never went past the house, Rena. Do you know what it's like way down in the canyon?"

"I never went past the trees, but I know that they bought the entire canyon. Mark said it was more than two sections. Does that sound right?"

"Two sections? It's only about eight hundred yards wide at the mouth, so that means it would have to be four miles long. I reckon we'll have to look at the map in the land office when we get a chance."

"We have to get married one of these days too, Mister Hayes. You did promise."

"I suppose so. But that means you can't shoot me before then."

Rena laughed and swatted him on his shoulder, but his thick coat deadened the impact.

As they neared the house, neither of them gave a moment's thought that Max or anyone else was inside. Tex had told them that Joe Wolfson and his deputy had checked the place the day before and found no signs of the last outlaw.

Max had finished his coffee but didn't bother washing his mug before setting it in the sink and walking back to his chair in the front room.

He had just set his butt on the hard seat when he shot to his feet again.

"Son of a bitch!" he exclaimed as he snatched his Winchester.

But it was too late to try a shot by the time he'd even spotted them. As soon as he grabbed his repeater, the buggy was gone from view as it passed between the house and the barn.

For just a few seconds, Max could have raced to the side window and taken a shot as the buggy rolled past, but he was close to panic after seeing that bounty hunter and Monique sitting in the buggy's seat.

He forced himself to regain his senses and calm down to figure how to handle that bastard. He knew he'd have to wait for him to enter the house and that would mean a pistol fight. Max wasn't happy with the idea, but he didn't have a choice anymore. He set the Winchester down and walked to the hallway.

When he realized that they'd be coming through the back door, he slowly began to step toward the kitchen before he stopped. It would be too risky to be standing in the kitchen even with his pistol cocked. *What if Monique entered first?* She'd scream and then that bounty hunter would pull his pistol and Max knew he wouldn't win the gunfight.

He took six long strides and entered the first bedroom and left the door open. He could see part of the kitchen, so he'd wait for them to enter the house and when he saw the bounty hunter, he'd shoot the bastard.

Max could only see the table chairs and the edge of the cookstove but knew that he'd get his shot soon.

———

Tabby pulled the buggy to a stop near the small back porch and set the handbrake.

Rena exited first and gingerly set her bad ankle on the ground before limping around the back of the buggy while Tabby slowly climbed out from the other side.

"We'll start unloading the rest in a minute," Tabby said as he lifted the bags from Philly's saddle and hung them over his shoulder.

"You're starting already, sir," Rena said.

"I knew this wasn't heavy, ma'am," he replied as he took her arm.

They were both all smiles as they stepped onto the porch and Tabby opened the door to let her enter.

Rena passed over the threshold, took two steps into the house where she'd lived for more than two years, then turned and waited for him. She was standing just a foot from the cookstove's firebox door.

Tabby entered and before he dropped the bags to the floor, Rena noticed some spilled coffee on the cookstove's surface. She almost dismissed it but then realized that it shouldn't be there at all. It should have evaporated by now.

When Tabby dropped the bags, she quickly pulled off her left glove and touched the cookstove.

C.J. PETIT

Tabby was smiling at her when she loudly said, "Well, now that we're finally alone, Thom, it's time I showed you just how good I really am."

He looked at her in surprise and was about to ask her what she meant when she put her finger to her lips and shook her head.

He still had no idea what was happening when she asked, "Do you know that I'm not wearing anything under this dress?"

Tabby may have been confused, but Max wasn't. As he listened to what Monique said, even though he couldn't see either of them, he didn't doubt that she'd soon drag the bounty hunter into a bedroom. He stared at the kitchen expecting to see her pulling him down the hallway in just a few more seconds. Then he'd have an even easier shot at the distracted bounty hunter.

Rena was almost certain that Max was just down the hallway with his pistol ready to fire, so she reverted to her most practiced skill set to draw him out.

She began unbuttoning her new coat as she stepped closer to a puzzled Tabby.

"You've been driving me to distraction for that entire ride with your roving hands and I can't wait any longer."

She shrugged her coat from her shoulders and tossed it back to the kitchen table just before she reached Tabby.

312

Max saw the coat fly past the end of the hall and began to think that Monique wasn't going to waste time in bringing the bounty hunter to a bed.

Rena put her lips closer to Tabby's right ear and whispered, "I'm sure that Max is in the house. The cookstove is still warm."

Tabby looked at the hallway entrance before whispering back, "We'll sneak out the back door and I'll come back in the front."

"No, no," she quickly replied, "I'll draw him out. Just don't say anything."

"I don't want you to put yourself in danger!" he exclaimed in a hushed voice.

"I won't be in danger. Just be ready. Okay?"

He nodded and wondered what Rena was planning to do. He should have gotten a good idea by her first loud announcement.

She then used a sultry, deep voice when she said, "Let's get rid of your coat first."

Tabby wasn't sure of his part in Rena's play, so she quickly unbuttoned his heavy coat then tossed it onto the floor near the doorway.

She was still wearing her gunbelt with the heavy Colt Walker as she said in her seductive voice, "You won't be using this weapon, Thom. I'd rather you use the one that God gave you."

She then unbuckled her gunbelt and let it drop to the floor with a loud thump.

Max heard the noise and almost stepped out of the bedroom knowing the bounty hunter was disarmed but decided to wait until he was even more vulnerable. He knew it wouldn't be long before his britches hit the floor but even when they did, he'd still wait until they were in the throes of unbridled lust.

Even before the bounty hunter's britches fell, he found himself becoming aroused as he listened to Monique and pictured what she was doing.

Once Rena dropped her pistol, Tabby finally realized how she had planned to draw Max into the kitchen.

He released his Colt's hammer loop and pulled his pistol.

Rena was in between him and the hallway and he was about to nudge her out of the way when she moved onto the second act in her play.

She suddenly turned and backstepped to the wall where she began to act out the part of a passionate woman being ravished by her lover.

Tabby was finding it difficult to concentrate as she began moaning and crying out demands for satisfaction as if he was running his hands all over her naked body.

Max was in even worse shape as he listened to her ever more passionate and lusty cries and sounds.

Rena had performed this play many times in her life, so it was almost second nature to her. She was the only person in the house who was unaffected by her impressive performance.

She'd been emitting every conceivable utterance and guttural creation she had within her for almost five minutes before she began slamming her behind against the wall in a rhythmic pounding that told Max that she and Tabby were finalizing their act of passion.

Max knew it was time. The bounty hunter was probably in such a distant mind that he'd never even hear him coming. He still didn't rush but moved quietly and with the confidence of a man who knew his enemy was unprepared for the fight.

Tabby had used Rena's loud cries to cock his Colt's hammer and even as distracting as she was, he kept his pistol's sights on the end of the hallway. He was wondering how long Max would take. It seemed like it had been an hour since Rena had warned him and he began to wonder if she had been wrong about Max being in the house.

He was beginning to worry about making the shot after holding the pistol level for so long that his forearm was growing tight.

Tabby was just about to shift his Colt to his left hand when he saw a revolver's muzzle slowly emerge from the hallway. Before he had arrived in Watson, he'd never even pointed a gun at another man. Even when he'd been firing at the other outlaws, it was a long range and he hadn't really seen their faces. Now he'd have to shoot a man just six feet away and he hoped he didn't hesitate. Rena's nearby voice gave him the determination to protect her just as he had when he'd slid on top of her to keep her safe.

Max heard what he assumed was the bounty hunter slamming Monique against the wall and had already imagined the sight that would soon become real.

He'd been keeping his boiling need to end this in check during his slow approach. But now he sprung his surprise as he burst into the kitchen and swung his Colt to the right to shoot the distracted bounty hunter.

His pistol's iron front sight hadn't even passed the cookstove when his eyes revealed the truth of what awaited him, and it wasn't anything close to what he'd imagined.

His mind had barely registered the shock of what he saw when Tabby's Colt blasted its .45 caliber slug across the seventy-four inches of space. In the smallest fraction of a second, it ripped into the right side of his chest as he turned before the bullet drilled through his lung's right lower lobe, clipped the top of his still beating heart and then barely cracked through the ribs on the left side of his chest.

In a strange balance of energy, after crossing through Max's chest, the bullet lost all of its power and simply dropped to the floor.

Max was still in shock as he fell to his knees. His heart had stopped, so very little blood left his chest before his brain lost its oxygen and he collapsed face down onto the floor.

Rena had stopped her act the moment Tabby fired and turned just as Max flopped forward.

Tabby took one long stride to where Max lay sprawled across the floor and kicked him once to be sure, even though it was obvious that he was no longer a threat.

He holstered his Colt then turned to Rena and said, "Turn around and I'll drag him out of the house."

He should have known better by now when Rena snapped, "I'll move him. I don't want to see blood on your shirt."

As much as he wanted to handle it, he knew she was right.

"Alright, but just pull him onto the back porch."

Rena didn't pick up her gunbelt or jacket, but simply grabbed Max's left wrist and began dragging the body across the floor. What made it even worse for Tabby was that she was limping as she slid his body toward the door. Max was bigger than he was, and Tabby itched to help her, but knew he couldn't.

Once she'd gotten the body onto the porch, she stepped over the streak of blood on the floor and wrapped her arms around Tabby, making sure her arms were above his wound.

"What do we do now?" she asked quietly with her head pressed against his chest.

"If you can throw some water on the floor, I'll start unloading the buggy and packhorse. I don't want to get his blood on either of the saddles, so we'll need something to cover them before we put the body over it."

"I'll get one of the dirty sheets. Just don't get too ambitious unloading."

"No, ma'am," he said as she released her grip.

She walked to the pump as Tabby grabbed his coat and after putting it on, he picked up her gunbelt and set it on the table before leaving the kitchen.

Rena had pulled the body far enough away from the door that there was enough room to avoid having to step over it. It also gave him a clear path for bringing in what he could from the buggy and packhorse.

It took him almost ten minutes to carry in most of the supplies and only finished that quickly because Rena helped after she had cleaned the floor.

They led Philly and the packhorse into the barn and after unsaddling them, left them in adjoining stalls and headed back to do the hard work of moving the body.

After folding the sheet to cover the saddle on Rena's gelding, it took a joint effort to get Max's body draped over the horse before they boarded the buggy and made a U-turn to head back to Watson.

Until the buggy was moving, they hadn't spoken of the unexpected confrontation in the house but only of the work that needed to be done in its aftermath.

As they rolled toward the canyon mouth, Tabby said, "You're an amazing woman, Rena. You realized that Max was in the house and then almost instantly figured out what needed to be done. I didn't have a clue what you were going to do even after you told me that he was there. If you hadn't come up with your act, I probably would have done something stupid that would have gotten us both killed."

"I almost missed the significance of the spilled coffee, but once I realized that someone was in the house, the rest came naturally."

"Naturally?"

"I guess that's not quite right. It's just that as soon as I knew he was there, I assumed that he had seen us and was waiting for us to come down the hallway. I knew we couldn't surprise him, so we had to bring him into the kitchen. My experience with men led me to the idea of luring him out of the hallway by letting him believe that we were occupied, and he could sneak up on us."

"You can call it whatever you want, Rena, but I think it was brilliant. The only flaw in your instant plot was that your performance was so impressive that I found it hard to concentrate."

"I've had a lot of practice, Thom."

"I hope that this is the last time I ever have to shoot someone, Rena. I'm not some gunman or even a lawman. I'm just a cowhand."

She was holding tightly to his arm as she said, "You're my man, no matter what you are."

Tabby smiled at her as they reached the mouth of the canyon then turned left to pick up the trail to the road.

––––

Forty minutes later, they pulled the buggy to a stop before the sheriff's office with more than a few townsfolk beginning to gather nearby.

Tabby wearily climbed out of the left side of the buggy as Rena gingerly stepped to the ground.

Leaving the trailing horse with Max hung over the sheet-covered saddle, they walked onto the boardwalk and Tabby opened the door letting Rena limp past.

John Lee was at the desk sorting reports when he heard the door open and was surprised to see Rena and Tabby back in town so soon.

"Tabby, did you forget how to find the canyon?" he asked with a grin as he stood.

As soon as he heard his deputy's greeting, Sheriff Smith shot to his feet and rapidly left his private office. He knew that there was only one reason for the couple to come back to town this early. His mistake was that he believed they had just spotted Max Johnson and returned for help.

Just as Tabby was preparing to tell Deputy Lee, he spotted Tex trotting past the cells.

"What happened?" the sheriff asked as he neared the front desk.

"Max was in the ranch house," Tabby replied, "His body is outside."

Tabby guided Rena to a chair as John stared wide-eyed at the open door.

"We didn't know he was inside and almost found out the hard way. He was set up in one of the bedrooms watching the kitchen because we came in the back way. Rena noticed that there was some spilled coffee on the stove and that the stove was still warm. If she hadn't been so quick to realize that Max was there, he'd be well on his way to Bannack by now and we'd both be dead."

"How'd you get him?" the sheriff asked.

"Once Rena told me he was there, I was going to go around the front of the house and try to get behind him, but even when I said it, I didn't like the odds. I may have been lucky to get the other ones but facing a man like Max Johnson with pistols was a whole different story.

"Rena already had figured out a way to trick him into coming into the kitchen before I even knew he was there. We pretended to be making love and he figured that I was too busy to see him. I had my Colt cocked and aimed at the hallway when he showed up with his pistol. I suppose that I should have yelled at him to drop the gun, but I couldn't take that chance, Tex."

"No, you didn't have to warn that bastard. He was wanted dead or alive and if you had so much as said a word, he woulda ducked back down that hallway and you know what most likely would happen after that."

He then looked at his deputy and said, "John, take that body down to Walker's."

"Yes, sir," Deputy Lee replied before trotting toward the open door before spinning around, grabbing his hat and pulling it on then leaving the office.

"He's a good boy, but sometimes…" Tex said as he watched his deputy untie the horse.

He then asked, "Can each of you write out a quick statement?"

"I reckon we can, but I hope you don't expect too much detail about Rena's performance."

"I don't figure that would be a good idea. John would probably spend too much time readin' it."

He took out some blank paper and set it on the desk with some reasonably sharp pencils.

Rena was able to just start writing from where she sat, but Tabby had to follow the sheriff to his office to borrow his desk. As he wrote, he narrated the full story to Tex.

When he finished, Tex said, "You know, if Bill Carroll hadn't been killed in Dilly's, I don't think you would have run into that bastard."

Tabby looked up and asked, "Do you think he would be more thorough in his search than Sheriff Wolfson?"

"No, sir. It's just that Joe and his deputy had make that long ride back to Virginia City. Bill Carroll and John wouldn't have had to leave town so early and I know that Bill woulda probably spend a long time searchin' the house but not just for Max. He would probably be hopin' to find more stolen cash somewhere. By what you just told me, it sounds like Max showed up yesterday and I'm pretty sure he woulda bumped into Bill Carroll and John. I mighta lost both deputies, but you wouldn't have had to shoot him. Of course, Max woulda disappeared again once he had their horses."

"And if that happened, he'd know that you were the only lawman in town. You'd be sitting in the jail by your lonesome and you'd be expecting your two deputies to return. He could have just walked in, killed you and had free reign to do whatever he wanted to do in Watson. At least until some of the citizens knew what was happening."

Tex had his arms folded as he looked down at Tabby and knew that he was right. Men like Max Johnson took advantage of every opportunity to cause mayhem.

"I reckon so," he said as Tabby slid his report to the corner of the desk and slowly stood.

"How's that back of yours?" he asked.

"It's okay."

He followed Tex Smith to the front office just as Deputy Lee was entering. Rena had already finished her statement and was quietly sitting near the desk looking at Tabby.

"El Walker said he'd charge the county for buryin' Johnson, but he'd give 'em a discount."

"He's not gonna have his boys dig a very deep hole anyway."

He then looked at Tabby and said, "You've got another reward comin' your way, Tabby. I reckon you'll be able to buy yourself a whole herd of cows with just this one. He and his boss had big prices on their heads. I'll have 'em all in a couple of days or so if you want to stop by."

Rena stood and took Tabby's arm as she looked into his eyes and smiled.

He smiled back then looked at the sheriff and said, "I don't reckon we'll be coming back so soon, Tex. We are going to spend at least a week on our honeymoon."

"Honeymoon? When did you two have time to get married?" he asked in surprise.

Tabby returned his eyes to Rena whose eyes had never left his face and said, "I've been married to Rena ever since I figured out that there was more to life than just being a cowhand."

Neither of them even glanced at the two lawmen as they slowly walked and limped out of the office.

They climbed into their buggy and after waving to Sheriff Smith and Deputy Lee, Tabby turned the buggy back down street to leave Watson.

They were going home.

CHAPTER 7

May 21, 1879

Rena rode beside Tabby as they passed by the grazing horses. After they'd settled into their ranch house, they made a trip to the Slant 6 where Tabby bought a bull and eight cows. Two of the cows had just calved. He also bought a young stallion and six mares and fillies.

As they passed the horses, Rena said, "It looks like Copper has been pretty busy. Do you think that they're all carrying his offspring?"

"I'd be surprised if they weren't. He's a strong boy. I just hope some of those colts are as handsome as he is."

"I'm still surprised that you didn't buy a big herd of cattle. I always thought that once you finally accepted getting married and being a ranch owner, you'd fill this canyon with cows."

"I thought about it for a week or so, but I realized that there was still that part of me that wanted to avoid too much responsibility. If I'd built a big herd, then I'd have to hire men and I wasn't sure I'd like telling them what to do. The thought of a cowhand calling me 'boss' didn't sit well."

"We'll be almost self-sufficient when those vegetables come in. Even if you only sell a couple of cows or horses each year, we'll have enough income to have the canyon to ourselves. We still have over four thousand dollars in the bank, too."

"I've always been a bit of a tightwad, ma'am."

As they passed the small herd of cows, Rena noticed that four already were already bulging with a growing calf. The two that had calved when they brought them to the canyon were kept in the barn for milk.

She pulled her gelding to a stop and after Tabby walked Philly back a few feet, she asked, "Thom, I know that you've told me often that it doesn't bother you that I can't give you a child, but I still wonder if you'll always feel that way."

"I can't promise you that, Rena. But I do want you to know that I've never played you false about what I feel. I'm perfectly happy being alone with you on our ranch. I'm still in awe of you as a woman and my friend. You are my life now, Rena."

"But what about when we're old and gray? We won't be spending nearly as much time entertaining ourselves and we'll need to start thinking about what happens when one of us is left alone and then when the ranch is only populated by four-footed creatures."

He smiled as he pushed his Stetson back on his head before saying, "We're still young, Rena, and we have a lot of work to do to make our home even better. But I know that we'll have to have someone join us sooner rather than later. You can't keep listening to my droning voice for so long without trying to shoot me with your Walker. When we go into town and I see you talking to Ros or some of the other women who don't still turn their snooty noses up at you, I can see the pleasure it gives you."

"I do enjoy talking to her. When I was out here with Mark Tinker and that bastard Jimmy Parsons, what made it tolerable was having Sharon with me. When she left, I felt so horribly alone."

Tabby looked into Rena's wistful eyes and said, "I'll admit that I'd like to have another man around so we could shoot the bull, too. I may not want to have a bunkhouse full of cowhands calling me 'boss', but if we build a small house nearby and found some young couple to move in, then we'd have instant neighbors. I'd have to pay him for his work, of course, but we'd still be in good shape as long as we don't build a palace."

Rena's eyes lit up as she excitedly said, "Why don't we build a nice new place for us and give the old one to them?"

Tabby smiled then replied, "I was thinking the same thing, Mrs. Hayes."

Rena laughed before saying, "We still haven't made our marriage legal, Thom."

"It's always been legal, Rena."

With their solution to at least part of Rena's question, they turned their horses back toward the ranch house.

————

They arranged for construction of the new house even further back in the canyon about four hundred yards from their current home. The house was completed and furnished in just eight weeks.

Finding the couple who would join them was actually made before the ground had been leveled for the new house. When they had made their visit to the Slant 6 for the horses and cattle, Thom had met with his friend, Steve Askov who had become enamored of a young woman in Virginia City. Steve didn't have anything to offer Viola Chester and he bemoaned that fact to Tabby during their visit.

Tabby and Rena made a second visit to the Slant 6 shortly after construction began. Steve jumped at the chance but had to be sure that Viola would accept him and be willing to move away from her family. She was thrilled with both offers and had to meet with Rena for her approval before everything was settled.

They moved in almost exactly a year after Tabby had ridden to the front of the ranch house and met Rena.

Their presence was a welcome addition to the ranch and even Viola's almost instant pregnancy didn't seem to affect

Rena as the two young women helped each other with their daily chores.

Rena was never expecting a miraculous pregnancy but was more than happy for Viola as her belly began to bulge. She spent time in Watson with Mrs. Jackson, who was one of the town's three midwives. If there was enough warning and the weather was agreeable, then Tabby would take the buggy into town to bring her back to assist with Viola's delivery.

Viola became less able to help Rena with the chores, but Rena didn't mind. She handled the daily work but also pickled and canned the vegetables from their large garden, churned butter and still found time to ride out to the back of the canyon with Tabby to inspect their growing herds.

Viola went into labor on June 17th around six o'clock in the evening. Tabby quickly drove the buggy into town to fetch Mrs. Jackson while Rena helped her friend and Steve paced in the kitchen.

As Rena wiped her sweating forehead, she looked at her friend and said, "Rena, I'm afraid. I don't want to die."

"You'll be all right, Vie. You're strong and everything is going well."

"I know, but still, I'm scared. My sister died having a baby. But if I die and my baby survives, will you raise her as your own?"

"Vie, you'll be fine. In a little while, you'll be holding your baby and be happier than you can ever imagine."

"How do you know, Rena? You've never had a baby."

Rena didn't respond as those horrid memories of her one pregnancy and the even more terrible ending to her child's life ripped through her mind.

She blinked then said, "I haven't been blessed as you have, Vie. I wish we could trade places but pretty soon you'll be a mother and that's something I can never be."

"I'm sorry, Rena. I shouldn't have said that, I…"

She stopped talking as she grunted when a strong contraction took command of her body.

Rena just continued to wipe her brow as Viola grimaced.

Tabby returned with Mrs. Jackson two hours later and she joined Rena in the birthing room while Tabby stayed with Steve in the kitchen keeping the coffee fresh and pots of hot water filled.

It was in the wee hours of the morning when Viola gave birth to a baby boy. There had been no complications and after cutting the cord, Rena laid the squirming child into Viola's arms.

"He's so beautiful," Viola whispered before she kissed her son's forehead.

"Yes, he is," Rena said as she stretched her back.

She looked at her friend's ecstatic face and tried not to let the jealousy inside her boil to the surface. She was ashamed of herself when she'd let that brief hope that Viola would die after giving birth so she could have the baby. It had been such a disgusting thing that she'd allowed to appear in her mind that she almost felt sick when it did.

After smiling at an exhausted Viola, she left Mrs. Jackson in charge and left the birthing room.

When she reached the kitchen, she smiled at Steve and said, "Congratulations, Steve. You have a son and Viola is fine."

Steve took a few whirls around the kitchen before asking, "When can I see them?"

"Mrs. Jackson will let you know."

He then kissed Rena on the cheek as Tabby approached her and softly said, "Sit down, Rena. You're worn out."

"I'll agree with you, sir," she replied before sitting down at the kitchen table.

Tabby poured her a cup of coffee and set it on the table in front of her before sitting beside her and taking her hand.

"Are you okay, Rena?"

She smiled weakly at him as she nodded then lifted the cup and took a sip of the newly brewed coffee.

Steve was preparing to pour another cup for himself when Mrs. Jackson told him he could see his wife and son. He set the coffeepot and unfilled cup down and trotted down the hallway.

After he disappeared, Rena said, "He's a handsome baby, Thom. I don't think you'll get much work out of Steve for a while."

"He hasn't been worth much for a couple of weeks now, ma'am."

She took another sip of coffee and after she hadn't spoken for almost a minute, Tabby asked, "Seeing the baby hurts; doesn't it?"

Rena didn't answer, but just nodded.

Tabby wasn't sure if he could help her. He knew that she could never have Viola's experience and it would have been bad enough if she'd just been barren. But she hadn't been barren. She'd had her unborn child taken from her and then lost the ability to have any more babies. He failed to fully understand all of the reasons for Rena's depression.

He said, "I'll tell Steve that we're leaving."

She nodded again as he rose then walked down the hallway. He wasn't sure if he was supposed to see Viola and the baby as he approached the open door, but as soon as Mrs. Jackson spotted him, she beckoned him inside.

He smiled at her as he entered then turned to look at Steve, Viola and their new son. Steve was all grins as he looked back at him. Viola was soaked in sweat but seemed even happier than her husband.

"I'm glad to see that your boy doesn't take after that ugly father of his. He's a handsome boy, Viola."

Viola surprised Tabby when she replied, "I know. He looks just like you, Thom."

Tabby laughed as he showed his palms in denial of her allegation, then looked at Steve before saying, "Congratulations to both of you, Steve. Rena and I are heading back to the house to get some sleep."

"Thanks for everything, Tabby. Viola and I couldn't be happier and it's all thanks to you and Rena."

Tabby nodded then waved before leaving the room.

He soon reached the kitchen and took Rena's hand as she wordlessly looked up at him.

"Let's go home, Rena," he said quietly as he almost lifted her from the chair.

———

335

The predawn had arrived by the time Rena and Tabby had slid beneath the quilt and blankets covering their new bed.

Tabby was hoping that Rena would almost instantly fall asleep, but after more than five minutes with her eyes wide open just inches from his, he knew he had to at least try to comfort her.

He pulled her even closer before saying, "I wish I could do something to make you feel better, Rena, but I'm at a loss. I may have made significant improvement since I first rode into our canyon, but I still feel totally inadequate to help you as a good husband should."

Rena felt his warmth from his body and his compassionate soul before she whispered, "You are helping me, Thom, but I feel ashamed more than regret or even jealousy."

"Why would you feel shame, Rena?" he asked quietly.

"Because…because of what I thought when Viola was early in her labor. She was afraid that she might die giving birth because she'd seen her sister die having her baby. She asked me to take care of the baby as if it were my own if that happened. Even though I kept telling her that she'd be fine, I actually had a horrible, despicable hope that it did happen. What kind of monster am I to even think it?"

He suddenly understood why she was so upset and gently kissed her forehead before replying, "You're not even close to being a monster, Rena. You're a human being and one of the very good ones. You were hurt and lost much more than just your baby. You were deprived of the ability to have another child. After all you've been through in your life, you finally have a man who loves you completely and a home where you could raise a family. When Viola asked that question, how could you not have that thought? When you looked at Viola, you saw what you could never have, and it wounded you more than any bullet could."

"What can I do now? I can't stop seeing her with her baby and I don't want to keep having those feelings of jealousy."

"I don't know, Rena. We could adopt a child, but I'm not sure it would be the same. Do you?"

"No. I've already thought of that after we learned that Viola was expecting. I was going to ask you about it but didn't want to pressure you into facing the responsibility of being a father. You know how you've always told me that you were almost happy that I couldn't conceive."

Tabby ran his fingers though Rena's long sandy brown hair as he said, "At first, I told you that because it was already difficult for me to accept the responsibility to provide for you then I had to deal with having to take care of a ranch. But then I continued to tell you that because I knew you couldn't have a baby and I figured it would make you feel better if you didn't feel guilty for not giving me a son. You do remember asking me that; don't you?"

337

"Yes, I remember. But are you telling me now that you wouldn't mind being a father, even if the child wasn't ours?"

"We've been together for almost two years now and each day, I get more comfortable with my new life. I'm a much better man now because of you and I'm sure that if you wanted to add a child or two to our home, I'd be a good father."

Rena began to cry as she hugged Tabby then began covering his face with kisses before saying, "I'd be happy with just one to start."

He was happy that he'd been able to help Rena and even though there was some remaining trepidation about being responsible for a child, he promised himself to be the best father he could be. His first goal was to keep their adopted child's mother as happy as possible.

———

Two weeks later, after finally getting officially married to speed the adoption process, Tabby and Rena returned to their ranch with a baby boy they named Michael James. He was the unwelcome child of one of the working girls at Dilly's. Because Tex knew that they wanted to adopt a child, he had brought the boy to his house until Rena and Tabby could pick him up.

Rena had fallen in love with the infant the moment she laid eyes on him and couldn't imagine feeling any happier than if she'd carried the baby inside her for nine months.

TABBY HAYES

Tabby was more than surprised when he felt a swell of pride fill him as he looked at Rena holding their new son.

With Viola nursing her son, little Michael became Sam Askov's feeding companion.

For the rest of the summer and into the early fall, the two babies grew rapidly and as more calves, colts and fillies arrived in the pastures.

The ground was littered with clucking chickens who had free reign over the ranch but didn't wander too far. They did attract a few coyotes and foxes now and then, but there were more than enough wild turkeys in the canyon to make it a less common occurrence.

Tabby and Steve had built a smokehouse so there was never a shortage of meat available. The variety was also pretty impressive, but both former cowhands refused to allow pigs or hogs to enter the canyon. They kept several slabs of bacon in the smokehouse, but it all came from Croker's butcher shop in Watson.

Life on the ranch had settle in to a placid routine that didn't involve any gunfights or serious threats. There had been a scare when little Sam had a fever, but he recovered quickly.

An unexpected result of Steve and Viola's arrival was that Tabby and Steve began to engage in competitive target practice. It had started when Tabby had tried to shoot a fox who was chasing a panicked chicken. He'd fire eight shots with his

Winchester '73 and had only been able to scare the fox away. He took a lot of ribbing from Steve, so they started to practice. They mostly used the '73s because of the higher cost of the .45-75 Express cartridges but practiced with their pistols as well. Now that there was a good selection of handguns, Tabby was using a .44 chambered Colt rather than his .45 for the same reason.

By the time that the spring of '81 arrived, both men were much more proficient with their weapons than they had ever been. The women felt safer when they heard their men firing their weapons.

It was just before summer arrived that their skill with their Winchesters and Colts were put to the test.

Tabby hadn't had to fire at another man since he'd put Max down and didn't think that it would ever happen again. Steve had never even come close to shooting anyone.

Viola was already heavy with her second child and was resting her feet as she sat in the rocking chair on the front porch as the two baby boys napped inside.

Rena was gathering eggs from the protected nests near the barn. Even though she never had fired the Walker, she still wore the heavy pistol at her hip. She didn't have a wedding band on her finger but believed that the gunbelt and pistol had the same significance.

TABBY HAYES

Steve and Tabby were about a mile behind the original ranch house as one of the mares was preparing to foal.

Rena had just placed another egg into her basket and was standing when she heard Viola shout, "Somebody's coming!"

Rena picked up the basket and walked quickly around the barn and looked at the canyon's mouth. It wasn't unusual for them to have visitors now, so she wasn't concerned and walked at a normal pace toward the front porch.

Viola had stood and had her eyes shielded by her hand as she watched the four riders approaching.

Rena spotted them and didn't recognize any of their horses which raised an alarm in her mind. They were still more than a half a mile from the house and knew that Tabby and Steve were even further away.

She set the basket on the edge of the porch and said, "Viola, go inside and get the shotgun. Don't come back outside but just set it near the front door. Go and stay with the boys and close the bedroom door."

Viola felt a wave of fear but quickly turned and entered the house. After taking the shotgun from the rack above the fireplace, she left it by the door and hurried into the bedroom and closed the door.

As soon as she heard the door close, Rena pulled her Walker and aimed it to the right side and cocked the hammer. She had never fired the big pistol and wasn't sure it would even work but pulled the trigger.

The old Colt fired and bucked in her hand making her almost lose her grip, but the loud report echoed off the canyon walls.

Tabby and Steve both jerked their heads around and without saying a word, ran to their horses and leapt into the saddles.

They set off toward the house and Tabby pulled his Winchester '76 from his scabbard as Philly tore up the ground beneath him.

Fred Dixon, Irv McLaughlin, Carl Thibodaux and Joe White had heard about the canyon ranch when they'd passed though Watson. They weren't in the same class of outlaw as Cash Locklear's bunch, but even though they'd heard the tales of how Tabby had taken them all down, they paid more attention to his oft-repeated claim of being just a lucky cowhand.

Even though there were now two men living on the ranch, Fred's crew didn't expect much of a problem because of the confidence they shared in their marksmanship and ruthlessness. Their actual position on the criminal scale was nowhere near the exalted place they believed that they deserved.

Fred had told them that if they just rode casually to the ranch house, they'd be able to get close enough to surprise the two cowhands. After that, it would be all over in seconds.

But they hadn't realized that even though the gunfight that had made Tabby Hayes well known had happened more than two years ago, that memory was so embedded into Rena's mind that she wasn't about to allow strangers to get within two hundred yards of her house without having Tabby beside her with his Winchester cocked.

When they heard the Colt's loud announcement, Fred was stunned but still didn't change their approach.

After a few seconds with no change, Joe White sharply asked, *"Why are we still goin' so slow?"*

"That woman was probably just tellin' her hubby that she's got visitors. We'll be in Winchester range pretty soon, so just get ready to move."

Joe and the others weren't happy with Fred's answer and nudged their horses into a slightly faster pace anyway. Fred had no choice but to match their speed.

Tabby and Steve were passing the new house when Tabby spotted the four riders. They were about the same distance from the house now and even though he didn't know who they were, he wondered why they were there. They weren't riding very fast and they didn't have their Winchesters out which would have at least warned him of a potential danger. He may have been puzzled, but just like Rena, those horrible memories pushed him to believe that they weren't good men just looking for a job.

Carl was the first to spot Tabby and Steve and shouted, "There they are, and they've got their Winchesters ready!"

Fred felt sick when he realized that this wasn't going to be the simple job he'd expected and yanked his Winchester from his scabbard as the others did the same.

He cocked his hammer and realized that they weren't going to reach the house before those two faster-moving cowhands did.

"Head for the barn!" he shouted as he angled his horse to the right and kicked him into a gallop.

As the others turned and matched his speed, Rena stepped backwards through the doorway, slipped the Colt back into its holster and grabbed the shotgun.

She then backed further into the front room but didn't reach the hallway. She stood where she could watch through the open doorway, the front window and then the side window. The side window gave her an unobstructed view of the barn.

When Tabby saw the four men pull their repeaters and then turn to hide behind the barn, he knew that he'd lost his advantage. But now his only concern was for Rena and Michael.

He shouted, "Steve, go to the front room through the kitchen! I'm going to pull up and make sure they don't get past the barn."

"Okay!" Steve yelled back and shifted his gelding's direction to the back of his house.

Tabby slowed Philly and turned him more to the left to keep a safe distance from the barn and their Winchesters.

Steve pulled up behind the house and slid from the saddle with his Winchester then hopped onto the short porch. He suspected that Rena was armed now and after opening the door, he stopped.

"I'm coming in the kitchen! Tabby is staying near the barn to keep 'em pinned down!"

Rena had whipped her shotgun's muzzles to the hall when she heard him on the back porch and as she lowered the scattergun, she shouted, "I'm in the front room, Steve!"

He entered the kitchen then headed for the hallway. Viola opened the door as he passed just to let him know where she was and that she and the boys were safe.

Steve just nodded to her as he trotted by and when he reached the front room, Rena said, "You can see them through the side window. I'm sure that they haven't seen me because I'm so far back."

"Okay. I'll take over here. Do you want to cover the back door with that shotgun?"

"Alright," she replied before walking quickly to the kitchen.

Viola watched her pass by and hoped that those four men just left.

The four men had already dismounted when they had lost sight of the two cowhands but hadn't heard Tabby's shouted instructions to Steve. As far as they knew, both men were on the other side of the barn.

Irv McLaughlin was looking at the house and asked, "What do we do now, Fred?"

Fred had no idea but replied, "Those two gotta be sittin' there on the other side of the barn waitin' for us to stick our heads out."

Carl snapped, "That ain't a plan, Fred! What do we do?"

Fred snarled, "What do you reckon we oughta do, Carl?"

Joe White said, "I don't like just sittin' here like this, Fred. It ain't nothin' like you said it was gonna be."

"Why don't you stick your head out there and get it blown off, Joe? I'm ready to just make a break for the end of the canyon."

Joe glared at Irv and said, "Go ahead and I'll watch you get shot out of your saddle. Can I have your horse?"

Fred knew that the longer they stayed put, the worse their situation would become. They were already starting to fight among themselves and he knew his own nerves were already stretched too tight.

"Okay," he said loudly, "Here's what we're gonna do. I'll slide over to the house side of this wall and Joe, you slide the other way headin' to the canyon wall. Irv, you cover me and Carl, you watch Joe's back. I'm gonna wave my hat in front of the barn and see if somebody fires. Joe you do the same. As soon as they fire, we'll know where they are and can go the other way."

Not one of them, including Fred, really thought it would work, but they were already getting desperate.

As they talked, Steve watched them through the window. He'd moved a little closer than where Rena had been to get a better view and could see them arguing. He could have taken a shot, but for the same reason that Tabby had when he was watching Max exit the hallway, Steve hesitated. He didn't know if he could shoot a man.

Tabby had dismounted and stood about a hundred yards from the barn. Now that Steve was in the house and he knew that Rena and Michael were safe, he felt free to stop those men. The question was how he could do it.

He could almost feel them on the other side of the barn but from where he stood, he could only see the front side of the barn. He had chosen this spot because he didn't want them to make a break for the house or enter the barn. But they could come around the back of the barn without being seen. It was a spooky feeling knowing that they could pop out from the back of the barn and start shooting him before he had a chance to bring his Winchester to bear.

347

But knowing that he was spooked led him to believe that those four men would be just as nervous as he was if not worse. At least he knew where Steve was, and they had no idea that they could be seen.

He briefly thought of jogging to the house to help Steve but didn't like the thought of giving them the opportunity to surround the house. They wouldn't need to fire their Winchesters if they decided to toss some burning branches onto the roof.

It was almost a standoff and just as Tabby was ready to walk to the back of the barn, he saw a hat appear on the far corner of the barn and then quickly drop out of sight.

He found it hard to believe that experienced outlaws would resort to such a silly notion, but he kept his eyes on the distant wall expecting to see one of the men appear after he hadn't fired.

Fred pulled his hat back on his head and turned to look at Joe at the back of the barn. He had just put his hat back in place and put out his hands asking what to do now that neither motion had attracted a gunshot.

Steve had watched them as they waved their hat and was even more confused than Tabby because he'd seen them both do it.

The entire confrontation had been ongoing for just ten minutes as the four men remained huddled on the side of the barn.

TABBY HAYES

Tabby finally had enough of just waiting for something to happen, but the sorry ploy of the waving hat had made him believe that those four men weren't nearly as bad as Cash Locklear's crowd. They may have intended to attack the ranch, but even that idea was ludicrous considering that they decided to launch their assault in broad daylight.

He began walking slowly toward the back of the barn. He was trusting that Steve had them under his Winchester now and if they tried to get into the house, he'd be able to stop them cold. His only concern now was that the chickens might let them know he was coming.

As he approached, the four outlaws were huddled near the center of the barn wall.

"Do we rush the house, Fred?" Carl asked, "Those women are in there and if we can keep 'em hostages, we can make those two cowboys toss down their rifles."

In reply, Fred quickly asked, "Would you?"

"No, but I ain't some cowhand who cares about his woman, Fred. If we tell 'em that we just need food and horses, they'll do it."

"You reckon they're gonna believe that?"

"Well, I don't hear you comin' up with a better idea."

Fred snorted but knew he didn't have a better idea. In fact, he had no idea at all.

Tabby had reached the back wall of the barn and after finding it clear, began walking to the other side passing chickens who didn't seem to pay him any attention at all. He heard their voices and could sense their desperation. He just hoped that he didn't screw up.

They were still loudly arguing to come up with a solution that had even a small chance of getting them out of this mess when Tabby suddenly stepped out from the back of the barn with his Winchester pointed at the tight bunch.

"Drop your guns, boys!" he shouted.

Even though their repeaters were all cocked, each of them knew that even if they managed to squeeze a trigger, it would be a rushed, inaccurate shot.

Without a word four Winchesters dropped to the ground.

Tabby was incredibly relieved as he said, "Now I don't have any reason to shoot you boys, but I'm not going to give you a chance to come back either. I want you to climb back onto your horses and I'll follow you out of my canyon. You'll have your pistols, but if I see any of you come back, I'll fill you all full of lead before you get close."

"Okay, mister, we're leavin'," Fred said.

"And just so you know you shouldn't show your faces in Watson again, I'll be riding right behind you until you reach the road and then I'll watch you head to Bannack."

Fred didn't comment again but mounted his horse before the others climbed into their saddles.

Steve had watched the takedown and was even more relieved than Tabby. Once they started boarding their horses leaving their repeaters on the ground, he left the front room and trotted to the kitchen.

Rena hadn't seen Tabby after he disappeared behind the barn, so when Steve suddenly appeared, she asked, "What happened? Where's Thom?"

Steve grinned as he passed and replied, "They're all disarmed and riding away. I'm going to mount Poker and get Philly for him."

Rena was elated as she lowered the shotgun and Steve left the house. She turned to tell Viola the good news and found Viola already standing in the hallway entrance.

"It's over," Viola said softly, "and the boys never even woke from their naps."

Rena laid the shotgun on the kitchen table and hugged Viola.

"I'm glad that the only shot that was fired came from my Colt."

———

After claiming Philly from Steve, Tabby kept his promise and followed the four men all the way to the road and watched them disappear toward Bannack before turning around and taking the trail back to the canyon.

As he rode, he still glanced at his backtrail, but he knew that they wouldn't be back.

He thought how ironic it was that when he'd had to fight a life or death battle with a much more violent group of men, he'd been woefully inadequate in his shooting prowess. Now that he was very good with his weapons, he hadn't had to pull a trigger.

As he had Philly moving at a medium trot, he smiled. It was almost three years ago when he'd made this same ride. He was terrified that he might be caught and hanged by a posse for something he hadn't done. Then he'd found that ranch house and thought he'd at least find a job.

What he'd found was a new life. A new life that began when a young woman stepped out onto the porch with an empty shotgun.

This time, as he rode toward the house that was now the home of his friend and his growing family, he saw that same young woman on the porch waiting for him. Only this time, she wasn't holding a shotgun in her hands. She held their son in her arms and wore a big smile on her face.

EPILOGUE

The four men who had invaded the ranch with intent to do harm, found a bigger problem when they arrived in Bannack. It wasn't because they had done anything wrong in town, but because Sheriff Wolfson had sent a telegram to other law enforcement offices three days earlier. They had robbed the Highwater Saloon in Virginia City and obviously believed that no one would care because it wasn't a bank.

They were arrested and sent back to Virginia City where they were tried and then stunned when they were sentenced to five years in prison.

Life returned to normal in the canyon after the tense, but not violent confrontation. The only real change was that four more Winchesters were added to the ranch's arsenal.

Viola gave birth to another baby boy in August and Rena hadn't felt a bit of jealousy. If anything, she was relieved that she hadn't had to endure the process.

She had thought of asking Tabby about adopting a little girl but realized that she was already being worn down by the very active little boy in their house and decided that she'd devote all of her time to Michael. They could always adopt again after he became less of a handful.

Michael was in his room napping while Tabby and Rena sat on their front porch on their large double rocker. It was a Sunday afternoon, and the air was already crisp with the promise of the much colder weather to come.

Rena was incredibly content as she snuggled under Tabby's right arm.

"Are you as happy as I am?" she asked.

"Maybe even happier. I couldn't have imagined this life five years ago. Even after I agreed to marry you, I still couldn't conceive of things turning out this well."

"I agree with you, sir. But what if I hadn't asked you to marry me when I did? Would you have asked me anyway?"

He looked at her and replied, "I'm really not sure. I mean, I was so set in my ways and didn't have any ambitions or dreams beyond minding cattle. I was definitely impressed with your, um, femininity, but that didn't mean I was ready to get down on my knee to beg for your hand."

"You never did ask me, and may I remind you that we didn't even become husband and wife in the eyes of the territory until we had to so we could adopt Michael?"

"I'm aware of that, Mrs. Hayes, and I apologize for the delay. But you know that I always thought of you as my wife almost from the first. Having that piece of paper didn't really change anything."

"I'm just teasing you, Tabby."

He smiled at her and asked, "Now I'm Tabby again?"

She kissed him and grinned when she answered, "I told you before that I could always start using that first nickname your cowhand friends gave you if you gave me grief about calling you Tabby."

"And I'll give you the same answer I gave you before that I'm fine with Tabby. It's still a better moniker than the other one. But do you know what I think I'll start doing in retaliation?"

"What?"

"I'll start calling you by that name."

Rena leaned back and laughed before replying, "Actually, I like it. If you want to start calling me Kitty, you go right ahead."

Tabby was still grinning before he kissed his wife.

———

1	Rock Creek	12/26/2016
2	North of Denton	01/02/2017
3	Fort Selden	01/07/2017
4	Scotts Bluff	01/14/2017
5	South of Denver	01/22/2017
6	Miles City	01/28/2017
7	Hopewell	02/04/2017
8	Nueva Luz	02/12/2017
9	The Witch of Dakota	02/19/2017
10	Baker City	03/13/2017
11	The Gun Smith	03/21/2017
12	Gus	03/24/2017
13	Wilmore	04/06/2017
14	Mister Thor	04/20/2017
15	Nora	04/26/2017
16	Max	05/09/2017
17	Hunting Pearl	05/14/2017
18	Bessie	05/25/2017
19	The Last Four	05/29/2017
20	Zack	06/12/2017
21	Finding Bucky	06/21/2017
22	The Debt	06/30/2017
23	The Scalawags	07/11/2017
24	The Stampede	07/20/2017
25	The Wake of the Bertrand	07/31/2017
26	Cole	08/09/2017
27	Luke	09/05/2017
28	The Eclipse	09/21/2017
29	A.J. Smith	10/03/2017
30	Slow John	11/05/2017
31	The Second Star	11/15/2017
32	Tate	12/03/2017
33	Virgil's Herd	12/14/2017
34	Marsh's Valley	01/01/2018
35	Alex Paine	01/18/2018
36	Ben Gray	02/05/2018

37	War Adams	03/05/2018
38	Mac's Cabin	03/21/2018
39	Will Scott	04/13/2018
40	Sheriff Joe	04/22/2018
41	Chance	05/17/2018
42	Doc Holt	06/17/2018
43	Ted Shepard	07/13/2018
44	Haven	07/30/2018
45	Sam's County	08/15/2018
46	Matt Dunne	09/10/2018
47	Conn Jackson	10/05/2018
48	Gabe Owens	10/27/2018
49	Abandoned	11/19/2018
50	Retribution	12/21/2018
51	Inevitable	02/04/2019
52	Scandal in Topeka	03/18/2019
53	Return to Hardeman County	04/10/2019
54	Deception	06/02/2019
55	The Silver Widows	06/27/2019
56	Hitch	08/21/2019
57	Dylan's Journey	09/10/2019
58	Bryn's War	11/06/2019
59	Huw's Legacy	11/30/2019
60	Lynn's Search	12/22/2019
61	Bethan's Choice	02/10/2020
62	Rhody Jones	03/11/2020
63	Alwen's Dream	06/16/2020
64	The Nothing Man	06/30/2020
65	Cy Page: Western Union Man	07/19/2020
66	Tabby Hayes	08/02/2020

Made in the USA
Monee, IL
14 August 2020